לדבורה

My Other Half

by

David Isaacson

AOS Publishing, 2024
Copyright © 2024

David Isaacson

ISBN: 978-1-990496-86-8

Cover Design: Chanelle Poupart

Visit AOS Publishing's website:
www.aospublishing.com

Dear Rachel,

I am so sorry for what happened here in Jerusalem. I realise that you won't forgive me for a long time, if ever. In the meantime, please allow me to explain myself.

It all began last year on a late-summer's night in Stancombe Woods. On our way to the woods, Skunk, Boney and I stopped off for a drink at the Dead Duck, which served Cardinal's Blight and had a fire in a hearth, horseshoes nailed to black beams and hunt scenes framed in brass. There was a food counter, a darts board, a shove-ha'penny table and lamps dressed in tasselled shades but no sign of Norm the landlord or Val, his grumpy wife, nor the wizened regulars who drank stout or pale ale and smoked roll-ups round games of dominoes.

Boney was waiting for Norm, or Val, to serve him, or at least appear behind the bar. Boney was a geography student who had a long black beard, a hangdog mien and a jungle-camouflage jacket. He had just returned from a week of solitude on a deserted Orkney island, which was Boney's idea of a holiday. Now bored by waiting, he approached the blackboard by the food counter. 'Scampi and chips or shepherd's pie, strawberry ice cream or apple crumble with custard,' he read out loud before erasing the menu with a dishcloth and proceeding to fill the void with a self-portrait in chalk. It was like *fin-de-siècle* Paris, though we didn't have whores, or absinthe, or any drinks come to that. Boney's self-portrait turned out to be Africa, with a yellow Sahara Desert, a blue Lake Victoria and green Congo Basin. Boney stepped back, tip of his tongue poking through his beard. He closed an eye and held up a thumb for perspective. The rest of the world was to come.

'Excuse me!' Norm didn't think much of Boney's handiwork. 'Can I help you?'

'No, no. I think I can manage.' Boney was halfway up Italy.

'Do you know how long it took Val to write up that menu?'

'Five minutes?' guessed Boney.

'Probably at least ten,' I argued. The letters were coloured in, with shadows for a three-dimensional effect.

'Does it matter?' asked Skunk, on returning from the bogs, where he had no doubt been to snort a line of speed. 'All we want is two pints and a half of Cardinal's Blight. Please.'

I was the half.

'Get out, all of you!' Norm strode across the pub and opened its front door to see us off the premises.

'You don't have to shout, like,' said Boney as Skunk gathered our bag of accessories, I put our ghettoblaster on my shoulder and we took our sorry leave.

'You're banned!'

An unseen bird chirped evensong over clicking crickets and a hum of distant traffic. Swallows darted between haystacks' silhouettes. A pink and lilac sky drew a glorious summer's day to a close.

We traipsed across a field of long grass, Boney staying close to an overgrown hedgerow to avoid cowpats the size of landmines, Skunk veering off like a mongrel chasing butterflies. I shuddered at a weird presentiment of the night ahead.

'Feesh.'

A late shaft of sunlight caught a gaunt, lanky figure in a beret and white smock sitting astride a wooden stile. Fysh, our resident artist, had been to Cadaques in Spain, where he hoped to show his portfolio of psychedelic landscapes to Salvador Dalí. After a couple of weeks camped outside Dalí's home with no sign of the master, Fysh sold his paintings and headed south to Morocco, to which he vowed never to return following an unsavoury incident with a young lady who wasn't young or a lady.

'Follow me, guys.' Fysh' plaited ponytail bounced over his back as he led us into the woods.

Way above our heads, birds' nests clotted the topmost twigs. Sturdy oaks, elms and horse chestnuts appeared in crazy postures as they faded into darkness. One tree bent over backwards as though beseeching the sky. Another lay prone, its cavities and twisted roots exposed for all to see. A blasted deadwood carcass spewed sawdust and bugs.

We hacked at brambles and nettles, circumvented a crater and leaped over a dried-out stream. By the time we reached our clearing, the sky had turned black and the trees were invisible.

Skunk dashed this way and that like a manic boy scout on manoeuvres. He piled branches on a patch of scorched earth and before long we were warmed by a raging fire. Skunk stood back and folded his arms.

'Do you think we'll need more wood?' he wondered out loud.

'Where do you get it?'

'You're not really the outdoors type, are you, Jake?'

'Where's Casey?' asked Fysh. 'Does he know where to find us?'

'Is Casey coming?' I hadn't seen Casey since the start of summer when he let me have a go on his Harley-Davidson, which I crashed into a bush, to the amusement of his biker mates, who were watching from the roof of Guevara House.

'Stop worrying,' said Skunk. 'He'll be here.'

A waft of patchouli announced a new arrival, one wearing safety-pins and costume jewellery, Siouxsie Sioux warpaint and hair bunched in little pyramids. Evie made straight for Boney, who was heating a pair of tongs in the fire.

'Hey, Boneyman! How was the Orkneys?'

'Have you never been?'

'No, funnily enough, I never have.'

'"This bloody town's a bloody cuss, No bloody trains, no bloody bus, And no-one cares for bloody us, In bloody Orkney."'

'Sounds like where I come from,' said Evie.

'Where *do* you come from?' asked Boney.

'It's all the same fucking place, man,' laughed Evie.

On seeing Boney drop a smidgen of hash onto a red-hot tong, I put our hollowed-out milk bottle to my mouth. Boney squeezed the tongs as he positioned them under my bottle and I inhaled thick, whirling smoke. Then I fell over.

Stars twinkled. Leaves rustled. The earth felt firm. A bassline rumbled, a guitar wailed, a high priestess broke into song.

'*Sssssummer tahm, and the living's easehhhhhh. Fish are, fish are jumpin nah and the cotton, ohhhhh, the cotton's hiiiiiiiiigh, Lord so hiiiiiiiiigh...*'

When the music ended, I put on a Grateful Dead bootleg tape. Everyone else was too stoned to move. Boney used to say, 'the Grateful Dead are shite, it's a well-known fact,' and the others called me a Deadhead but the band had become our default accompaniment, especially on trips into the unknown.

'So *this* is the promised land.'

His American twang evoked an image of a Wild West gunslinger, a cool, taciturn loner riding into town and staying to save its God-fearing settlers from marauding bandits. He had the chiselled jaw and flinty eyes, gleaming white teeth and dimpled cheeks of a bona-fide Hollywood hero. In Casey there was no music or intimacy, just a presence. He was sitting on a low branch like he'd been there all along.

'Casey! How was the land of the free?' asked Evie.

Fysh jumped up and flapped his arms. 'Land of the freaks. Furry freaks.'

'How's the acid?' Skunk wanted to know.

'It's liquid.' Casey reached into a pocket for a crust of bread and a tiny bottle. He counted heads, broke the bread into six pieces and dripped a drop from the bottle over each piece of bread. Every outstretched hand received a crust.

'Good trip, everyone,' said Evie. It's going to be one for the annals, I can feel it.'

'Hey, yours is bigger than mine,' complained Fysh.

Skunk took his crust with nonchalance, as if he did a crust of bread every day.

Boney looked at his askance as though reminded of something else. Then he stuck out his tongue and the crust was gone.

I took mine with a wordless prayer.

'Ladies and gentlemen...,' announced Casey in a mock Home Counties accent. 'This is your captain speaking. I'd like to welcome you aboard Cosmic Air, flight 101, and wish you a pleasant journey. We expect to be taking off any time now. I'm glad to say that weather and flying conditions are set fair and the outlook is fine. We'll be cruising at a height of thirty thousand feet and... fuck knows where we're going.'

We laughed nervously. An owl hooted. Someone hooted back. The fire declined into embers. Quietly, imperceptibly, reality slipped away.

Evie stood very still, head raised, arms extended.

'What's going on with you, like?' asked Boney, who had been clomping around like an ape at the dawn of time.

'I'm an old oak tree,' said Evie. 'I cast spells on travellers who pass this way.'

'I don't see any travellers.' Boney scanned the darkness. 'And you're not an old oak tree. You're Evie, remember?'

Evie looked down at her body in amazement. She wasn't a tree, she was a person. She cackled at her mistake, flopped down beside me and tried to roll a number. On looking up, her mouth fell open. Fear of a bad trip always lurked somewhere under the surface. Now it was written on Evie's face.

A bloodied hermit was standing beyond the fire. 'This is hell,' he said, and I realised it was Skunk.

'No, no, no,' said Boney. 'Hell doesn't exist. It's a lie told by priests to scare us.'

'Here.' Evie got up and handed Skunk a bottle of water, which he poured over his head. 'Take deep breaths.'

'You're just freaking out,' said Fysh.

'What happened?' I asked. He looked like he had fallen out of a tree.

Skunk took a deep breath. 'I was strolling down a trail, minding my own business, when I heard a movement. I thought it must be an animal. Then it stood up, a big, furry goblin with pointed ears and ugly little eyes.'

'Weird,' said Evie.

'It was horrible. He said it was time to die. I was really scared.'

'Hang on, Skunk,' said Casey. 'Let's get this straight. You're saying a goblin spoke to you?'

'He's possessed,' said Fysh. 'Skunk's been possessed by a goblin.'

'This just gets worse.' Evie lit a cigarette.

'I reckon we're looking at an exorcism.' Fysh began to pace. 'Don't worry, Skunk, I know about this stuff. I've studied Aleister Crowley. The best way to exorcise an evil spirit...'

'Will you shut the fuck up?' Evie aimed a kick at Fysh. 'Nobody's going to be exorcising any evil spirits.'

'I expect he's still looking for me,' said Skunk. 'He could turn up at any minute.'

'Let's kill the goblin,' I heard myself say.

'What?' Skunk thought I was crazy.

'Yup,' said Casey. 'That's just what we'll do.' Casey was cradling a wooden stake like a homesteader on a veranda.

'I'm not going back in there,' said Skunk.

'I'm staying with Skunk,' said Evie.

'I'm going back to campus,' said Boney, and Fysh, who reckoned he could gauge their position by the stars, headed off with him.

'That leaves just us.' Casey jumped off his branch. 'We're not scared. Come on, Jake, let's go.'

A full moon beamed. Branches swayed. A breeze whispered in my ear. 'Turn back. You're not made for blood and gore, especially when it's your own. This isn't a dream.'

I forged on, through thick foliage, arms cut by thorns, ankles stung by nettles, hands outstretched as protection from unseen trees, wishing I had a torch, and a compass, and a gun. At least I had Casey. Casey had probably confronted rattlesnakes in deserts or cougars on the high ground. Casey knew how to approach a deadly adversary. And that was in silence. Still, you'd think he'd hoot or give some sort of sign of his whereabouts.

'Say, Casey, do you think it knows we're here?'

Silence.

'Casey?'

Maybe he was fooling around, just to scare me.

'Casey...'

Maybe he'd gone on ahead.

'Casey!'

Where the hell was he? Wherever I looked, I saw only goblins and shadows. Then it dawned on me. The goblin had killed him. And it was about to ambush me. Stumbling in the darkness, I tripped over Casey's body. The goblin had turned Casey into a fallen log. Nobody heard me scream.

I became he and my fear subsided. He pressed on through the woods. Warm, sticky blood appeared on his fingers but he couldn't feel a thing. The woods began to thin and a light appeared between far-off trees.

A Palladian mansion appeared in a large clearing, its bright lights shining over a silver lawn. Partygoers in black tails and elegant gowns were fanned out across a raised terrace. A carousel whirled on the lawn. Ceramic horses went round and round in circles, bobbing up and down without moving, bearing new riders on every reappearance.

Inside the mansion, in a ballroom overlooked by a trinity of august stained-glass windows, a fancy-dress ball was in full swing. Cave-dwellers in bearskins were roasting a pig on a spit, gladiators sparred with tridents and nets. A washerwoman was wringing linen and scolding a sullen urchin. 'It's a Long Way to Tipperary,' sang a regiment of tommies. Everyone was acting in character.

Embarrassed to have arrived without a costume, I left the ballroom to explore. At the end of a plush corridor were three adjacent doors, each with a plaque in gothic script.

Pleasure. Guilt. Redemption.

I couldn't decide on a room. Who was I to commit to a choice? 'You are a young man in twentieth-century Britain,' I reminded myself. As such, I was bound to opt for *Pleasure*.

Disco lights flashed. Naked bodies writhed. Spectators masturbated without shame. A girl carved in ebony sashayed towards me, licking her lips, pearl necklace swinging between sumptuous breasts and hard, dark nipples. She turned her back, bent over and beckoned me into her *anus mirabilis*. Throbbing so hard I was fit to explode, I unscrambled my clothes. I held her raised buttocks, I clasped her bosom and came prematurely. Disgusted and disgraced, I dressed in shamefaced haste.

In *Guilt* next door, a dozen hooded monks were shuffling in a circle like manacled convicts, whipping each other's backs in synchronised time. Orange smoke and acrid fumes trailed by an overhead thurible stung my eyes, nose and throat. I backed into an alcove, where a hippy in a loincloth was being crucified. I was in the wrong place for sure.

In *Redemption*, a chamber quartet were playing behind black curtains. A chandelier shone over a polished parquet floor, over head-high plinths arranged in a circle, each mounted by a skull holding a scarlet rose in its teeth. The skulls faced inwards, towards a coffin laid open on a bier. I climbed inside and lay in its silk interior, wrists crossed on my chest.

'You're too early.'

'Who's that?' I sat up and looked round but couldn't see anyone.

'You haven't fallen in love yet. Come back when you're ready.'

I returned to the corridor and found a winding staircase lined by brass balustrades that led up to a landing so long neither end could be seen. A bedroom door was ajar. A full moon shone through tall windows on partygoers lying higgledy-piggledy on the floor, draped over armchairs and snuggled together on a four-poster bed. Snoring, sniffing and gibbering deliriously, they made me feel at home.

I settled down between a clergyman and a milkmaid and, looking forward to meeting everyone in the morning, I yawned, closed my eyes and rolled over.

'*Allons-y!*'

I knew it was you at once. I recognised your soft voice and sweet face, your black beret and Star of David necklace. You hauled me up and we tiptoed between sleeping bodies. We skipped down a winding staircase and danced across the terrace, like angels.

A glowing dawn beckoned a new day. Woodland trees awoke and flexed their branches. Songbirds welcomed us to the world.

'Where are we?' you asked.

'This is England. I live here.'

'You live here,' you echoed in derision. 'Don't you know we are outsiders? Here, there and everywhere, we are phantoms stalking the earth.'

'I'm not a phantom,' I said. 'I might be having a spiritual experience but I'm still a human being.'

'You have it the wrong way round. You are not a human having a spiritual experience but a spirit having a human experience. I've come to take you home.'

We arrived at a clearing, where a bonfire's embers were smouldering and three people were sleeping. On seeing my friends, I turned to introduce you before realising I didn't know your name.

'What's your name?'

You had disappeared.

'Look, it's Jake.'

A trio of bodies stirred. Evie pulled at a blanket to rouse a groaning Skunk.

'How's it going, Jake?' Casey sounded concerned, like something was amiss.

'I met my lover from a previous life.'

Skunk scrambled to his feet then peered into my eyes, one after the other, like a doctor examining a patient. He whispered his diagnosis to Evie, who relayed the news to Casey.

You'd think they'd want to know about my lover from a previous life. You'd think they'd want to meet you. But no. They gathered our stuff and we headed back to campus in silence.

Letter 2

I was hemmed in between Evie and a wall. Half-expecting to find Skunk there too, I was pleased to see it was just the two of us, both under Evie's duvet. In such close proximity, and without makeup, Evie looked like a stranger. Jim Morrison was glaring at us from a poster. Break on through from the wardrobe door.

'Hello, Jake,' she said. 'Have you recovered? You were in a right state.'

'Why, what happened?' I vaguely recalled yearning for a girl in Stancombe Woods.

'You kept saying, "Love is all there is"'.

'Love *is* all there is. Everyone knows it but no-one admits it. Love is the only reality.'

'You're such a hippy, Jake. Do you remember the long walk?'

'Chairman Mao?'

'That's the long march. I'm talking about last night, or this morning, when we got lost.'

'How do you get lost coming back from Stancombe Woods?'

'Oh, I like that. If it wasn't for me and Casey, you and Skunk would still be there. Did you see me in that garden? I was squatting down for a piss, arse out to the world, when suddenly a dog started barking and an upstairs light went on. I was expecting a farmer with a twelve-bore... Jake! Did you hear a word I just said?'

I was looking for you on campus. In dawn's cool light, the lecture halls and library, coffee shop and residences all rested in eerie silence. Lumumba Slope resembled a spaceship that had landed in a green valley. Ordinarily I would have made for my room in Flat 22, but here I was in Flat 7, waking up with Evie.

We kissed and our bodies entwined. Cuddling, coupling and grappling, upside out and inside down, we lost ourselves in ecstasy.

In those last long days of summer, languid evenings in central space were followed by hot, steamy nights in Flat 7. Evie would catch my eye before heading off to her place down the Slope then twenty minutes later I followed suit and no-one was any the wiser. Meanwhile the leaves were changing colour, darkness was coming earlier and at night the air turned bracing. Twenty minutes became thirty, then forty, then sixty. As summer came to an end, we didn't need words to call time on our affair.

Evie was sitting at my desk in the first week of a new academic year. Above her shone a gallery of stars: Bogart being tough, Marilyn on a windowsill, Cary Grant in a tux; Cagney snarling, Dietrich dancing, the Marx Brothers at a racetrack. Most luminous of all, stately on a galleon's prow, Greta Garbo sails away, leaving forever the man she loves. She was holding a chocolate digestive – Evie that is, not Greta Garbo – and sipping tea from a mug. 'What if God is a false concept?' asked the mug, which originally belonged to Emily, an American student who formed an ill-advised attachment to Skunk before returning home no longer wanting a homecoming-queen reception nor adjusted to a life in Knoxville, Tennessee.

'*Da na, na na Na, na na, na na....*' A whooping and hollering was doing my head in.

Top of the Pops was starting next door in Flat 24, which meant it must be 7:25 on a Thursday evening. I pulled back a curtain to see a trail of orange tail-lights dotting a black sky.

'Are you going to get up?' Evie had let herself in while I was asleep. People were always doing that, especially during the day. Evie's painted face, spiked hair and chainmail skirt anticipated a night out. She whipped off my duvet and cackled at my nakedness.

Then someone opened the door.

'As you can see, there are three rooms per corridor.' It sounded like the vice chancellor taking parents of prospective students on a tour. 'In this corridor, there's Boney at the end,

Faye in the middle and... here's Jake, who's wrestling with Evie.' Fysh was showing off to a girl dressed in a sombrero, a poncho and black pantaloons.

I grabbed my duvet and resettled in bed, embarrassed in front of Fysh's new friend.

'Hey, guys,' said Fysh. 'Look what I found. A first-year.'

'I'm not a "what" and you didn't find me. I'm Kitty,' she said. 'Pleased to meet you.'

'Pleased to meet *you*.' Evie re-positioned her chair. 'What are you studying?'

'Philosophy.'

'Oh, God, not another one.' Evie had had her fill of philosophers.

Kitty took off her sombrero and tossed back her hair. She had a high, handsome forehead and sky-pale eyes set wide apart in a weathered, English-rose face. A turquoise nose-stud seemed less adornment than self-laceration. She sat cross-legged on the floor and looked around at Hollywood's stars and the Indian-cotton canopy that sagged over our heads, a traveller taking in her new confinement. Then she set about rolling a joint as if making a contribution.

Fysh fidgeted, pulled faces and gurgled like an unctuous court jester. He put on Kitty's sombrero and cocked his finger and thumb. 'Your money or your wife?' He was handing Kitty an ashtray when the door knocked him sideways.

It was Skunk, dressed in an old velvet jacket whose lining was ripped and ankle-length corduroys. A big toe protruded through a hole in his trainers. He paused to consider Kitty then sat beside Fysh, cross-legged, chin on fist, like The Thinker with a hangover.

'Hi, Skunk.' Fysh did his best to act normal. 'When you wanna go shrooming?'

'Not any time soon, I shouldn't think,' said Evie. 'Not after last time. The grass was the wrong colour, the dew wasn't wet enough, a cow was giving you a dirty look... Then you threw a strop when the bus stop wasn't there.'

'Oh, that,' said Skunk. It could happen to anyone.

Next to arrive was Gordon, who gawped at Kitty like he'd never seen a newcomer. Gordon was a mature student who had worked in the real world, in a plastics factory in the Midlands. There he discovered John Stuart Mill, whose Victorian utilitarianism inspired Gordon to sign up for a degree in Intellectual History. At Wessex he fell in with us and in no time he became an enthusiastic user of consciousness-expanding drugs while his appearance went from clean-cut to uncut. He lost the will to study and questioned his own existence, though that might have been Freud's fault. Gordon's Freudian bummer first surfaced on a trip to Arundel. We were in sight of Arundel Castle when Skunk and I realised that Gordon was missing. We found him back at the station, taking photos. 'Did you see that train go into the tunnel? You know what that symbolises, don't you? There'll be another one in a minute.' We reminded him that we had come to see to the castle and we retraced our steps, either side of Gordon, but in Gordon's mind, every blackbird was a vagina, every tower a penis, so we changed course and went to the cathedral, hoping some sacred silence would release poor Gordon from Freud's heinous grip. Yet it was there in Arundel Cathedral, over a bottle of red wine provided by Skunk and a joint I rolled discreetly in the pews, that Gordon first blamed his father for failing to identify with him at that crucial phallic stage of his psychosexual development.

'How are you, Gordon?' asked Fysh.

'Have you got a quarter, Jake?' Gordon looked like he had just woken up. 'I've got to go to the bank tomorrow anyway.'

Evie laughed. Gordon always had to go to the bank tomorrow but never made it because the bank closed at 3:30, long before Gordon was out of bed.

'It's in the top drawer,' I said.

Gordon took a quarter of Leb from my top drawer and squeezed in next to Skunk, half under the desk, to roll a joint.

'Have you been to Mexico?' Skunk asked Kitty.

'No, I was on a kibbutz. The volunteers were having a Castenada phase.'

'Kitty had a gap year,' boasted Fysh.

'My grandfather founded a kibbutz.' I wished I knew its name. 'Maybe it was the same one.'

'I was at Kibbutz Galuyot,' she said. 'Right in the middle of Israel. Halfway between Jerusalem and Tel Aviv.'

'Did they have good hashish?' asked Fysh.

'Not as good as in Egypt.'

'You went to Egypt, too?' She was like one of those intrepid women adventurers you read about in the Sunday papers' books pages. 'Wasn't it dangerous?'

'It was. I nearly got raped by a cop.'

'What a scumbag,' said Evie.

'What happened?' Skunk wanted to know.

'I told him I understood his impression of Western women as cheap slappers, but this was just capitalist bullshit, just TV and advertising. I said I was an ordinary girl. I asked him to think of the women he knew – his mother, his sisters, his cousins. He wouldn't want this to happen to any of them, would he?'

'Too right,' said Evie.

'He went off the idea and went away. I was just glad I had good karma.'

'Karma?' repeated Skunk. 'Give us an example of this "karma".'

'That was an example.' Kitty's cheeks turned pink.

'Give us another.'

'Alright then. I was on a trip down south, to Luxor, and I got talking to the bus driver. He wouldn't let me buy a ticket. He was like, "That's okay, it's on me, man".'

'And that's it?'

'On the bus back to Cairo, there was this guy sitting next to me. He was friendly and cool, so at one of the stops I shared a doobie with him. At journey's end we said *salaam*, and he planted a little Judas kiss on my cheek. Seconds later, two cops appeared. They knew I was carrying ganja and said they were going to take me in. I gave them my money and luckily they got bored and waved me away. I binned my ganja and wondered how I was going to get to Cairo with no money. Then a bus pulled up. It was the same driver. He recognised me and let me travel free again. If that's not karma, I don't know what is.'

'That *is* karma,' Fysh confirmed.

'Has anyone seen my undies?' I needed to get up, to pee.

'I don't wear them,' said Skunk.

'Urgh.' Evie was disgusted.

Kitty got up to look for my undies and cast a furtive glance at Skunk. I tried to see Skunk's wild green eyes and Laurence Olivier nose, his defined jawline and athletic physique through Kitty's eyes. And still he looked like an angst-ridden ragamuffin.

'Come on,' said Fysh. He passed what was left of Kitty's joint to Skunk, handed Kitty her sombrero and put on his beret. 'You haven't seen my room in the top corridor.'

'Hold your horses.' Kitty wasn't to be rushed. 'I'm looking for a friend.'

'Welcome to the club,' said Fysh. When Fysh fancied a girl, self-pity and resentment were never far away. If she turned him down, he would blame someone else for queering his pitch. And if he did have his wicked way, he became obsessive and jealous.

'She's about my height, has blonde hair and dresses like a hippy chick,' said Kitty. 'We're both doing philosophy.'

'Sounds like your alter-ego,' said Skunk. 'Are you sure you're not imagining her?'

'Who is she?' Fysh liked the sound of another hippy chick. 'What's her name?'

'No, I'm not *imagining* her. She went to Dharamsala. She should be back by now.'

'She'll turn up.' Gordon passed his joint to Kitty. 'A person can't just disappear, can they?'

'Of course they can.' I was still thinking of you.

'She hasn't *disappeared*,' said Skunk, if only to contradict Gordon. 'You can't disappear if you haven't appeared in the first place.'

'Maybe she's still navigating her way round campus,' suggested Fysh.

'I don't think so,' replied Kitty in a withering tone. 'If she travelled to Dharamsala, on her own, I think she can find her way around a university campus.'

'Let's put out a missing-person bulletin.' Fysh cupped his hands into a megaphone. 'Hippy chick gone AWOL. Hippy chick gone AWOL.'

'Who are we talking about again?' I had lost the thread.

'My friend, Diana,' said Kitty.

'Diana' came out in a cloud of smoke.

Letter 3

You reappeared in Amsterdam, when I was down and out.

I was in the red-light district where a model in silk lingerie was exhibiting her charms in a small scarlet room halfway up a tall, gabled canal house, its French windows opened wide to an early-autumn night. She paced to and fro, attracting punters on the street below. The longer I gawped the harder my desire grew. 'You're here on business, not for pleasure,' I reminded myself. It was a Saturday night and the streets were packed. Red lights rippled in an inky canal, narrow residences wobbled. A humped bridge stood above its watery reflection to form a shimmering brick circle. The sounds of a bottle smashing and jeering voices prompted me to check I hadn't lost my passport. I was already worried about dodgy dealers and plainclothes cops. 'Pull yourself together,' I told myself. 'The biggest idiot could do it.' That's what Dad always said, though not about scoring a quarterweight of hash in Amsterdam. Soon enough I'd be back in Flat 22 having a laugh with my friends. It seemed like a long time since our crisis meeting in central space.

'I called a mate in Huyton and he said it's dry up there, too,' said Boney. Liverpool too was suffering a drought.

'Looks like I'll have to go to Amsterdam, then.' As Lumumba Slope's resident dealer, I had responsibilities to my customers.

'That's a great idea.' Evie put down her knitting and aimed a kick at Gordon, who was foraging at our feet for morsels to put in a pipe. 'Can I come?'

'Yeah,' I said. 'We could make out we're on honeymoon to put Customs off the scent.'

'I'll come,' said Skunk.

'No, you won't,' said Evie.

'You're broke,' I pointed out. 'And besides, you look too suspicious.'

'Hmmm. Well, bring back some smack while you're at it.'

'So what's the plan?' asked Evie.

'You don't need a *plan*,' tutted Skunk. 'Buy the hash, stash it in souvenirs, bring it home.'

'I'm looking forward to it already,' said Evie, and her knitting needles resumed their clicking.

Tick tick. Tick tick. Tick tick, went the cooker's little clock while I waited for Evie. I hadn't seen her all day and neither had her flatmates. At last, the front door opened. At last, we could get going.

'Thought I'd come to see you off,' said Vincent. 'What's wrong?'

'If Evie doesn't get here soon, we'll miss the ferry.'

'You been let down by your bird?'

'She's not my bird.'

'Story of your life, that is. Here, you'd better take this.' Vincent handed me his flick knife, which he had shown me how to use when we were flatmates.

'I'm not taking that.'

'You're such a pacifist, Jake.' Vincent pocketed his knife and gave my shoulder a 'bon voyage' punch. 'Don't come back empty-handed. We're relying on you.'

Tick tick. Tick tick. Tick tick. At last, the front door opened. At last, we could get going.

'You got an eighth, Jake?'

'No, John, I don't have an eighth. Nobody has an eighth. Come back the day after tomorrow, when I'm back from Amsterdam.'

Tick tick. Tick tick. Tick tick. Evie wasn't late. She wasn't coming at all.

'Speakeasy,' announced a nameplate above a narrow doorway to a converted warehouse. Murky orange light seeped round the edges of blackened windows. I was half-expecting to be asked for a password, to be uttered through a head-level grille, but the door pushed open and I descended a steep stairwell to a brick-walled basement. There I was met by a stoned buzz and Pink Floyd's spacey screams. Psychedelic patterns floated over dancing hippies, beatniks lolled on bean bags, chess players pored over a game. It was like a Dutch version of Flat 22.

A barman with a tattooed neck and rings in his nose handed me a menu. Silver haze sativa. Sinsemilla gold. White Russian indica. Durban poison. Thumbnail photos showed glistening buds dripping white and purple crystals.

'This is grass.' I didn't fancy smuggling a quarterweight of bulky, smelly grass through Customs. 'Don't you have any hash?'

He turned the menu over. Nepalese temple ball. Afghan black. Turkish black. Indian manali. Indian charas. Slate Rocky. Red Leb. Blond Leb.

Now we were talking. 'Hmmm.'

'What short of high you have in mind? Shoporific or pshychedelic? Hare Krishna or William Blake?' He pulled out a tray of samples that made my mouth water.

'It's not for smoking now. It's for export.'

'What?' The barman withdrew his samples. 'You want me arreshted? I don't know you. Get out of here!'

How many times had Vincent told me not to show my hand? Now I had done just that. Shocked by my stupidity, barely aware of an outside world and the strangeness of its people, I pounded ill-lit backstreets and crossed dainty bridges in search of another coffee shop.

A scent of burning hash drew me to a hidden doorway. Before I knew it, I was sharing a joint with two young Arabs. I coughed like a novice but carried on to be polite.

'That's good stuff.' To be honest, I was too disorientated to say whether it was good stuff or not. 'Do you know where I can get a quarterweight?' I was a serious player, not some kid after an eighth.

Never score from a dealer on the street. That was one of the first things you learned. You would wind up with an eighth of shoe polish or henna instead of a quarter of hash, or your 'dealer' would be an undercover cop. On the other hand, you weren't supposed to look a gift horse in the mouth. Opportunities had to be grasped. And besides, it was better to trust people than to go around in a constant state of suspicion. Better and more convenient.

My new pals invited me to join them. They seemed friendly enough, and they knew where they were going. Red lights and canals gave way to a concrete, residential neighbourhood.

'Where are we going?'

'You have dollars?'

'No, I have guilders.'

'How much guilders you have?'

I didn't want to tell them because that would be showing my hand. And besides, I hadn't figured out my budget. I still had to pay for accommodation, and a model in red. 'How much does a quarterweight cost?'

'What else you like, besides hash?'

'Acid. Coke. Opium.' I hoped I wouldn't have to sample them all.

'Where you from?'

'London. What about you? Are you twins?'

They exchanged glances. 'You have British passport?'

'Sure.' I checked my inside pocket.

'Show us.'

They flicked the passport's virgin pages, stopping to grin at my mugshot. 'They're going to run off with it,' I thought. 'Or they'll kidnap me and hold me to ransom.' When your fears are too preposterous to be plausible, you know you're being paranoid. They returned my passport like mates having a laugh.

'You have place to stay?'

'I don't, actually. Could I stay at your place?'

'Why, of course you may' was, it seemed to me, the gist of their response. The fraternity of stoners knew no strangers.

'Do you live nearby?'

We entered a deserted pedestrian underpass. I was surprised to see my friends checking the exits. I thought we were going to their place. Surely they didn't intend to do such a big deal out here, in a public space?

'Run!' A voice screamed in my head. But I stood my ground, to let fate take its course.

'Give us your wallet, and passport.' One of them held a knife between my legs.

I gave them my wallet and passport.

'And your shoes.'

'My shoes?' I screamed.

'Give them to us.'

'Why do you want my shoes?'

The knife between my legs twitched.

I hurled my shoes at them. Then I turned and ran faster than I'd ever run, stopping only when I reached a well-lit parade of shops, where I vomited on a pavement. Tears ran down my cheeks. I had almost been castrated, or murdered. Yet here I was, alive and unscathed. A moment of elation gave way to guilt. How feckless I was to arrive, at night, without sorting accommodation in advance. As for wilfully walking into an underpass with a pair of muggers, that was too shameful to think about. I had to focus on the present. I took off my socks and the road felt cold. I looked through shop windows, at a bakery's loaves and pastries, at a jewellery store's watches and rings and a hair salon's mannequins, all representing a world from which I was now excluded. I was facing a night full of tramps, drunks and junkies who would fight over scraps of food or a bench in a public park.

'Excuse me,' I began as a solitary, late-night pedestrian approached. 'I was wondering whether...'

He broke into a trot, as though scared of being mugged, or catching what I had.

'Come back! I need help!'

What I needed was help from the British consulate which, I hoped, would replace my passport, lend me some cash and provide me with a pair of shoes. All being well, I would be out of here in the morning. How good it was to be British!

My optimism diminished as a night of aimless wandering wore on. Britain's consular staff were hardly likely to treat a drugs tourist who has come a cropper as a matter requiring their urgent attention. I would have to wait my turn in a bureaucratic labyrinth. I could just see how it would go.

'Her Majesty's foreign office does have a policy of lending money to those who, through no fault of their own, find themselves stranded, but we are not a charity and we do need to be satisfied that the claim is genuine, and that the claimant is a bona-fide subject of the Crown.'

'My claim *is* genuine. And I *am* a bona-fide subject of the Crown. I've lived in England all my life. Can't you tell by my accent?'

'Furthermore, to be confident that the claimant is sincere in their stated intention of returning immediately to the United Kingdom, we need proof that they will embark on the first available passenger ferry or aeroplane...'

'Well there's nothing to keep me here. I've got no shoes, no money and nowhere to stay.' I didn't have any hash either.

'...pending prior approval from the relevant authorities, which is to say, Customs and Excise, the Home Office and...'

'Hang on a minute. How long's all that going to take?'

'That depends on the queue ahead of you.'

'How long is the queue?'

'It's not the queue's length so much as the complexity of individual cases that slow things down. One complex case can take longer to resolve than numerous straightforward cases.'

'How complex are the cases ahead of mine?'

'I am not at liberty to discuss other cases. That would be most improper.'

'Well how complex is my case?'

'We won't know that until it's processed.'

'When will that be?'

'That is hard to predict. We'll need a police report to verify your story. And we will need to interview you in person.'

'You can interview me now.'

'That would be jumping the queue. Now, why don't you leave a contact address with my secretary...'

'I don't have a contact address!'

'There is really no need to raise your voice.'

I had to lower my expectations, too. 'I don't suppose you could lend me a pair of size eights?'

They appeared as if from outer space, a pair of public phoneboxes. Zero called an English-speaking operator, who agreed to reverse the charges. Hearing the ring tone, I steeled myself for recriminations.

'Jacob! Is that you?'

The alarm in Dad's voice brought a lump to my throat. My eyes welled. How lucky I was to have my parents!

'Hi, Dad.' Stifling sobs, I tried to sound calm. 'I'm in Amsterdam.'

'What are you doing in Amsterdam?'

'Having a weekend away. Thought I'd check out some galleries and museums. Trouble is...'

'You're buying drugs, I suppose.' Dad always suspected the worst, even when half-asleep. Mum was busy fussing in the background, wishing I'd stick to the straight and narrow. She tried to wrest the phone from Dad, to ask where they went wrong.

'No, what happened was, I got mugged. Don't worry, I'm fine.'

'It's the company you keep. You've fallen in with a bad lot.'

'My friends have nothing to do with it. I'm here on my own.'

'You need your head examined.'

'They took my wallet, which had my money and boat tickets in it. So I was wondering whether you could wire the funds to get me home, please. Maybe if I got the address of a local post office, you could send a cheque or something.'

'Alright. But the bank's closed till Monday. And even then it might take a while for the transfer to clear. What about your passport?'

A flash of blue and white caught my eye. I said goodbye, hung up and dashed out of the booth to wave my arms. Never had seeing a police car made me so happy.

Two taciturn constables took me to their station, where I waited in a sterile room. After a while, a desk sergeant called me over to make a statement. Unfortunately I hadn't noticed my muggers' distinguishing features, I couldn't find the underpass on a map and I didn't know what I was doing there. The sergeant sympathised. Muggings were becoming more and more common, he said. It was normal. I had no cause for concern.

'I haven't got anywhere to stay.'

'You can stay with me.'

I could have wept at his hospitality. Until he led me down a flight of steps to an empty cell. A bright neon striplight illuminated a bare mattress and an iron bucket.

'I don't suppose you could switch off the light?'

'You don't suppose right. Go to sleep. You will feel better in the morning.' Then he locked me in, to make sure I wouldn't escape.

There was nothing to see through the bars except a big, round clock.

'4:07,' said the clock.

I lay on the mattress, closed my eyes, and was back in the underpass. I opened my eyes and I was there again, a knife between my legs. I got up and shook the bars. A cold floor rattled my bones. I went back to bed and tried to sleep, only to be mugged in the underpass. I was stuck in a loop of eternal recurrence.

'4:08,' said the clock.

If this were a novel, divine providence would intervene on my behalf. The desk sergeant would come down with my wallet and passport. Or I'd get a cellmate who had opium and a pipe. Or I'd wake up. But it wasn't a dream, it wasn't a novel and God was dead. And I had only myself to blame.

Then I heard your voice.

'In a cell, on a street, in central space: what does it matter where you are?'

You were so right. Suddenly I was free. I flew out of my cell and soared, over memories seen anew through your eyes.

Letter 4

'It's a beautiful day.'

There was hardly a cloud in the sky. The sun gleamed on silver train tracks, it shone on a quarrystone cottage, on hawthorn hedges and rambling shrubs, on magnolia blossoms and on Skunk, who was sitting on a bench, reading a Penguin Classic. A cat was sleeping under a signpost for Stancombe station. A blackbird sang from a sycamore tree.

'Yes, it is,' agreed Skunk.

'I wonder when the train's going to come.'

'What difference does it make?'

'We don't want to wait here all day.'

'Why not? It's as good a place as any.'

'Aren't we supposed to be going somewhere?' We had come here for a reason, surely. I went inside and rapped the ticket-office window. 'Hello? Is anyone home?' I was talking to my reflection. The place was deserted. Back on the platform I found a noticeboard filled by columns of numbers lined up in adjacent rows like a mathematical puzzle. 'What do these numbers mean?'

'It's a timetable,' said Skunk. The numbers represent arrivals and departures.'

'Oh. Well we haven't seen any arrivals *or* departures.' Still, I understood the principle. To know how long you had to wait for your train, you had to find its time of arrival then subtract the current time. I wondered what time it was.

An elderly gentleman was sitting on a bench, spine ramrod straight, fingers clasping a standing umbrella. His moustache bristled as he glared at my jacket. It was a cut-away Royal Navy jacket whose three gold chevrons made me a captain, if not an admiral.

'Excuse me. Do you know what time is?'

He must have thought I was having a laugh.

'I mean, do you know what *the* time is?'

'Do you not wear a wristwatch?'

'I gave it up, to be free.'

'For your information, it's 11:20.'

I returned to the timetable. Each column had a heading. *Monday to Friday. Saturday. Sunday.* In other words, you had to know what day it was.

'What day is it?'

'Good God, man! Do you mean to say you don't know what day of the week it is?'

'He gave up the calendar, too.' Skunk was being funny.

'It's all the same fucking day, man.'

'It's Sunday,' said the elderly gent, who evidently didn't like Sundays. 'June the twenty-second. Nineteen eighty...' The year was drowned out by a freight train.

'Oh, that's right. It's my birthday. Twenty-one today! Happy birthday to me, happy birthday to me. Happy biiirthday, dear Jay-ache...'

Were Skunk a normal friend, he would have joined in. But he wasn't, so he didn't. We had toasted my birthday that morning, celebrating in central space with a blotter of green-dolphin acid each. But I didn't get cards or presents, we didn't have a cake and nobody wanted a singalong.

'Waiting is hell but heaven is waiting,' said Skunk, looking pleased with his new aphorism, though neither half made much sense to me. If he was hoping to initiate a friendly chat with the elderly gentleman, he was out of luck: the old boy was ignoring us. Unperturbed, we smoked a joint and watched a middle-aged couple with matching shoulder-bags arrive.

A short, plump woman in a beige cardigan, laced shoes and a tartan skirt secured by a giant safety pin showed their tickets to the guard. Her partner, who was wearing an anorak and slacks, was trying to sneeze into a handkerchief. 'Ah, ah, ah...' Nothing. He put his hanky away, scratched a head of receding frizzy hair and caught up with his companion.

'Morning.' Skunk's salutation was premature. They hadn't got to us yet. 'Morning!' This time it sounded like a rebuke.

'Good morning,' replied the woman. 'It's a beautiful day.'

'That's what I said! I'm Jake. This is Skunk.'

'I'm Daphne. This is... Brian.' She didn't sound very sure about Brian, though they seemed well enough acquainted.

'Where are you going?' asked Skunk, with too much emphasis on the 'you'.

'Are you going to watch cricket?' Their matching bags were just the type of accessory people took to cricket. 'Are Wessex playing at the county ground? Hey, Skunk, do you fancy watching some cricket?'

'No, we're going to visit my sister-in-law in Poole,' said Daphne. 'She's been poorly for a while now. Where are you two off to?'

Skunk smiled vapidly, as though a grin were as good as a destination. He leaned over sideways to catch the sun round Daphne and Brian but leaned too far and fell off the bench.

'You have to make yourself stupid,' I said, to explain Skunk's behaviour. '"*Il faut s'abêtir.*" That's Pascal.'

Daphne checked her watch and Brian muttered something about a cup of tea.

'I could do with a cup of tea,' said Skunk, once he had resettled on his bench.

'We saw a kiosk on the forecourt, didn't we, Brian?'

'Well, then.' Skunk put down his book. 'Why don't you wait here while I get the teas?' He squinted at the exit as though sizing-up enemy lines.

'Oooh, I don't know,' said Daphne.

Brian was more forthright. 'You really shouldn't bother.'

'It's no *bother*,' said Skunk.

'We can get a cup of tea at Westbourne, or in Poole,' Daphne assured us. 'It's not as if we're dying of thirst.'

'Well I'm getting the teas in.' Skunk's mind was made up. 'But if you insist on being martyrs to politeness, I won't get any for you.'

'There's no call for that.' Brian stiffened his neck.

'Alright.' Daphne was game. 'White, no sugar please.'

'White, no sugar,' Skunk confirmed.

Brian cocked his head. 'A train's coming.'

The train's approach gave Skunk a dilemma. Make a dash for the kiosk, where a queue of punters, a chatty vendor or a slow-boiling kettle could mean missing the train, or play safe and stay where he was. Skunk sold the guard a dummy before disappearing through the exit.

The train ground to a halt and Daphne and Brian clambered aboard, without a 'goodbye,' a 'nice to meet you' or, my least favourite, 'take care'. Now *I* had a dilemma. Take the train or wait for Skunk?

He returns in time to see us depart, then gives chase along the platform like a ragged Anna Karenina. I extend my arm through a window. If only he could run a bit faster, our fingertips would touch. The platform gives way to a rubbish-strewn verge as the train gathers speed. The scenery turns verdant and Skunk recedes from view.

The guard's whistle brought me back. A carriage door slammed shut, an engine shrieked and the train shunted off. The last carriage was rounding a bend when Skunk reappeared, empty-handed.

'I thought you were getting the teas in?'

'Hmmm? I didn't have any money.'

'Where are your trainers?'

'Oh, I got rid of them.' He returned to his bench on bare feet and picked up his paperback.

'First Love. By Ivan Turgenev,' said a cover that pictured a nymph or dragonfly hovering over a lily pond.

'"Beware of love,"' read Skunk. '"Beware of the love of women. Beware of that ecstasy – that slow poison."'

Skunk's view of love was warped by his experience with the L-woman at school. Elle was his best friend's girlfriend, before Skunk inveigled himself into a menage-à-trois, which he thought would be a lasting arrangement, 'until I got hammered'. Regardless of Skunk and the L-woman, it was a nemesis in my own destiny that I glimpsed in Turgenev's warning.

A bespectacled jogger in a tracksuit stopped jogging on reaching us.

'Hello,' he said, smiling cheerfully.

'Hello,' we replied.

'Let me ask you a question,' he said. 'Have you ever thought about the kingdom of God?'

'Don't tell me. Jehovah's Witness, right?' Skunk sucked his cheeks. 'I don't fancy your chances in these parts.'

'Oh, you'd be surprised.' The jogger seemed buoyed by Skunk's pessimism. 'Lots of people are sceptical to start with but they do want to hear good news. That's what we do – we spread the good news.'

'What's the good news?' I asked.

The jogger's smile widened. 'Jesus is coming.'

'Oh. I thought you were going to say we're in for a hot summer. Or they've raised the student grant.'

He had more good news. 'And there is still time to repent. Now is the time to cast off Satan's influence. Now is the time to join our congregation of true worshippers in the kingdom of God. Before Armageddon engulfs us all.'

Skunk winced. 'You know the trouble with Christianity?'

'Well, Nietzsche calls it "a slave morality".'

'It preys on the vulnerable,' said Skunk.

'I wouldn't call it *preying* on the vulnerable.' The jogger was happy to correct Skunk's misconception. 'A lot of vulnerable people find comfort in Jesus.'

'That's just it,' argued Skunk. 'You exploit their loneliness. Convince Miss Homesick Student that Jesus loves her and before you know it she renounces her mum and dad. You know what Jesus said about setting son against father and daughter against mother? "He that has greater affection for his father or mother than for me is not worthy of me."'

'That's what a leader of a dodgy cult would say.'

'He also said, "Whoever hears my word will have eternal life,"' said the jogger.

'I don't *want* eternal life.' Skunk sounded like a child refusing a bribe.

Realising that Skunk was a lost cause, the jogger turned to me. 'Jesus is the light,' he said.

'How do you know that?' I felt compelled to make a stand for reason. 'Belief isn't knowledge.'

'It says so in the Holy Scriptures.'

'That's hardly empirical evidence.'

'Only through the ministrations of Jesus Christ will you be admitted to the Kingdom of God.'

'Imagine you've got it all wrong,' I said. 'And Christianity isn't the one and only truth. Then you'd be colonising souls for no reason.'

The jogger's smile wilted. 'Well... I...'

'How would it feel to have *that* on your conscience? All that time, you were conning vulnerable people.'

'There's no "con". I'm merely inviting you...'

'And I'm inviting you to focus on your own soul.'

The jogger sighed like a balloon deflating. He looked so crestfallen I thought he was going to throw himself on the tracks. I was relieved to see him settle for the waiting room.

'Well, he left with a flea in his ear,' said Skunk.

But the flea was in *my* ear. 'Now I feel guilty.'

'I don't see why. I'd have thought you more than anyone would resist proselytising Christians.'

'Because I'm Jewish, you mean?'

What was I, a spokesman for my ancestors? Judaism was a backward, superstitious cult. My parents identified with this secret society only when a Jewish name made the news, whereupon they'd take pride if it was a positive story or feel shame if that name was up to no good. I had no such allegiance. I was an existentialist.

I *was* an anarchist. The anarchists called me 'Hebrew Jake' because they already had Jake the Gnostic, who manufactured LSD in Wessex University's chemistry laboratories, and Punky Jake, who pushed EP Thompson off the stage, mid-speech, at a CND rally in Trafalgar Square. We convened on Monday evenings in an abandoned student-union office in a group consisting of compulsive-activist speed freaks, who plotted nocturnal raids on the university's secret research facilities, bourgeois utopians, who argued over the ideologies of Proudhon, Kropotkin and Malatesta, and Dada surrealists who put performance art before politics. We had anarcho-syndicalists, who occupied Stancombe House on behalf of Stancombe's homeless community, anarcho-feminists who screamed, 'You've got clitoris envy' at anyone wearing a necktie, and an existential nihilist faction, which was me. 'Let's picket high-street banks,' I said. 'And places of worship. And London Zoo.' Unfortunately we didn't have the operational capacity to put my visions into practise, but when Dr David Owen, former foreign secretary and co-founder of a notorious Gang of Four, addressed Wessex's student body in Steve Biko Hall, I led the way in hurling a fusillade of rotten tomatoes at his well-coiffed head. Dr Owen chased me out of the hall and down the stairs, yelling, 'Come back here, you little Trotskyite'. Dr Owen had it all wrong. 'I'm not a Trotskyite, I'm an anarchist!' I shouted back. The incident made national news and I would have been expelled had Wessex's administration or security officials identified me as the culprit. In my second year, when I lived in Westbourne with Vincent, my zealotry waned and one day I woke up to find I was no longer an anarchist. For what did I need a fixed conviction? I was a free man.

'4:09,' said the clock.

Letter 5

My parents' gramophone cabinet took me back. Sing Something Simple. Gracie Fields' Greatest Hits. The Pirates of Penzance. They were all lined up in a compartment under the record player but none ever saw the light of day. Likewise, on either side of a brass-framed mirror, a collection of leather-bound books that never left their shelves. My parents had gone on holiday, leaving Great-Aunt Flora upstairs with a minder and, in the kitchen, a well-stocked fridge.

The doorbell rang and there was Malcolm, in an Afghan coat. I had invited him over and forgotten all about it.

'You called earlier,' he said. 'You spoke to my mum. Said you were at Damsel Lane for the weekend.'

You'd think he was talking to an idiot, but I let him in and was helping him take off his coat when I pricked my thumb on his CND badge. I showed him the bead of blood and Malcolm reciprocated, both thumbs up.

'So, what brings you home?' he asked as we settled in the lounge. 'May I?' He picked up a lump of hash I'd left on the coffee table. 'Are you going to the Rock Against Racism rally?'

'I didn't know there's a Rock Against Racism rally.' I tried to imagine Skunk rocking against racism and wondered where he was. 'Where is it?'

'I thought Wessex was supposed to be radical. It's tomorrow morning, in Hyde Park. The Clash, Buzzcocks, Stiff Little Fingers... It's gonna be massive.'

I made us both a cup of tea and returned to find a stoned Malcolm.

'Sometimes I get paranoid,' he said. 'You know what I mean? I can be walking down the road and every taxi that passes, I think it's the pigs. Anyone who saw me running away would think I'm a right wally.'

'You'd better not do acid, then.'

'I've always wanted to try acid. My mate Steve did it once, said it was amazing. Have you got some?'

I showed him a blotter of two green dolphins, which he held in his palm as though expecting it to jump. Then, before I could stop him, he tore the serrated line and put a green dolphin in his mouth.

'This is the first time I've done acid,' he said.

I was going to wait for Skunk, but if Skunk wasn't going to make it, Malcolm would have to do. So I swallowed the remaining green dolphin and for a while we traded reminiscences and anecdotes about the old days.

Then Malcolm started to feel funny. 'How long does it last?' he wanted to know. 'My nan said LSD makes you crazy. And you're never the same again.'

'Oh, I wouldn't worry about that,' I advised him. 'I've done it loads of times.'

Malcolm ruffled the carpet and recoiled. 'Woahhh! The carpet's moving. How do you make it stop? I knew I was going to have a bad trip. It's too intense.'

'I'll see if we've got some orange juice,' I said.

'Ding dong, ding dong.'

I took my head out of the fridge and heard my parents' doorbell. It was probably a neighbour wanting a cup of sugar. I tried to remember the neighbours. They were probably someone else by now.

'Don't let them in,' pleaded Malcolm as the letter-box clattered.

I opened the front door and there he was, wild eyes darting this way and that, hair stuck to his scalp, cycling shorts falling apart. Skunk hauled his rucksack off his back, locked his bike and smiled triumphantly. Our embrace I kept brief on account of his sticky coating.

'Where have you been?'

'I didn't have a ticket,' he said, while making himself comfortable in an armchair. 'And a guard was checking everyone's legitimacy. So I biked it. All in all, it didn't take as long as I thought it would. I did get stuck in Croydon, mind. Or it might have been Penge.'

'Who are you?' asked Malcolm, from behind the coffee table. 'I don't like you.'

'That's good,' said Skunk.

'It's good to be honest,' I explained, though it sounded like an advertising slogan. 'This is Skunk, so called because of a hair dye he once tried, not because he smells. This is Malcolm. We were at school together.'

'Hello, Malcolm,' said Skunk.

'Why don't you leave?' Malcolm asked him.

'Why don't *you* leave?' Skunk was thinking of that parlour game where you're all in a balloon and you have to justify your presence before everyone votes on who should be thrown out of the balloon.

'I can't leave,' said Malcolm. 'I wish I could leave.'

'Nobody gets out of here alive, right?' Skunk tried to sympathise. 'Fuck, these green dolphins are strong...'

'No, no, no,' I said, with Malcolm – or Boney – in mind. 'They're weak as Watneys.'

'I can't tell the two of you apart,' moaned Malcolm. 'You're like two halves of the same person. I'm going to call Steve. Steve said I could call him if I'm tripping, any time.'

I showed Malcolm to the phone in the hall.

'How does it work?' he asked.

'Well, everyone has a number.'

'They do?' Malcolm didn't like that idea at all. 'What is a number, anyway?'

'Numbers are like letters,' Skunk explained from the lounge. 'But where letters form words, numbers form other numbers. And they go up and down instead of sideways.'

'What's Steve's number?' I asked, but Malcolm hadn't the foggiest. 'Well whose number do you know?'

'I know my mum's number. Three oh three, three nine, four nine.'

'*Now* we're getting somewhere.' If I sounded like Oliver Hardy, nobody seemed to notice. Malcolm repeated the digits, one at a time, while I dialled.

'Who are you calling?' Skunk had joined us at the phone stand, to lend a hand.

'Malcolm's mum.'

'Let me talk to her,' said Skunk.

'Oh, that'll help.'

We were several digits in when, distracted by Skunk, Malcolm lost his place and we had to start again. 'Three, oh, three,' Malcolm began, with Skunk repeating the numbers lest I hadn't heard them.

The call went through and after Malcolm shied away in horror, I held the handset to my ear and listened to it ring.

'What's your mum's name?' Skunk was still helping.

'Doreen.' Malcolm's face lit up.

'Doreen what?' Skunk wanted to know.

I tried to rehearse my conversation with Doreen but it was hard to concentrate with a ringing in one ear and Skunk in the other.

''ello.'

'Hello?'

'Ooza'?'

'Ah. You don't know me. I'm a friend of Malcolm's.'

'Fuck off!' The phone went dead.

'Who was it?' asked Skunk.

'He didn't say.'

'Let's try someone else.' Skunk fancied another go. 'Who else could we call?'

'How about the Samaritans?' I suggested.

'You can't call people from the Bible.' Skunk rolled his eyes at my stupidity.

'Not *those* Samaritans. It's a helpline for people who want to commit suicide.'

'Does Malcolm want to commit suicide?'

'Why would I do that?' asked Malcolm.

'Could be any number of reasons,' I said. 'You've been sucked into a vortex of dread? You're depressed by life's futility? You've fallen in love with the wrong girl?'

'The Torture Never Stops,' said Skunk, in reference to a Frank Zappa album.

That gave me an idea. 'How about some music? We've got Gilbert and Sullivan, Gracie Fields, Val Doonican...'

The lounge floor was tilting up and down like a small boat in a storm. The coffee table was rolling, side tables were sliding away from their moorings. A distant cabinet looked like shipwrecked flotsam. Still, I made it to the far side and opened the records compartment.

A golden hayseed couple were riding a wagon under a tangerine sky. 'Oklahoma!' proclaimed the sleeve in large, joined-up script. I put it on a dusty turntable and, hand trembling, placed a delicate stylus on track one.

Click, click, click. I must have scratched the vinyl. Undaunted, I replaced the stylus on track two.

'There's a bright golden haze on the meadow.
There's a bright golden haze on the meadow.
The corn is as high as an elephant's eye...
And it looks like it's climbing clear up to the skyyyyy...'

I took a deep breath and joined Gordon McCrae.

'Oh, what a beautiful moooorning,
Oh, what a beautiful daaaaaaay,
I got this feeling insiiiiiiiiiide me...'

All set for a contented '*Everything's going my waaaaaaay,*' I noticed a pitiful figure slumped over the coffee table.

'Malcolm! Malcolm!' I shook his shoulders, slapped his face and tried to find his pulse. I hoped he wouldn't need mouth-to-mouth resuscitation. Malcolm opened his eyes as if struck by the same fear. I was so relieved, I could have kissed him.

'Give him some of this.' Skunk pulled a bottle of Bushmills from his bag.

'Oh, that's a brilliant idea.'

Malcolm rose, a zombie from the dead, and walked out.

'I hope he comes back,' I said. 'If anything happens to him, it's on me.'

'Where have you been?' asked Skunk on Malcolm's return.

'Lots of places.' Malcolm cracked a crooked smile. Having got one over on Skunk, he settled down beside the coffee table and was soon holding his crotch, sucking his thumb and humming tunelessly.

'*Chicks and sheep and geese better scurry,*
When I take you out in the surrey...'

I was bobbing along to Oklahoma! when I perceived a stranger in our midst.

A matronly woman in hair rollers, dressing gown and slippers was standing in the doorway with an arms-folded, 'what's all this, then?' demeanour. Surely we couldn't be in the wrong home? No, it was matron who was in the wrong home. The weird thing was, I had no memory of letting her in. She must have shimmied up a drainpipe then climbed through an upstairs window. I was wondering whether I was hallucinating when it came to me. My parents had gone on holiday, leaving Great-Aunt Flora with a minder. Matron was the minder.

'I'm Mary,' she said.

'Hello, Mary,' said Skunk.

'Sure your parents said you might be paying us a visit.' She thought Skunk was me. 'Lovely couple, your parents, lovely.'

'They're *my* parents, actually. I'm Jake.'

'Oh, it's you, is it?'

'Mary's looking after Great-Aunt Flora, aren't you, Mary? How is she doing?'

'What's wrong with your friend?'

'You mean Malcolm?' Usually it was Skunk.

Mary cocked her head at Skunk. 'What's that you're hiding there? Is it a bottle of holy water?'

'Well, it's a bottle of Bushmills.'

'Why didn't you say so? I'll get some glasses from the kitchen. Would you all be having ice or do you take it straight?'

'On the rocks, please,' said Skunk.

'I don't drink whisky.' Alcohol made me dyspeptic, and drunk.

'Don't be so soft,' said Mary. 'What sort of idiot doesn't drink whisky?'

Mary fetched glasses from the kitchen and poured trebles, or quadruples, all round, though not for Malcolm. 'I daresay he's had one too many as it is,' she said. 'To peace on Earth.'

'Your health,' said Skunk.

I drained my tumbler in one, lest Mary think me an idiot.

Mary switched on the TV, turned up the volume to drown out Oklahoma! and plonked herself next to me on the sofa. 'Oooh, I don't like him,' she said of Bruce Forsyth. 'Too smarmy by half. And would you look at those dancing girls? Have they no shame?' We watched the shameless dancing girls complete their routine then Mary got up and changed the channel. 'Oh, that's... whathisname. I can't stand him. What time does the snooker start?' Mary consulted her watch. 'I want to see Hurricane Higgins. I mean the other chap, the other fella, he might be world champion but Hurricane Higgins is the people's champion. He's overcome a lot of adversity to get there, so he has. Who's ready for another?' Mary switched off the TV and poured herself another. 'All the girls like Hurricane Higgins.'

'What girls?' asked Skunk.

'My pals in the convent.'

'Are you a nun?' Skunk was like a little boy meeting a fireman.

'Sure I was Sister Bernadette at the Convent of the Holy Mother of our Lord Jesus Christ for thirty-seven years. Then...'

Malcolm belched. 'I want to go back to the womb.'

'What did he say?' Mary leaned forward. 'I didn't catch it.'

'He wants to go back to the womb,' said Skunk, as though Malcolm was planning his summer holidays.

'It's all my fault.' I felt nauseous. 'I gave him a green dolphin.'

'I don't know why you blame yourself,' said Skunk.

'Look at him! What if his nan is right and he never recovers?'

'You are your brother's keeper,' said Mary. '"Where is your brother?" That's the question God will ask.'

'You'd think God would know,' said Skunk.

'Is that how you speak of our Lord? You are a blasphemous young man, so you are. God asks the question because He wants to hear what Jake has to say for himself. God knows where Malcolm is.'

'You can say that again,' said Skunk.

'And unlike you, Jake accepts his guilt.'

'Jake doesn't *accept* guilt. He *acquires* it, like a collector. But a court of law can't find you guilty if you're not of sound mind.'

'What's wrong with his mind?' Mary gave me a once over for signs of mental cracks.

'He feels guilty, that's what's wrong with his mind. He lets his conscience bully him instead of standing up for himself.'

'A good man listens to his conscience. Your conscience is the voice of God.'

'No, it's not,' said Skunk. 'If you have a conscience, you put it there yourself.'

Mary pulled a face. 'What are you saying? Have you no sense of perspective? Your conscience... it's God's way of telling you right from wrong, good from evil...'

'*If* God exists...,' argued Skunk, 'then the difference between good and evil is His problem. And if He doesn't exist, there *is* no difference between good and evil.'

'Would you wash out your mouth with a bar of soap.'

'If you insist on being good, do so for its own sake, not to stake a place in God's favour,' Skunk continued. 'If goodness is simply a means to ingratiate yourself with God, then it's not good, it's evil.'

'Have you considered repentance?'

'Why should he repent?' countered Skunk.

'Not him, *you.*'

'What have *I* done?'

'The sinner who repents is closer to God than the man who has never sinned.' Mary got up and refilled her glass. 'A nightcap for the road,' she said as she yawned with arms outstretched, though she was only going upstairs. The argument was over, much to Skunk's disappointment. 'I trust you'll be having a peaceful night,' she added doubtfully.

'Goodnight, Mary,' said Skunk. Then he turned to Malcolm. 'This should be easy to resolve. I can't help feeling, there's a solution just round the corner.'

A sickening silence was amplified by a click, click, click as Oklahoma! went round and round. My parents' lounge, that went round and round too.

I awoke in a stuffy bedroom that reeked like a dormitory. My mouth was parched, my head ached. For a moment I thought it was winter, and I'd forgotten to switch off the radiator. No, I was fully dressed, in my parents' bed, with Skunk. I looked again, and there behind Skunk, was a sleeping Malcolm.

'What are we doing here?'

'Depends what you mean by "here,"' said Skunk. 'I didn't know where else to put us after you threw up on the rug and passed out, leaving me to clean up the vomit. I'm going to make coffee.' He clambered over me and went round the bed rather than disturb Malcolm.

I was inspecting a fuzzy face, blurry eyes and cracked tongue in a split-screen mirror courtesy of Mum's dressing table when Skunk returned with three steaming mugs on a tray.

'How's he doing?'

'Shhh. He's still asleep.'

'No, I'm not,' said Malcolm. 'I can hear every word you're saying.'

'And how are we this morning?' asked Skunk. 'How about a nice mug of coffee?'

Malcolm threw off the blankets, almost knocking his mug of coffee off Dad's bedside table. For all his wan, red-eyed dishevelment, Malcolm exuded a new sense of purpose. 'I'm going home.'

'You're not drinking your coffee,' scolded Skunk while Malcolm got himself together. 'What about some breakfast? I was thinking of a fry-up.'

Malcolm didn't want a fry-up or anything else for breakfast. Nor would he let me help him on with his coat. And to my offer of an eighth of hash, 'to take home as a souvenir,' as Skunk put it, he said, 'I never want to set eyes on drugs again.' In which respect you might say I had performed a good deed.

On sunny summer mornings, while our ivy-clad residence cast its shadow over barely visible bushes beneath lounge and kitchen windows, the front garden showed off. Butter-yellow daffodils and blood-crimson tulips, fiery orange hollyhocks, lavender hydrangeas and pink rose trees formed a carnival of colours around an antique black lamppost that stood erect as an ornament to propriety on a circular lawn. A horseshoe drive glistened in the sunshine.

'It's no good,' said Malcolm of the gravel at his feet. 'It's still moving.'

We followed him to a bus stop down the road, where we hid behind an advert for Harmony hairspray. 'I hope Doreen's home,' I whispered to Skunk. 'We don't want to leave him on his own.'

'She should be home on a Sunday morning. Unless she goes to church.' Skunk turned to the Harmony girl. 'Hey, Malcolm. Does your mother go to church?'

Malcolm flagged down a bus and vaulted up its stairs. We sat a few rows behind him. When we stopped at traffic lights on Feltbridge Broadway, Malcolm got up to get off and we tumbled down the stairs in warm pursuit.

I wished he wouldn't walk so fast as we crossed the high street and headed down a tree-lined avenue of terraced houses. I was getting indigestion.

'Anyone would think he was trying to lose us,' said Skunk, before Malcolm disappeared at a break in a row of front-garden hedges.

We ran the final straight and found a woman in an apron standing outside an open front door.

'You must be Doreen,' said Skunk.

'And you must be Jake. Did you have a good night?'

'"*Oh, the farmer and the cowman should be friends...*," I began but my stomach was playing up, Skunk was too self-conscious to join in and without instrumental backing it wasn't the same.

'I thought you were going to the Rock Against Racism concert,' said Doreen. 'What's wrong with Malcolm? He looked queasy.'

Skunk laughed amicably. 'I'm amazed he looks as good as he does.'

'It's drugs, isn't it? Malcolm!' She called up the stairs then turned back to us. 'What happened?'

'Well,' said Skunk. 'Malcolm was catatonic, Jake was paralytic, and Mary was nowhere to be seen. So I put us in Jake's parents' bed, though not Mary, obviously. Mary's a nun.'

'I wish you boys wouldn't experiment with drugs. I've seen what damage they can do. I don't know how many times I've warned Malcolm to be careful. Drugs can make you schizophrenic.' Doreen lit a cigarette.

'Have you got any chicken soup?' I asked. 'Not for me. For Malcolm. Give him a bowl of chicken soup and he'll be right as rain.'

'What's right about rain?' Skunk couldn't let a cliché pass unchallenged.

'You'd know if you lived in a desert.'

'The desert is Jake's metaphysical habitat,' Skunk told Doreen.

'Skunk's habitat is a swamp,' I said.

'If this is what you've done to Malcolm...'

'It's because I'm from Africa and Jake's an Israelite,' Skunk explained.

'You can say "Jew,"' I said.

'Yes, I can say "Jew". But you're less a shtetl-dweller than an ancient Hebrew, crossing a wilderness in search of Israel.'

'You should see a doctor,' said Doreen.

'Oh, it's just a hangover,' I assured her. 'Could I use your toilet?'

'He won't be long,' promised Skunk. 'It's not as if he's going to be jacking up heroin. Tell you what,' he said. 'Why doesn't Jake have a shit, I'll put the kettle on and we can all have a nice...'

'You're stark staring crazy, both of you.'

'Hang on,' said Skunk, to a firmly closed door. 'We haven't had coffee! And Jake hasn't had a shit!'

Back at Damsel Lane, Hurricane Higgins was compiling a break, barely pausing between pots in an atmosphere thick with tension.

'How about some breakfast?' asked Skunk.

'Shhh.' Mary was concentrating on the snooker.

Skunk lowered his voice. 'Eggs and bacon?'

Higgins missed a long red and Mary jolted back in her armchair. 'Now look what you've done,' she said, as though Skunk's idea of breakfast had put Higgins off his shot, but Skunk was already in the kitchen, slamming doors and clanging pots and pans. When Steve Davis, the other fella, took his place at the table, Mary took the opportunity to stare at me.

I tried to think of something to say but it was too early for a theological argument and I was too hungover for small talk.

'You possess a special power,' said Mary. 'One day you will be called upon and a great responsibility will fall on your shoulders. And when the time comes, I hope you will have the gumption to act as a leader of men.'

I wasn't one to ponder over my future, and Mary was barely qualified to predict it, but her words prompted a rush of questions. When would the time come? What sort of gumption did I need? Who was I going to lead?

For a second opinion I went to the kitchen, where Skunk was trying to adapt to electric hobs.

'Mary's off her head,' he said admiringly. 'She thinks you're going to be the messiah.'

Flat 22 was a picture of domestic bliss. Up in the kitchen, Junkie Simon was cooking a curry while Faye cut up a line of speed. Down three steps in central space, Boney was dozing, Evie was knitting and Gordon was playing chess. I could tell from the smell they'd been smoking black hash. They were listening to one of my Grateful Dead bootlegs (Rainbow Theatre, October 3, 1981, a rare UK show and scene of my first acid trip), even though I wasn't there. Dirty mugs and full ashtrays, torn Rizla packets and open books, naked cassette tapes and a bottle of ketchup, an art pad, an ordinance survey map, a hairbrush and a bicycle lamp were scattered across the table as if to welcome me home.

'We thought you were dead,' said Junkie Simon, after a slow double-take. A drugs peddler of no fixed abode and Flat 22's most honoured guest, Junkie Simon turned up at any time, day or night, spouting incoherently. He jacked up in central space, or in Gordon's groovy pad if he wanted some privacy, and passed out wherever he happened to be. He didn't want to hear the Grateful Dead when we could be listening to Joy Division, and he didn't know how we could live in such a pigsty, but he stayed for days and was happy to pitch when there were chores to be done.

'I'm soooo sorry,' shrieked Evie. 'I got my days mixed up. Are you alright?'

'I got mugged.' At last, I could say it.

'I *knew* it.' Evie rushed up the steps for a hug.

'*I* got mugged,' said Junkie Simon. 'About a year ago. In Gladstone Square I think it was.'

'Occupational hazard,' said Boney.

'It was my own fault,' I had to admit.

'When you didn't come straight back, I felt so guilty I went to see Father O'Malley,' said Evie. 'I told him all about you.'

'What d'you do that for?' I had never heard of Father O'Malley.

'I didn't know if we'd ever see you again. Father O'Malley told me to pray for you.'

'Makes it all worthwhile, like,' muttered Boney.

'He invited me into his living room and we sat in armchairs round the fireplace,' said Evie. 'It was really nice, actually. Father O'Malley got out a bottle of brandy and read passages from the Bible. I never knew there were so many crazy characters in the Old Testament.'

'Where's Skunk?'

Nobody had a clue.

I found him in Kitty's room in Luxembourg Village, reading a paperback on her bed to a breathy backdrop of Peruvian pan pipes. It was typical Skunk: befriend a gullible first year, exploit her goodwill and occupy her space. Kitty was too naïve to see through him and too polite to kick him out. She was studying at her desk in a long white T-shirt that said, 'Just Visiting' over a spacey picture of planet Earth. A framed photo on the windowsill showed Kitty in sunglasses alongside a tanned, horsey-faced athlete.

Skunk rolled onto his side. 'Where have you been?'

'Amsterdam.'

'What, all this time?'

'I got mugged.'

'How did that happen?'

'I was testing a theory.'

'What was the theory?'

'It's better to trust people than be suspicious.'

Kitty nodded in agreement.

'And it isn't, I take it?'

'The world's a dodgy place. I'm not going back there in a hurry. I was lucky to find a Salvation Army hostel. Then at least I could kill time playing chess with my fellow-dossers. The worst thing was sharing a dormitory at night. It could have been a TB ward, there was so much coughing and gurgling, to say nothing of non-stop snoring, and wanking. Plus I was worried that someone would steal my shit. Then I remembered: I didn't have any shit to steal.'

Skunk laughed. 'Sometimes nothing's a mighty cool hand.'

'I did get these, from a cupboard in the hostel.' I raised a foot to show off my new, second-hand Dutch loafers.

'Very nice,' said Kitty.

'Do you fancy a game of tennis?' I asked Skunk.

'Tennis?' echoed Kitty.

In the summer holidays we played several times a week on a court in Luxembourg Village, hoping that Junkie Simon's cocaine would enhance our game. In reality it only enhanced our edginess and Skunk's tantrums. On the other hand, the joints we smoked to remove the edge had us playing shots in slow motion or laughing at random absurdities, which was not conducive to good tennis.

'It's going to rain,' said Skunk.

'It's not going to *rain*.' Kitty had caught the habit of contradicting Skunk.

'It's bound to rain if we play tennis,' said Skunk.

Kitty looked through the window. 'They're not *rain* clouds, are they?'

In lieu of a game of tennis, I flicked through Kitty's records. 'English hippy,' said The Hangman's Beautiful Daughter. 'International bohemian,' said the Liberation Music Orchestra. 'Borrowed from Fysh,' said The Twelve Dreams of Dr Sardonicus. A portrait of Napoleon illustrated Beethoven's Emperor concerto. A landscape of rolling fields advertised Vaughan Williams. 'To Kitty, love Diana,' read an inscription on Death and the Maiden.

'What's this?' I asked of an album that pictured Mahler gazing into space. The sleeve notes of *Lieder eines fahrenden*

Gesellen were too small to read. And even if you had a magnifying glass, it was all in German.

'Songs of a Wayfarer,' said Kitty. 'Shall we put it on next?'

'Anything would be better than Peruvian pan pipes,' Skunk was saying when he was interrupted by a knock on the door.

'Come in!' Kitty adopted the proprietorial posture of an expectant hostess, to Skunk's evident irritation. The door opened and she screamed in delight. 'I thought you'd got stranded, or lost, or kidnapped. When did you get here? Does Verity know you're here?'

Diana was very pretty. She had tropical blue eyes set off by a nut-brown tan, exquisite cheekbones that matched a well-defined jawline, a straight, perfectly angled little nose and a resolute, no-nonsense chin. Her lips pouted as though forming an involuntary kiss. Honey-blonde tresses cascaded around a long, aristocratic neck. A scarlet shawl and maroon sari clothed a slender figure in an exotic outfit that added a transcendental aura to her intensity. From pink bandana to orange clogs, she was dressed in shades of red. Even her mirror-studded bag was violet and crimson. She looked like she'd stepped off a magic carpet.

'Skunk, Jake... meet Diana.'

She sat on the floor, her stoned eyes barely acknowledging Skunk or me but staking her claim to Kitty's attention while disregarding her old friend's fuss. 'Carlos sends his love,' she said while rolling a joint, her elegant fingers moving impatiently.

'Carlos!' echoed Kitty. 'How *is* Carlos?'

'Same as ever. Said he'd get me a job in Barcelona if it doesn't work out down here. He drove me down in his car.'

No magic carpet, then.

'Where are you bivouacked?' asked Kitty.

'What's it called, again? Guevara House?'

'I lived in Guevara House in my first year,' I said. It was fate dressed up as coincidence. 'What's your room number?'

'Twenty-nine.' Diana threw me half a glance.

'I used to be in thirty-seven. That's just round the corner. And I heard you're doing philosophy. What course are you on?'

This, said Diana's face, was exactly the sort of student bonhomie she had hoped to avoid. 'Metaphysics (Descartes to Kant), with Leonard Cricklemore,' she said. 'And a supplementary course on European Theology.'

'*I* did Metaphysics with Cricklemore. He used to be a monk. Now he's a neo-Platonist.'

'I didn't *want* to do Metaphysics but it was all they had left.'

'Me neither. We had to write about John Locke's theory of personal identity with particular reference to his Essay Concerning Human Understanding. I wrote about Michelangelo Antonioni's theory of personal identity with particular reference to The Passenger.'

'Jake's a movie buff,' Kitty told her thoroughly disinterested friend.

'According to Cricklemore, I do a lifelike impersonation of an idiot,' I boasted, primarily to Skunk, who knew what he meant.

'*Boomshanka, boumboulay,*' said Diana, to bless the joint. She inhaled through her fist, chillum-style, then passed it to me, with no eye contact. 'It's Manali,' she said.

A single toke knocked me sideways.

'How was India?' Kitty wanted to hear all about it. 'It must have been amazing. Did it match your expectations?'

'Oh yes, India,' said Skunk. 'That explains the uniform.'

'Uniform?' echoed Kitty, in sing-song indignation. 'It's not a *uniform.*'

'Uniformity is good,' said Diana. 'Uniformity reminds us we are one. Everyone wears red in an ashram.'

'Why red?' asked Skunk.

'Red is the colour of passion,' said Diana, with cold certainty.

'What's an ashram?' Two hits of Diana's joint left me lagging behind. A third launched me into a new here and now. I looked up and found a stunningly beautiful girl sitting in front of me, just inches away. I'd never seen such deep-blue eyes.

'It's a Sannyasin commune.' She was talking to me. 'I'm a Sannyasin.'

'Really?' I didn't know what a Sannyasin was but I recognised her misplaced zealotry. 'I was an anarchist.'

'Tell them about David Owen,' said Skunk.

'Who's David Owen?' Diana asked Kitty.

'Politician,' scoffed Kitty.

'Jake threw squishy tomatoes at him,' said Skunk.

'Why?' Kitty wasn't one for student politics.

'He already told you,' tutted Skunk. 'He was an anarchist.'

I gave them an account of the David Owen incident, taking in the history of anarchism, including quotations from Kropotkin ('Where there is authority, there is no freedom') and Proudhon ('Property is theft') and references to the Paris Commune and the Spanish civil war, with an aside on finding squishy tomatoes at the co-op, but for all Skunk's titters of support, Kitty wasn't interested and Diana was wondering where she was.

I was trying to remember *what* she was. 'What did you say you are again?'

'A Sann-yasin.' Kitty answered for her.

'What's a Sann-yasin?'

'Sannyasins are followers of the Bhagwan Shree Rajneesh.' Diana straightened her back. 'We travel from all over the world to Poona, to be with Bhagwan.'

'And you went to Dharamsala,' Kitty reminded her.

'That's up north. I trekked through Mother India for three days, on trains so crowded you had to sit on the roof or hang from carriage doors.'

'Have you got any photos?'

Diana pulled a face. I was so uncool.

'I mean photos of India. The Taj Mahal, Goa beach, the hell-hole of Calcutta...'

'It wasn't a package tour,' tutted Kitty.

'My camera was stolen. But that's okay. My pictures are in here.' Diana put a hand over her heart. 'Anyway, I'm going back as soon as I can.'

'But you've only just got here.' Kitty spoke my mind.

'My real life is in the Him-*are*-leeahs. Only Westerners say "Himalayas".' Diana smiled at our ignorance. 'I feel their pull.'

'What do you do there?' I could have been my dad.

'It's not about *doing*. It's about being.'

'I see...' I could have been my mum.

'How was Kibbutz Galuyot?' Diana asked Kitty.

'Excellent.' Kitty smiled at her memories. 'I worked in the orange groves, picking oranges, and there were some really *simpatico* volunteers. We had wild toga parties and went on a mind-blowing trip to the Sinai desert.'

'Oh yeah, you told me in your letter,' said Diana. 'Your *compadres* had magic mushrooms stashed in a jar of honey.'

'You don't get magic mushrooms in the Middle East,' objected Skunk. 'You're more likely to get...'

'Excuse me...,' frowned Kitty. 'Have you ever been to the Middle East?'

'You don't have to go to places to know about them.'

Kitty raised her eyebrows. 'You're only saying that because you haven't been anywhere.'

'Yeah, I have. I was born in the Tropics. I used to live in Kenya.'

'Only until you were two. That hardly makes you Marco Polo. You don't even speak any languages.'

My pounding heart took a new direction as I belatedly recognised the truth. Skunk and Kitty were sleeping together! I felt foolish for missing the signs and betrayed for not being told. Now I was an outsider, just when I wanted to show Diana I was an insider.

'Carlos left me the car.' Diana pulled a key on a fob from her bag. 'He said I could keep it.'

'You've got a car?' Skunk was all ears. A car needed taking for a spin. Skunk took Emily's Ford Fiesta for a spin and pranged it on a bollard. 'What make is it?'

'What? Mini Clubman, I think.'

'She's not going to let *you* drive it,' I told Skunk.

'Why not?'

'You haven't got a driving licence.'

'Driving's a piece of piss.'

'And you're not insured.'

'You're such an anarchist,' said Skunk.

'If you get stopped by the police, which is quite likely, they'll want to see your driving licence. When you say you haven't got one, they'll search you and find whatever drugs you're carrying. Then you'll get busted and Diana's car will be impounded. And Diana will get charged with something too.' And I would feel guilty for not stopping him.

Skunk flinched at my scenario while Diana remained unmoved. Kitty sighed and lit a Camel, a picture of forbearance. The pan pipes' dirge had finished but nobody felt like putting on something else. I tried to think of something to say to Diana, but nothing came to mind, or nothing appropriate at any rate.

'Well, I just popped in to say hello.' Diana gathered herself to leave. 'I've got to go to the library.'

'I could show you the library,' I thought, though I had never mastered the library's microfiche filing system and I couldn't borrow books because I lacked the right pass.

'Have you got a reading list?' asked Kitty. 'We're probably doing the same books in European Theology.'

'I don't care about reading lists,' said Diana. 'I want to see what they've got on Bhagwan.'

Kitty rose to see her out, they clasped in a half-hearted embrace and Diana was gone.

Now I could breathe, and review my situation. I fancied Diana so badly I couldn't think of anything else. Even Skunk's affair with Kitty seemed irrelevant.

'She didn't seem very pleased to see you,' Skunk told Kitty.

'It was *you* she wasn't pleased to see,' countered Kitty.

Skunk laughed and Kitty looked me in the eye, as though daring me to seduce Diana.

Letter 7

'Diana Farquharson' jumped out from a grid of pigeonholes. I was hoping to find her in person, though it was hard to imagine Diana among the Philosophy common room's Boy George lookalikes, Marxist literature and agitprop posters. She evidently hadn't checked her pigeonhole, which was stuffed full of flyers. Under my own name I found an envelope addressed by my personal tutor, no doubt lamenting my absence from tutorials. I put it back in its hole and bought a ham roll and cup of coffee from a booth in the corner.

Numerous Guardians were scattered across the common room, like it was a one-newspaper state. 'Israel's shame in Lebanon,' read a headline, beside a cartoon depicting Israeli soldiers as Nazi stormtroopers. Focused as I was on finding Diana, I didn't have the time, inclination or sense of self to consider The Guardian's calumny. Which didn't mean I forgot it.

The Tuesday market downstairs occupied both sides of a drag that stretched from Philosophy porter's lodge to Union Square, the whole area now scented by ganja, incense and samosas. The weekly market was a popular source of records and books, bongs and pipes, second-hand clothes and vegan cuisine. Skunk had asked me to look out for Coltrane's Africa/Brass after Boney had smeared Marmite on Skunk's copy and I was happy to comply because Africa/Brass was my favourite Coltrane album.

'Do you have anything by the Mahavishnu Orchestra?' I asked a leather-clad record vendor. 'Or Shakti? What about Ravi Shankar?' Diana was bound to like Indian music.

'Only what's in the box, mate. If it's not there, you can come back next week.'

'*You don't know what love is,*' wailed a bluesman.

Bertrand Russell's History of Western Philosophy stood out, in all its voluminous glory, among an array of books displayed, spines up, across a rectangle of tables. We disliked Bertie (as Skunk called him) because his small-minded rebuttals of Freddie (as Skunk called Nietzsche) tainted Nietzsche's reputation for two generations. Nonetheless, I flicked through his History of Western Philosophy in search of a pithy quotation for Diana. Finding nothing but long-winded exegeses, I tried to remember what I had learned from Prof Cricklemore's course in my first year. Kant's transcendental idealism... Berkeley's subjective empiricism... Hume's rational scepticism... They all led to the same conclusion: we don't really exist.

The sun caught her honey-blonde locks and bright scarlet shawl. She was standing erect across the rectangle, reading a small book like a woman at prayer.

I pushed my way through a crowd of browsers and sidled up to the gorgeous first-year.

'Hey, Diana. I was just thinking about you.'

'Hi there. Do you know where they're having a meeting for first-year philosophy students?'

'No, I don't. You should check your pigeonhole in the common room.'

'Doesn't matter. I'm sure my personal tutor can fill me in. I've got Remy Sachs. You don't know where he lives, do you?'

'I've no idea. Probably in Westbourne, or one of its bourgie suburbs. Why?'

'Don't tutors have, I don't know, cocktail parties for their students?'

Diana had fallen for a classic transference fantasy. She was in Remy Sachs's home, curtains drawn against an autumn wind, log fire blazing, sipping port with her tutor, hanging on to his every word. This, the prelude to her seduction, roused a jealousy I didn't know was there.

'I'd give Remy Sachs a wide berth if I were you.'

'Oh? And why is that?' She flicked her hair and closed her shawl.

'He's infamous for fucking his prettiest students.' So went the rumour at any rate. Either way, I had let Diana know that I fancied her. That was the main thing.

'Maybe I want to fuck him. I'd rather get involved with a mature academic than with some possessive student.'

I took her words as a compliment. We had only just met and she was already sharing her most personal misconceptions.

'"Love does not claim possession but gives freedom,"' she read from her little book. 'Have you ever read Rabindranath Tagore?'

'No,' I said, and I opened my History of Western Philosophy in search of a riposte. We were like spies in a Hitchcock movie, perusing second-hand books as a front for their undeclared love.

'Namaste.' The bookseller steepled his fingers at Diana. His stoned eyes, brown skin and old kaftan were those of a kindred spirit. 'I've got The Home and The World somewhere.'

Diana glowered. 'How dare you ingratiate yourself with me, you obsequious little man,' said her eyes. He could have been an urchin in a teeming Indian city drawn to her European eminence. She put down her book and merged into a busy drag.

'What do you reckon?' The bookseller turned to me.

'She's just got back from India.'

'Do you want it or not?'

He was talking about the History of Western Philosophy. 'Certainly not.' I had half a mind to tell him what we thought of Bertrand Russell, but the other half took priority.

'Where are you going?' I caught up with Diana at the porter's lodge.

'Why must I be going to someplace in particular?'

'No reason. A lot of people do, though. Go someplace in particular, I mean.'

'I'm just walking. That's when I get my best ideas.'

'I get my best ideas when I'm talking to someone.'

'I talk to myself.'

'Say, Diana. Have you still got some of that Manali?'

'For God's sake.'

'We could go to your room for a smoke.'

'You spend all your time smoking dope and sleeping around. It's such a cliché.'

'That's not all I do.'

'I wasn't talking about you so much as Kitty. She never used to be like this. It feels like I don't even... Do you know them?'

A cadre of Socialist Workers was milling outside the coffee shop. I didn't recognise their faces but the donkey jackets and lapel badges, Doc Martens and buzzcuts were the same every year. I glared at them out of habit; anarchists reserved particular contempt for the Socialist Workers Party.

'Yeah, they're Socialist Workers Party. Shall we go inside? They do good chips at the coffee shop.'

I looked through the window for a friend or at least an acquaintance to whom I could introduce Diana. A short, long-haired character in a shapeless jacket looked back. I tried to see my reflection through Diana's eyes, but Diana was inscrutable.

'I'm fasting,' she said, and instead of going to the coffee shop we resumed our stroll, crunching leaves underfoot.

'Why are you fasting? You're not Jewish, are you?' Autumn was the season of Yom Kippur. 'You don't look Jewish.'

'Once a week I go without food for a day. It reminds me of the excess and privilege into which I was born by a random act of luck, when so many people have no access to the most basic necessities. I call it Abstinence Tuesdays.'

'I don't get round to eating quite often.'

Diana quickened her pace. My dysfunctional attitude to eating had nothing in common with her principled sacrifice. Yet it seemed to me that our characters overlapped.

'We only eat because we have to, because we're animals,' I said. 'I'd rather be a spirit.'

Diana stopped still, to assess my sincerity. She too would rather be a spirit. We resumed our stroll in tandem, as though sharing a destination.

The Meeting House looked like a turret that wanted to be a rocket. Elevated on stone stilts, its round walls were marked by archers' apertures beneath a conical roof painted green to blend in with the local trees. Its stained-glass windows' abstract, nonecumenical design showcased a commitment to inclusivity and equal standing for all known religions. But the surrounding trees had grown so big they hid the nonecumenical windows, which could only be seen from the inside.

'Hare Krishna meetings,' read Diana from a free-standing noticeboard outside a pair of glass doors.

'Hare Krishna, Hare Krishna, Krishna Krishna, Hare Hare...'

A bald, ponytailed tambourinist in a tangerine robe leads a column of chanting, barefoot monks on a march, or rather amble, towards Piccadilly Circus. We're stuck on Regent Street, in a gridlock, on a sweltering August day. 'Can I join the Hari Krishnas?' I ask Dad, who swears under his breath and winds up his window.

'Meditation... Vegetarian food... Guest lectures...' Diana announced a list of attractions, her voice rising in excitement. 'This week it's "The Road to Enlightenment". I'm going inside for details. See you later.'

A grassy hill bisected by a wide flight of shallow steps led up to a three-storey, red-brick library. The building had a hyperbolic, paraboloid roof, to symbolise our mental contortions. Not that you could actually see the roof, unless you were flying.

The philosophy section on the top floor was known for its comfy armchairs and, under 'Ontology to Phenomenology,' its panoramic view of Stancombe Woods. You could spend hours here, gazing through the window, watching nature's colours mingle while mulling over life's challenges and meanings. Forest greens and aquamarines, golds and ochres, russets and coppers and clarets and plums brought Stancombe Woods to life. 'See you later,' she said. Unlike 'see you soon,' which pointed to a vague time that might never happen, 'see you later' carried a confident ring of certainty. 'Later' was sooner than soon. Rising and falling, the skyline of Stancombe Woods formed the contours of a woman.

Letter 8

The Rialto's illuminated twin towers rose above Westbourne's skyline like Notre-Dame over Paris. Its peeling colonnades and stucco walls recalled an Edwardian heyday of rowdy music halls and packed picture-houses. A faded burgundy carpet led through a once-magnificent porch to a pair of hefty doors. 'Repulsion' and 'Cul-de-Sac' were written in red plastic capital letters in the 'Now Showing' slot. Instead of a Polanski double bill, we should have gone to see An Officer and a Gentleman at the Odeon.

On a traditional first date you kiss and cuddle in fraught hopes of a night of passion. Such was the spirit in which I asked Diana out. But the way things transpired, our date fell short of the stereotype, though I did have the fraught hopes.

At the top of a rickety flight of stairs, an usher checked our tickets and parted a pair of satin drapes. A sloping crescent of antiquated seats faced a stage shut down by a heavy curtain. Kind of Blue accompanied a hush of anticipation. I acknowledged a couple of regulars, we found adjacent seats in the front row and I rolled a joint with Diana's super-strong Manali. Already-dim lights went out and Miles Davis faded into silence.

An attractive blonde holds an elderly client's hand. She's at work in a beauty parlour. The Girl nods off, mid-manicure.

Diana smiles at the Girl's absent-mindedness.

'Have you fallen asleep?' asks the client. 'I think you must be in love or something.'

'Ha!' Diana exclaims at an exterior shot. 'That's South Kensington High Street.'

The Girl treads the streets of mid-Sixties London sporting a free-wheeling mini-skirt. A leering workman importunes her for 'some of the other'. She flinches on a man's touch.

Diana is riveted by the Girl's other-worldliness. I pass her the joint.

A pushy suitor kisses the Girl. She wipes her mouth, brushes her teeth and goes to bed. We linger on a vagina-shaped crack in the pavement. A trio of old-time street musicians playing banjo and spoons cross a busy road. Nuns throw a ball in a walled-off garden. Clocks tick in her apartment.

Diana gives back the joint.

Her sister is fucking her fancy man. Hearing them through a wall, she smothers her face in a pillow. Left alone, she sees a man's reflection in a mirror. She barricades herself in her room, and hears footsteps.

Diana shifts in her seat.

She switches on a light. A wall cracks. Her imaginary intruder rapes her. Her suitor breaks in. He wants to be with her all of the time. He turns his back and she bashes his head with a candlestick holder, again and again. She receives a postcard showing a phallic Tower of Pisa and a reminder to pay the rent. Then her lecherous landlord arrives.

Diana's absence was ruining my concentration. I assumed she had gone to the loo. I hoped she wouldn't ask for an update on the action.

The Girl takes a razor blade to her landlord.

And still there was no sign of Diana.

She was downstairs, watching traffic through the foyer's double doors. She clocked my presence then turned her back. 'You could have warned me.'

'Come on. It hasn't finished yet.'

'Go watch the rest of it then.'

'And after Repulsion there's Cul-de-Sac. You might prefer Cul-de-Sac.'

'I need a drink.'

Seagulls squawked overhead as we crossed the road to the Crown and Anchor as though barely acquainted. Diana gave the barman a pound note for a lemonade with orange juice and waited for her change while I asked for a half of Directors and a packet of cheese & onion crisps. Her scarlet shawl, maroon sari and mauve tights seemed more conspicuous than ever.

'Oi, sugar tits,' leered a bloke whose naked bum was flopping over his trousers and onto his bar stool. 'Come over 'ere, luv.'

I showed Diana into a snug and directed a glare that was more of a glance at bum cheeks. I hoped he didn't want a fight. I was already hoping Diana didn't want a fight. She certainly didn't want a conversation.

There were no signs of a thaw as we returned to campus in Diana's Mini Clubman. I wanted to point out the snooker hall where Vincent and I used to play all night, and the bikers' café where we had fry-ups for breakfast, and the army recruitment centre, which the anarchists picketed during the Falklands War, and the Church of the Holy Trinity, where I was going to marry Fran Mullens in an anarchist wedding before we cancelled the ceremony, and our honeymoon in Berlin, due to Fran's homosexuality, but Diana was in no mood for my assortment of student reminiscences.

I tried to see the town through Diana's eyes: a typically rundown English seaside resort with a grand Victorian station and a mock-Tudor quarter of bijou shops, twisting lanes of gentrified cottages and, in a descending line to the seafront, tawdry 'Vacancy' signs flashing in bed-and-breakfast windows and gaps between promenade hotels that yielded nothing but darkness.

Back in Lumumba Slope car park, a chaste goodnight kiss signalled a sorry end to my fraught, misplaced hopes.

Letter 9

'I bumped into Self-Made Man in the library. "Aye-oop, lad. Where were you and t'other one on Fraaadeh?"'

'What did you say to that?'

'I said, "I am the other one".'

This was true. Skunk was supposed to be studying natural science, not philosophy, but he didn't see why he shouldn't attend – or not attend – the most interesting shows, so he accompanied me to my Modern European Mind tutorials. Prof Illiplay, or 'CM,' as Skunk called him, had trouble telling us apart, especially when we wore each other's jacket.

'He said CM's going to put us on the dean's list if we don't show up this week.'

'He can't do that to you.'

'I'm already on the dean's list, on the natural-science side. At least I used to be. I might be on another list now.'

'What is a dean's list anyway?'

'If you're on a dean's list, you have to go get your knuckles rapped. Not literally,' he laughed. 'It's not a Victorian workhouse. Your dean just asks why you haven't been writing any essays or going to any... oh, shit!'

'What?'

'It's Fraaadeh tomorrow.'

'Oh, shit!' I agreed. 'What is it this week?'

'The Brothers Karamazov.'

'Ha! It *would* be the longest book. Well there's no point going to the show if we haven't read it.'

'We've still got tonight.'

'I suppose I could read the first half and you could read the second half. Then we could tell each other...'

'It's not in two parts. It's not the Bible.'

'Well how are we going to read seven hundred pages before tomorrow morning?'

'I've got some sulphates.'

'Oh, great.'

'Come on. It'll take your mind off Diana.'

My mind *was* off Diana. It had been for about two minutes. I had knocked on her door, checked the Philosophy common room and spied on Remy Sachs, and still I couldn't find her. I asked Kitty whether she had seen her, probably several times, prompting laughter from whoever else was there. She had probably copped off with some pseudo-mystic chancer in her tutorial group or a fucked-up Sannyasin she'd met at the Meeting House. There again, she might have had an accident. She could be lying unvisited in a hospital ward, or dead in Westbourne morgue. She could have returned to the Himalayas for all I knew. Meanwhile I was pretending I didn't fancy her. 'It's nice to see you so enamoured,' said Evie.

'And we like Dostoevsky.'

'You know what will happen. We'll stay up all night, lose track of time and miss the show. Or we'll make it to the show and be too wired to remember our position.' Tutorials were like stage productions. You had to remember who you were supposed to be.

We left Flat 22 at 9:23 the following morning, pausing only to observe Skunk's stricken bike, whose wheels Fysh had mangled in a rage brought on by Skunk's alliance with Kitty – a self-defeating act of sabotage given that Fysh rode it more than anyone. Lightning cracked a ridge of black clouds. A growl of thunder preceded a splatter of rain then a downpour sent allcomers scurrying for cover, except Skunk, who was hallucinating.

'You just missed him,' he said, on a rain-lashed path behind the Meeting House. 'He went that way.'

'Who did?'

'The Devil. He's just round that bend.'

'Come on,' I shouted. 'We're going to be late.'

I found shelter alongside several steaming students at the Philosophy porter's lodge. It was then that I saw Grushenka, the prostitute, heading towards a Centre for Advanced Psychology. Clutching her crinoline and petticoats, holding her bonnet against wind and rain, she climbed a flight of steps then looked over her shoulder, doubtless in fear of Dmitry, who was out to give her a hiding. She stuffed into her cleavage Dmitry's promissory note, which old man Karamazov had gone to great pains to acquire as a gift to Grushenka in hope of winning her hand, despite her cruelty in playing father against son. Old man Karamazov had been murdered and Grushenka felt guilty. Lightning flashed, thunder rumbled.

'Grushenka!' I yelled. 'Come back! It wasn't your fault!'

Not hearing me in the storm, she entered the Sigmund Freud wing and that was the last I saw of Grushenka. Meanwhile Skunk was thrusting his way, against the tide, through a crowd of students who had covered their heads with books, folders and bags.

Prof Illiplay leaned back in his swivel chair, hands clasped behind his head, legs crossed on a desk too big for his study. He was dressed in his trademark uniform of plaid jacket with patched elbows, starched denim jeans and suede Hush Puppies. On this side of the desk, Self-Made Man, Jethro and Siobhan were sitting so close their knees almost touched.

'Sorry we're late,' we said.

'Sorry about the rain,' said Prof Illiplay, to be sympathetic. Or sarcastic. Or omnipotent. It was hard to tell.

'We don't mind getting wet,' said Skunk. 'Not if it's for a good cause.'

'Ehhh. Talk about drowned rats.' Self-Made Man retracted his chair to let us through, though not fast enough to escape our drips as we made our way to adjoining seats under a window battered by rain.

Jethro looked even more anxious than usual. He had probably been up all night at Nightline, where he provided company for lonely insomniacs in a padded hospitality suite in Luxembourg House. Jethro's shiny black slip-on shoes and trousers that extended halfway up his chest, his string vest and transparent lavender shirt, its armpits darkened by damp patches, added a series of sartorial eccentricities to his pudding-bowl haircut and lugubrious demeanour.

Siobhan hid behind a low fringe of long black hair and a full-sleeved, ankle-length dress. Siobhan wasn't one to speak, or even raise her head, but she wrote the best essays. Waiting outside Prof Illiplay's study before a show, Siobhan once told me about her life in the Plymouth Brethren. As Siobhan recalled her past in a barely audible voice, I couldn't help but notice her baby-blue eyes, crimson mouth and porcelain complexion. After that I regarded her, in private, as sexy Siobhan.

'We haven't seen you two for a while,' said Prof Illiplay. 'I take it you come prepared?'

'Oh yes.' My Brothers Karamazov was now filled with asterisks, arrows, circles and annotations. 'Oh, fuck!' I had left it in central space.

Skunk winced and ground his teeth. Busy conducting a dialogue of his own, he nodded at a thought then smiled at another. 'What?' He looked around to take in his whereabouts. 'Sorry. Caught napping in the trenches.'

'We were talking about humanism.' Self-Made Man was keen to get on. 'In the words of Thomas Mann...,' he ran a finger down a page of his notebook. '"We don't love qualities, we love persons, sometimes by reason of their defects as well as..."'

'Hang on a minute,' said Skunk. 'Why are we talking about humanism?'

'I don't mind talking about humanism,' I said, to make amends for forgetting my Brothers Karamazov. 'The highest form of humanism is...' I paused, for rhetorical effect, and forgot which of my sayings I was quoting.

'Misanthropy,' said Skunk in a loud whisper.

'Right. The highest form of humanism is misanthropy.'

'What *are* you going on about?' Self-Made Man threw a look of despair at Prof Illiplay.

'The humanist becomes misanthropic,' I argued, 'because real people don't live up to his ideal of humanity.'

'That's not a humanist, lad. That's a cynic.'

'One could argue it from the other end.' Prof Illiplay swivelled his chair and extracted a book from his shelf. 'In the words of Jonathan Swift, "I hate and despise the animal called mankind, but I like the occasional Tom, Dick, and Harry."'

'I wouldn't trust a humanist,' said Skunk.

'Go on, then.' Self-Made Man rolled his eyes. 'Why wouldn't you trust a humanist?'

'Humanism is just pity.'

''Ere we go. The Neechee boys are back in town.'

'And pity is just compassion, with a twist of empathy.' Skunk jiggled his foot. 'But the main attribute of pity is hypocrisy. The humanist feels superior to the sufferer. This superiority he calls "good fortune," as in, "there but for the grace of God go I". The humanist wants to salve his conscience and *advertise his virtue.*' Skunk raised his voice above Self-Made Man's objections. 'Humanists don't even have to know the sufferer to feel compassion. In fact it's the impersonal touch that gives compassion such a good name. Compassion means "suffering with". It's not by actual suffering but by "suffering with" that you affirm your humanity. (Though I must say, I don't see why tears are more human than laughter.)'

'Have you quite..?' Prof Illiplay tried to get a word in.

'Pity doesn't get out of the armchair. It doesn't *live.* It sends a cheque in the post. It's only through the suffering of others that pity experiences life at all.'

'Can we get back to the Mann?' Prof Illiplay tried again.

'Pity is Zarathustra's last temptation, it's... What man?' Skunk's foot stopped jigging.

'For our latecomers' benefit...,' Prof Illiplay induced a little bow from Skunk, '...we're looking at The Magic Mountain, with particular reference to Thomas Mann's humanism.'

I felt nauseous. 'What about The Brothers Karamazov?'

'That was last week. It's a pity you missed it, given your self-image as existential outlaws. We talked about Dostoevsky's place in the consciousness of modern Europe. Do you put the murder of Old Man Karamazov in a context of patricide in Freud, the death of God in Nietzsche or a prevailing anarchy which, according to Dostoevsky, invariably accompanies a breakdown of traditional, devoted lives? Do you think you can manage four thousand words by this time next week?'

Yes, we nodded.

'Good. Now let's talk about The Magic Mountain.' Prof Illiplay sat on his desk, legs dangling, Magic Mountain in hand. 'Some call it a *Bildungsroman*, confined though the hero is to a sanatorium. Would you agree that...?'

'I would rather not talk about The Magic Mountain,' I said.

'You haven't read it, have you?' Self-Made Man scented an early knockout.

'Oh, I've read it.'

'We read it in the summer holidays,' Skunk confirmed.

'I thought you'd like T'Magic Mountain. It's Neechee with a human faaace.'

'It's certainly true that Nietzsche was a big influence on Mann.' Prof Illiplay crossed his legs. 'Where do we see that influence in The Magic Mountain?'

Self-Made Man inhaled and leaned back to marshal his thoughts. 'The essence of T'Magic Mountain, the central message, is: master your suffering.'

'What do *you* know about mastering your suffering?' Skunk asked him.

'We're not talking about me, lad. We're talking about poor old Hans Castorp in the sanatorium.' Self-Made Man consulted his notes. 'Hans has to "accept life with joyful affirmation in spite of all its..."'

'The Magic Mountain isn't about mastering your suffering,' I said, with as much contempt as I could muster. 'It's about justifying antisemitism, at the dawn of Nazi Germany.'

All heads turned towards Prof Illiplay, who was stroking his chin. 'And how do you support this bold claim?' he asked me.

'He's trying to be controversial,' said Self-Made Man.

'There's no justification for antisemitism.' Jethro could have been at Nightline, where it was important to say the right thing.

'The Jews are God's chosen people,' said Siobhan. 'Jesus told the Samaritans, "You don't know who you're worshipping. We Jews know the God we worship, and through one of us, God will save the world."' Siobhan looked directly at me, as though it were through me that God was going to save the world.

My mind took me back to a decrepit little synagogue in south London. It was Yom Kippur and Papa was in his element, whether greeting fellow congregants in gravel-throated Yiddish, reciting responses to the cantor's choruses or belting out the big numbers like Mario Lanza in a prayer shawl. I stayed by his side, sitting when he sat, standing when he stood, turning the page of my *siddur* when he turned the page of his. At the same time I tried to make sense of prayers translated into English on alternate pages. Why would God want to be worshipped? Why would people want to worship Him? What was everyone thinking?

Papa put me in the picture. 'It is by the Almighty's benevolent providence,' he said, 'that we live at a time of our third Jewish commonwealth. King David's dynasty ruled Jerusalem for more than four hundred years. Then the Babylonians destroyed Solomon's Temple and took the Jews to Babylon as slaves. When

King Cyrus of Persia set us free, we returned to Jerusalem to rebuild our nation. This second Jewish commonwealth survived until the Romans sent their legions to destroy the Second Temple and expel us from our land. For two-thousand years after that we lived like nomads lamenting our exile. Now, by the greatest miracle, our ancient tribe is returning to Zion.'

Papa told me how he and his younger brother Isaac ran away from their home in a shtetl near Bialystok to escape the drunken peasants who murdered their parents during a pogrom. For month after month the two boys travelled by foot, through the Russian and Ottoman empires, two young Zionist pioneers, hiding from strangers, stealing fruit from orchards, washing in streams. 'Eventually we reached *eretz Yisrael,* where there were swamps to be drained, fields to be ploughed and fortified settlements to be built. It was while redeeming God's promised land that Isaac, may his name be blessed, died of malaria. Shortly after that I met Dina, a lovely Sephardi girl, in Haifa. When I put her in the family way, her father went berserk, even though I fully intended to do the honourable thing and marry her. There was no place to hide from her vengeful, powerful father and so, once again, I had to run for my life. I stowed away on a boat and, luckily enough, it took me not to Hamburg, Rotterdam or Marseille but to Cardiff. And there...,' he said with a proud smile, 'Chaim Grynberg became Henry Green.'

Papa told me too about his pals in the congregation. Morrie Gilbert, once a senior partner in an international law firm, did a four-year stretch for embezzlement. Benny Shapiro, once a pianist in Gene Krupa's big band, had his American visa revoked for associating with communists. Louis Ashkenazi was in Auschwitz.

'Are you alright?' asked Jethro.

I was trying not to cry. '*You* tell them.' I nudged Skunk in the ribs.

'Alright then. Tell them what?'

'Tell them about The Magic Mountain.'

'Oh, that's right. Climb the magic mountain, so to speak. Well, our hero, Hans Castorp, has two mentors, who represent the two sides of European civilisation. In the goodness-and-light corner there's Settembrini, who personifies virtue, wisdom and enlightenment. (The writer writing about himself, you might say.) In the darkness-and-evil corner, there's Naphta, a cunning, subversive Jew.'

'Hold up,' said Self-Made Man. 'As I recall, Naphta converts to Christianity.'

'A Jew is a Jew, whatever he converts to,' said Skunk. 'Ask the victims of Nazi Germany if you don't believe me. In this case he's actually a paradigm of the Jewish people. The way Mann writes it, Naphta's conversion represents a treachery innate in Jews. And that's just the start of it. The whole setup is a demonisation of the Jewish race.'

'Surely Mann's narrative illustrates Europe's historic antipathy to Jews, rather than any prejudice of his own,' suggested Prof Illiplay.

'Thomas Mann wasn't a Nazi.' Self-Made Man landed another blow. 'He went into exile in America to get away from the Nazis.'

I got up, took Prof Illiplay's Magic Mountain out of his hands and searched its pages for incriminating evidence.

'We didn't bring our Magic Mountains,' said Skunk. 'We thought it was The Brothers Karamazov.' He held up his Brothers Karamazov and a chunk of pages fell out. While Jethro helped pick up and collate the pages, Skunk took the opportunity to revisit some of his favourite lines. 'This is what Smerdyakov thinks of Ivan...,' he began, chuckling like a warm-up man distracting the punters during an unforeseen hiatus.

I took a deep breath and cleared my throat. 'Page four hundred and fifty. "*Naphta... began to speak of the devout excesses manifested by pious souls in the Middle Ages, astounding cases of fanatic devotion and ecstasy in the care of the sick: kings' daughters kissing the stinking wounds of lepers, voluntarily exposing themselves to contagion and calling the ulcers they received their 'roses'; or drinking the water that had been used for the cleansing of abscesses, and vowing that nothing had ever tasted so good."*

'"Settembrini made as though he would vomit. It was not so much, he said, the physically disgusting element in these tales that turned his stomach as the monstrous lunacy which betrayed itself in such a conception of the love of humanity."'

'And what conclusion do you draw from that?' asked Prof Illiplay.

'The Jew's love of humanity is enough to turn a decent man's stomach,' answered Skunk.

'The Jew is a monstrous lunatic!' I was shocked by Prof Illiplay's indifference.

'It's just a book,' said Prof Illiplay.

'You can't say that,' said Skunk. 'You might as well throw up your hands in resignation.'

'It's not as if we're talking Shahlock or Fehgin,' argued Self-Made Man.

'They're just outdated stereotypes,' I snapped. 'Naphta represents a universal prototype, which is far worse.'

'You can see what Mann's doing,' said Skunk. 'He's trying to absolve Christianity of its own sinful history by blaming the Jews, that is, the Christians' victims.'

'He vilifies the Jewish race by casting his Jew as the Devil,' I explained. 'Just like The Guardian vilifies Jews by portraying Israelis as Nazis. They're such cunts.'

'There's no call for that, lad.'

'Think of the zeitgeist,' said Skunk. 'Mann is writing in Weimar Germany.'

'I wouldn't have you down as a structuralist.' Prof Illiplay tried to lighten the mood. 'One could certainly argue that Mann's humanism is influenced by a stream of Christian mysticism that dates back to Meister Eckhart. In this context, the Christian world...'

'You mean the world whose calendar starts with the birth of Jesus?' I'd had enough of the Christian world. 'The world that counts its history backwards until it starts counting forwards? Some of us don't recognise that history. For some of us it's not the twentieth century at all.'

'When is it, then?' asked Jethro.

'It's the fifty-eighth century.' According to Papa, in the Jewish calendar the year was five thousand, seven hundred and twenty something, and that was several years ago.

Self-Made Man nodded ironically. Jethro looked confused. Siobhan bowed her head.

'Ehhh. The lad thinks the whole world's against him.'

'Have you ever considered positive thinking?' Jethro leaned forward and blinked nervously. 'Research shows that banishing negativity can be highly therapeutic.'

'I think we're getting off the point,' said Prof Illiplay. 'Have you calmed down?' he asked me.

'Yes, thank you.' Now my indignation seemed like an affectation, a contrived, overwrought performance like those of Dostoevsky's maniacs, staged for light entertainment.

'If you're so Jewish...,' said Self-Made Man, '...how come I've seen you scoffing bacon butties in t'coffee shop?'

'You are such a fucking idiot!'

The truth stung. Proper Jews didn't eat bacon butties. I was guilty, not of being a Jew, but of not being a Jew. All this time I had been carrying on like a free man instead of upholding the traditions of my tribe. My head throbbed, from a night of snorting sulphates, or the pull of my ancestral roots.

Letter 10

We were getting ready to host a party. Fysh was making magic-mushroom tea, Gordon was playing chess with a disinterested Boney and I was reading Remembrance of Things Past, or 'In Search of Lost Time,' as Skunk called it, though to be honest, Proust's blockbuster was easier to put down than it was to pick up, and I was thinking about Diana. Surely even a recluse such as Diana wouldn't miss a Bonfire Night party in Flat 22. At any moment she might appear in the kitchen, where Faye was dancing and Skunk was loitering in his underpants.

Gordon opened the window to a whiff of cordite. On every whoosh, sparkle or bang, Gordon craned his neck for a better view then reeled himself in. 'When I was a kid, we used to make a Guy out of old newspapers and shout, "Penny for the Guy!" at passers-by,' he said. 'You don't get that anymore. It's not even called Guy Fawkes Night anymore.'

'Guy Fawkes was innocent,' said Boney. 'The Gunpowder Plot was an anti-Catholic conspiracy. It's a well-known fact, like.'

'I loved her,' said Proust. 'I was sorry not to have had the time and inspiration to insult her, to do her some injury, to force her to keep some memory of me.'

A wave of nausea coursed through me, which was to be expected after a cup of disgusting mushroom tea.

'*Oh Lord, please give us a helping hand,*' sang Hendrix.

'This is Quasi.' Skunk sounded like a bashful schoolgirl presenting a new boyfriend to her parents. 'It's short for Quasimodo. Quasi used to be an enforcer for a Hell's Angels' chapter in Amsterdam.' Now he was Skunk's supplier of sulphates. Skunk beamed in admiration and pulled a wedgie out of his underpants. His own underpants, that is.

Quasi's pink eyes stared at Gordon's game of chess from a pock-marked face framed by greasy ginger hair. '*H, A, T, E*' was tattooed on his pork-sausage fingers. He leaned over Gordon and the hand of hate took Boney's pawn with a knight.

'I can't take his pawn.' Gordon angrily replaced Boney's pawn and his own knight. 'That would upset my whole strategy, which is to put pressure on the centre, thereby not ceding any ground to his fianchettoed bishop, which could pose a threat on the long diagonal if I don't negate it with my pawns.'

Quasi straightened up and collided with the ceiling. The whole flat shook. Crouching in the kitchen, he found a fellow speed freak in Faye.

'Do you live here?' asked a swirl of black lipstick, pink powder and purple kohl.

'Yes, he does.' Skunk, now dressed for the occasion in a Hawkwind T-shirt and cycling shorts, answered for me.

'I'm Tracy. This is Jackie.'

'Hell is other people.' Skunk's *bon mot* was premature. We were still on the small talk.

'Are you enjoying yourself?' asked Jackie.

'Why should he be enjoying himself?' answered Skunk.

'He doesn't look like he's enjoying himself.'

'Why are you playing chess?' Tracy asked Gordon.

'I often ask myself the same thing,' laughed Gordon. Encouraged by this unexpected interest, Gordon slid back his chair. Maybe Tracy, or Jackie, wanted to sit on his lap.

'It's not much of a party, is it?' said Tracy.

Skunk laughed so hard he scared the hell out of both of them.

'They're on drugs,' said Jackie, *sotto voce.*

'We'll come back another time,' said Tracy.

'That won't work,' Skunk shouted after them.

'Wait! Where are you going?' Gordon's hopes of a shag went with them.

Up in the kitchen, a flickering Nutty John was passing a pipe to Smiley Dave, who was laughing with Faye, who was talking to people I couldn't see behind Fysh, who was entertaining Penelope. You could tell it was Penelope by her ever-present Jackie Kennedy shades and cashmere cardigan, worn with its arms knotted loosely under her throat. A beautiful Greek alumna of a Swiss finishing school, Penelope was known throughout campus for her regal poise, voluptuous figure and seductive voice. High-society friends took her to premieres at the Rialto, to nightclubs patronised by celebrities and yachting galas at Westbourne marina. Low-society friends took her to parties at Flat 22.

'Woof,' I barked. 'Woof, woof. Woof, woof, woof.' I rose on my hind legs but nobody took any notice.

A flash of scarlet changed everything. Why did Diana have to appear right now? I couldn't speak to her now, not when I was a dog. What if she didn't like dogs? 'You're being ridiculous,' I told myself. 'Everybody likes dogs.' To be on the safe side, I locked myself in the toilet.

'Who's going to Stowe?' Evie was rounding up suspects. 'Come on, it's the biggest bonfire in Europe. There's a train in twelve minutes.'

'Not the train! Is everyone going? I can't move.' Gordon was caught in several minds.

The toilet wasn't what it was. Back in the day, a naked red bulb cast a festive, yuletide glow over Christmas cards on the cistern, a Santa Claus hat on the doorpeg and tinsel and balloons arranged in clusters overhead. You could practically hear, 'Hark the herald, angels sing, glory to the newborn king'. Now it was a purgatory in orange. The balloons were deflated like used condoms, broken streamers flapped in the draught and Santa's hat could have been a dead rat. The door didn't lock, the window wouldn't close and the temperature hardly rose above freezing. And above a stained basin, a cracked mirror could tempt you into a never-ending spiral of introspection.

Central space was quiet. Everyone had gone to the biggest bonfire in Europe, except Skunk. I joined him at the table, wishing I had gone too, with Diana.

'You're thinking about *her* again, aren't you?'

'Who?'

'You're in love, Jake.'

His words were charged with meaning. 'You' meant I was on my own. 'In' meant a sticky situation. 'Love' meant it was serious.

'You're a slave to the passions.'

'It's reason that's a slave to the passions, not me.'

'It wouldn't be so bad if she was your type. I mean, don't you think she's a bit... Aryan?'

'She's not Aryan. She's Apollonian.'

'She seems quite Teutonic to me.'

'Yeah, she's a regular Brünnhilde. You should hear her singing arias from The Ring Cycle.'

'You know what Freddie says about miscegenation.'

'I'm not planning on marrying her. I'm not going to have her children.'

'You can't be in love with someone who wears only red.'

'What's wrong with red?'

'You're deliberately missing the point. It's dressing to order that's weird.'

'Everyone dresses to some sort of order.'

Skunk rolled his eyes. 'Who is this Bhagwan, anyway? I've never heard of him.'

'He's a guru. That's short for "gullible are you". He's my new *bête noire.*'

'You should count yourself lucky to have one.'

'I checked him out in the library, with a first-year's help on the microfiche front. He looks like a right charlatan with his long white hair, straggly beard and knitted hat. According to a sociologist at the Sorbonne, he's a charismatic genius with a narcissistic personality disorder.'

'Typical mystic. What does he preach?'

'From what I could make out, it's Eastern mysticism with some Western romanticism added for cosmetic purposes.'

'What does *he* get out of it?'

'The Sannyasins give him all their worldly goods. He has a fleet of Rolls-Royces.'

'That's cults for you. How do people fall for it?'

'It's easy enough. I once had a free personality test in what I thought was a bookshop on the Charing Cross Road. The receptionist gave me a form with a hundred and twenty questions. She didn't say they were Scientologists. They projected my answers onto a graph that illustrated my personal development, with peaks representing happiness and troughs unhappiness. Apparently I suffered a traumatic experience in childhood.'

'And did you suffer a traumatic experience in childhood?'

'Not that I know of. (I might have suffered a traumatic experience before I was born but they didn't ask about your previous lives.) Anyway, if you deny it they'll say you're suppressing your memory, which is itself evidence of your trauma.'

'That's really devious. I thought cults were just an excuse for sex and drugs. I knew someone...'

'It's not like she's still in her ashram.'

'She is, in her head.'

'Out of her head more like. I've never known anyone so out of their head.'

Skunk sighed. 'You've really got it bad.'

'Naah. It's just an infatuation.'

'*Infatuare.* To make foolish.'

'Just because Nietzsche goes by a word's origin, that doesn't mean...'

'Infatuation takes up residence with those predisposed to suffer,' said Skunk, like an expert testifying in court. 'It usually stays dormant in the cellar, but if it comes upstairs, it will take over your life. It's an addiction, it makes smack look like Smarties. Only you can't see it, not when it's happening to you. You think it's love, so you invite it to stay. Then it enslaves you. You become a masochist to whom every indignity and self-abasement only proves the purity of your love. Gambling everything you have on a stranger, you shut yourself off to keep your love untainted. I mean, let's face it: infatuation is psychotic.'

'Haven't you noticed how beautiful she is?'

'Yes, she's very beautiful... But you have to stay your hand. If you're too besotted, you'll scare her off. You're not very good at hiding your feelings, Jake.'

'I know *that.* That's why I didn't talk to her earlier.'

'And you have to be a bastard.'

'Are you being a bastard to Kitty?'

'I'm not the one in love. Anyway, my point is, you don't want to get hammered.'

'Someone has to get hammered, I take it?'

'No, Jake. Everyone lives happily ever after.'

'I don't see why not.'

'Love is a state of constant conflict, with both yourself and your object.'

'You're just saying that because of the L-woman.'

Skunk held out his fists, not for a fight but a game of chess. I chose the fist holding a black pawn, we laid out the pieces and would have started to play were Skunk's thoughts not exceeding their remit. Only after I had rolled a joint and read almost a paragraph of Proust did he play pawn to king four, as he always did. On move seven, he left a bishop *en pris* then suggested he take it again. I consented for the sake of a good game but my magnanimity set an unfortunate precedent. If you can retract your last move while your opponent is considering his next move, then neither player knows whose turn it is. Stalemate had a new dimension.

Shrieks and laughter marked the others' return. In with a gust of cold air came Boney, panting like a poodle, Fysh, swaying and whooshing and Evie, who was shoving Boney. Here too, glory hallelujah, came Diana, her big blue eyes spacier than ever. My heart pounded as though trying to escape.

'Fuck me...,' cackled Evie. 'Have you been here all this time?'

'No,' I said, 'Skunk took me to a nightclub.'

Diana handed her pouch of hash to Boney, who doffed an imaginary cap and settled into the armchair to set about filling a pipe. Diana sat next to me.

'I met a Frenchwoman,' said Evie, and I wondered whether it was you. 'She said she was looking for Marie Antoinette. "You're in the wrong country, luv," I told her. "This is England. We're here to burn Guy Fawkes, not guillotine aristocrats." She didn't know what I was on about. I dare say she couldn't speak English.'

'Was it a good bonfire?' Skunk asked Diana.

Diana was too wasted to put her memories in order. 'There were Brahmins garlanded in marigolds and sadhus smeared in ashes in a procession of crazy floats. Everyone was wearing masks. Some said they were going to the Ganges to wash away their sins. Some said it's the Day of the Dead.'

'I don't remember that,' said Boney.

'There were rumours of a human sacrifice,' said Diana. 'It was mob rule. I tried to see what was going on but there were too many people. Above our heads, a cloud was burning in the sky.'

A pipe of pure Manali almost knocked me off my chair. I found myself with the Children of Israel, crossing a desert in search of the Promised Land. A pillar of fire rose towards the sky.

'It was God lighting up the way ahead,' I said.

'It wasn't God,' scoffed Boney. 'They were burning the Pope.'

'An effigy of the Pope,' Skunk assured Diana.

'Burn the Pope! Burn the Pope! Burn...' Fysh stopped mid-chant to check for a burning glow in the pipe he'd just smoked. Satisfied that it was dead, he passed it to Skunk, who didn't like pipes anyway.

'The whole world was on fire,' said Diana. 'I thought we were going to be burned alive.'

'What happened to Casey?' asked Fysh.

'Casey?' Diana returned to her senses. 'He said he was heading back to his ranch.'

The front door crashed open. Clack, clack, clack. A pair of stilettoes and fishnet tights, a short leather skirt and biker's jacket announced the coming of Lush Liz.

'Whezza party?'

'It went to the bonfire in Stowe,' said Skunk.

Lush Liz tottered over and looked down on our rump of revellers. 'What sort of party do you call this? Lookatchoo, bunch of dope-smoking hippies playing chess and prattling on with your pseudo-philosophy. You wouldn't recognise a real woman if you saw one.' A drop of mascara rolled down her cheek, like she'd been left out in the rain.

Lush Liz expected more from such a notorious flat. Where she had mastered the tenets of orthodox hedonism with ease, we fell woefully short. Touched though I was by her disappointment, I was pleased that Diana could see what we weren't.

Liz shrugged off her jacket, unbuttoned her shirt and clasped a naked bosom. She reached between her legs and, writhing and moaning as if about to give birth, she threw back her head. 'Oh, God. Oh God. Oh, God!' When she had finished, she mis-buttoned her shirt, grabbed her jacket and bounced off the kitchen counter. Her heels clacked and the front door slammed shut.

'Bravo.' Fysh broke into applause.

'Oo-err.' Evie wrinkled her nose.

'What was all that about?' wondered Boney.

Diana scowled through furious eyes. She had fallen in with a gang of sexual deviants who masturbated in the kitchen. And I was the ringleader.

'Thank you for such a... lovely evening.' She stood up and threw her shawl over her shoulder. The night was over, so too our friendship.

Diana's displeasure reverberated as her footfalls on the path outside receded into silence.

Letter 11

Guevara House was dark, except for a dim light in Diana's window. I climbed two flights of stairs and tapped on her door, quietly lest I wake her neighbours. I hoped she had crashed out, in which case I could head back to Flat 22 knowing I had done my best to put things right.

'I thought it would be you,' she said on opening the door.

Her room was devoid of student paraphernalia or anything pertaining to its current occupant. A candle's flame threw long shadows across bare walls and standard-issue furnishings. The candle's position mid-floor said she'd been meditating.

'I've come to apologise.'

She gestured to the floor, inviting me to sit, to participate in her ritual. She sat, cross-legged, expecting me to follow her example. We had to steeple our fingers and close our eyes: a posture that precluded rational conversation.

To show good – or bad – faith, I sat cross-legged on my side of the candle. I steepled my fingers, closed my eyes and purged my mind of random thoughts. But I couldn't dismiss its erotic visions of Diana.

After a couple of minutes that seemed much longer, Diana wrapped it up. 'All is *maya*,' she said, like a priest saying 'amen'. Then she fixed me in a trancelike glare, which would have been thrilling were she not mistaking my polite compliance for blind acquiescence. 'I see you are open to enlightenment,' she said.

'Go on, then, enlighten me.'

'The pyramid of enlightenment has three stages. First you must accept the world's unreality: everything is *maya*, or illusion. To confront your illusions, you must live in the moment.'

I tried to confront my illusions. I tried to live in the moment. Now she was wearing a red basque and suspenders.

'Secondly, you must strive to be one with the universe, knowing it can take years to reach such a high level of consciousness. Many drop out on the way up. But if you can truly respect every living creature, you are ready for Nirvana, which is to say, release from the cycle of birth, life and death.'

'Let's fuck,' I almost said.

'Finally, to attain true enlightenment, you must forfeit your ego and live an ascetic life. Only then will you know the truth. Only then will you be capable of... love.'

I was already capable of love. Very capable.

'To discover the secret of life you must be constantly aware, not for a short time each day, not just when you feel like it, but always. That's how you live an authentic life. When you know the secret of life...'

'There is no secret of life, Diana. There's no *maya*, no nirvana and no pyramid of enlightenment.'

Diana's jaw fell. A distant firework spluttered.

'Your self-denial is just an inverted form of self-indulgence. Your asceticism is the will to power in disguise. And you shouldn't let a Bhagwan tell you what colours to wear.'

'You mean you were just humouring me?' Her face reddened. 'If you're that unwilling to open your mind, why didn't you say so? Why did you let me carry on? I thought I could trust you.'

'You *can* trust me. It's Bhagwan you can't trust.'

'I thought you accepted me the way I am.'

'This isn't the way you are.'

'How do you know? You don't know me.'

'You've been brainwashed.'

Diana rose to her feet and switched on the overhead light. She blew out her candle, picked up its saucer and opened the door to show me out.

A wave of disappointment crashed over me, leaving a wash of dolorous anticipation in its wake.

'Don't say I didn't warn you,' Skunk was going to say.

'Never mind, Jake,' Evie was going to say.

'Penelope gave me the bum's rush at a similar stage,' Fysh was going to say.

'Here you go, have a line of speed' would be Skunk's idea of consolation.

Why on earth did I have to tell her she was brainwashed? How stupid could I be? I decided to snort Skunk's speed then score a whole gram, just to punish myself.

'Bye, then.' I turned for a last look and was thrilled to see tears in Diana's eyes.

'I think we need a doobie,' she said, with a brave smile. She poured us both a glass of water then rolled a joint on her bed while I made myself comfortable in her armchair.

'Where have you been this past week?' I asked her.

'You sound like my father.'

I took it as a compliment. Girls loved their fathers.

'He's a real bastard, my dad. He and Verity were always drinking and fighting. Then they got divorced. He disowned me for going on a CND march. Now he won't have my name spoken in his house.'

'Where is his house?'

'He lives in a mansion in Holland Park, with Cecily, my wicked stepmother, and God knows how many servants and marble busts. He's obsessed by the Greeks and Romans. (He thinks I'm studying Plato and Aristotle.) And money. He made a fortune in banking then moved into publishing. He'd hate you. You're a permissive degenerate.'

'"We are the people our parents warned us against," as the hippies used to say.'

'He thinks Kitty's a witch. She probably *was* a witch in a previous life. I can just see her stirring a cauldron. "Come here, little children... Look what I've got." She ran away from her convent school, you know. Verity picked her up off the streets and moved her in with us. My own mother! She thought Kitty would be a good influence on me.'

We didn't talk about our past experiences like that. We were *sui generis*, free from our contingent backgrounds, free to be ourselves. And I detected an element of malice in her airing of Kitty's misfortunes. But I said nothing, preferring discretion to valour for fear of another row.

'Kitty's dad died when she was a baby in a sailing accident in Saint-Tropez. Kitty and her brothers were supposed to be with him on the yacht, but at the last minute they stayed behind with Susan, Kitty's mum. Susan couldn't cope after such a tragic accident so she sent her sons to boarding school and Kitty to a convent. One time when we were home alone, we did some acid and Kitty just sat there, crying, "Daddy, Daddy".'

'Poor Kitty.'

Diana snorted. 'She's lucky to be alive. Her dad was a baronet, so she's actually the *Honourable* Katherine d'Abo. She never tells anyone that. You'd think she'd appreciate her good fortune.'

'No you wouldn't.'

Diana threw me a look. 'Where's her self-respect? I mean, all this sleeping around on the sly. First it's with Carlos, one of my oldest friends. Then she comes down here, and having slept with Fysh, who's obviously quite round the bend, she moves on... to Skunk! Why does she have to be so promiscuous?'

'She's looking for love.'

'She only chose Wessex because of me. Same with doing philosophy. I told her it would be a waste of time.'

'It's not a waste of time.'

'Yes it is. All Remy Sachs cares about is having his books published. It's not what I expected at all. I thought philosophy professors were supposed to teach us the truth.'

'Tutors aren't gurus. They're just academics with sinecures who make a nice living writing books and articles that nobody else understands. What do they care about truth?'

'It was stupid of me to imagine I'd find truth in Western philosophy anyway. Western philosophy is a spiritual wasteland.'

'No it isn't. Philosophy sorts out your head. Hegel teaches you to think dialectically. Marx explains our alienation. Nietzsche explains what it means to be human.'

'I thought you were a rebel.'

'You can't rebel against philosophy. That would be like rebelling against music.'

'Why don't we study Eastern philosophy?'

'That's not our heritage, is it?'

'Compared with Eastern spirituality, Western individualism is totally shallow. There's no understanding of Sanskrit concepts such as *maya,* there's no focus on the here and now or living an authentic life.'

'Your *maya* is what Kant calls "phenomenon," that is the mere appearance of reality. Noumenon, or true reality, is unknowable to human minds. "Living in the moment" is Sartre's antidote to *mauvais foi* (or bad faith). And Heidegger shared your quest for authentic being.' Heidegger was a Nazi, but this I was too ashamed to mention.

Diana softened. 'I did read some Nietzsche in Dharamsala. According to Nietzsche, you're either a master or a slave.'

'You're a master by birth, Diana.'

'To be a master means to master desire.'

To be a master meant to act. A slave would be too scared. I lunged forward, lips first.

Diana recoiled. Then she got up, crossed the room and opened the door. She was kicking me out, again.

Out in the corridor, I faced an obvious truth. Diana didn't fancy me. What did I care? I was well rid of her stupid mysticism and self-deceptions, her pretty face and Roman-goddess name. I should have given her a piece of my mind while I had the chance.

I tapped on her door, quietly lest I wake her neighbours.

91

A squirrel on a heap of brown leaves was contemplating an acorn. Two motorbikes parked in adjacent bays were kissing. A bell tinkled as I entered the co-op.

'Afternoon, Jimmy.'

Jimmy was writing up price tags with a marker pen. A postgraduate in applied mathematics who wore wire-framed spectacles, denim dungarees and peaceful sandals, Jimmy was the co-op's manager and sole worker. And when he wasn't manning the co-op, he was pulling pints in Luxembourg Village bar. You had to love Jimmy.

'You're the salt of the earth,' I told him. 'Weird saying though, isn't it? What good is salt to the earth?'

'Are you taking the mickey or just uttering the first thing that passes through your mind?'

'Oh, the latter, I'm sure. Say, Jimmy, you sell spices, right?'

'Over here.' He showed me to a row of big plastic containers filled with twigs and leaves, purple pulses and maroon beans, green seeds and saffron powders.

'I was thinking of cooking a romantic meal for two. Maybe a vegetarian curry. What do you think?'

Jimmy screwed up his face.

'I know. Curry gives you the shits, doesn't it? But she's just got back from India and I want to make her feel at home. The problem is, I don't know how to cook a vegetarian curry, or anything else for that matter.'

'Why don't you ask your friend to help? You know, the one I always see you with.'

'What, Skunk?' Skunk would turn our romantic meal for two into an abstract argument for three. 'Maybe I should aim for something less ambitious, like beans on toast. Or a takeaway from the coffee shop.'

Seeing as I was here, I decided to do some shopping, a chore made simpler by Faye's rules. Bread: granary, unsliced. Rice: brown, long-grain. Eggs: free-range. Vegetables: locally sourced. Not that Faye was ever at Flat 22. And when she was there, she was too sped out to eat, whatever the food's provenance.

'Maybe I should take her to a fancy restaurant in town.' I placed a full basket on the counter. 'Or do you think that would that be pushing it? I don't want to seem besotted.'

'Who are you talking about?' asked Jimmy while putting my environmentally sound groceries through the till and into a large brown paper bag.

'Diana Farquharson. She's a first year. Lives upstairs in Guevara House. You've probably seen her around. Very pretty, blonde hair, only wears shades of red.'

'Is she your girlfriend?'

'I've been wondering the same... Oh, shit!' I didn't have any cash. 'You mind if I run to the bank? I'll be right back.'

'The bank's closed.'

'Why, what time is it?' An overcast sky gave no hint of the time. Autumn's misty air was still smarting from last night's fireworks. The day hadn't time to get going before evening descended. Darkness at mid-afternoon.

'Nearly ten past four.'

'Tell you what. Why don't you put it on my slate?'

'We don't do slates. If everybody had a slate...'

'How about an IOU?'

'You could always go to Bettabuys. They accept cheques.'

Bettabuys was conveniently located behind the coffee shop. They had special offers on mass-market products and two-for-one deals, printed cardboard signs over well-stocked aisles, branded carrier bags and a loop of piped muzak interrupted by Nineteen-Eighty-Four-style announcements. The scent of industrial disinfectant demonstrated a high standard of hygiene and there were young, female cashiers who wore name tags on their gingham-pinafore uniforms because nobody knew anybody's name at Bettabuys.

'I'm not going there.'

'Shall I take that as an expression of your appreciation?'

'You know we love you, Jimmy. By the way, are you going to be here over Christmas?'

'Why, are you inviting me for Christmas dinner?'

'Well, you're welcome to join us. Though to be honest, I might not be here this year.' I was hoping to spend the holidays with Diana and was entertaining visions of making love under a Christmas tree when a tinkling bell interrupted me.

'Jake!'

'Sally!'

A jolly-hockey-sticks, deputy-head-girl type, Sally was a neighbour in Guevara House in my first year. She used to complain when a cloud of smoke wafted through my open door and gathered under the corridor ceiling. She complained when she found anarchists in the bathroom and toilet and was particularly put out when a journalist from The Daily Express came to rake muck following the David Owen incident. Later that term, on her birthday, I slid a card signed with a kiss under her door. After that, she giggled at my jokes and made me cups of tea, she introduced me to her friends and invited my anarchist associates to our bathroom and toilet. Now she looked different. She had trimmed eyebrows, coloured eyelids and an androgynous buzz-cut and, in place of tennis shoes and tracksuit she wore pixie boots and a ruffled mini-skirt that clenched her wasp-like waist. After two years at Wessex, Sally had become trendy, and pretty.

'You're looking well,' she said, sounding surprised as much as pleased, before leaning in for a kiss on both cheeks, in the manner of a sophisticated European. 'Tim and I were talking about you just the other day. Tim will be sorry he missed you. We haven't seen you for ages. How are you?'

'I'm in love.'

'How exciting! I want to hear all about it. What's her name?'

'Diana.'

'Like Princess Diana!'

'Oh, I didn't think of that.' The name I declared as mine wasn't even Diana's.

'Is she a hippy chick?'

'Not exactly. She's a first-year.'

'Ohhhh. I expect she sees you as her mentor.'

'I shouldn't think so. She already has a guru.'

'Why don't you bring her round for dinner? We'd love to meet her.'

'Thank you.' I wondered what Sally and Tim would think of Diana's pyramid of enlightenment. 'Listen, I gotta go. It was nice catching up.'

'Take care of yourself, Jake. Hey, aren't you forgetting something?'

Diana had asked the same thing. I thought we'd stay in bed all day, making love, smoking hash and exchanging sweet nothings but I awoke to find Diana, dressed in a maroon sari and cerise tights, studying at her desk as though our night of passion hadn't happened. Bypassing the pleasures of foreplay, we'd headed straight to a climax, a rushed sating of desire that I took to be a quick practice, a warm-up before the full flowering of our love. Then Diana fell asleep.

'What are you writing?' I asked her.

'"Are Aquinas's proofs of God's existence cosmological or teleological?"' Diana raised her eyebrows at the question's absurdity.

'Aquinas's "proofs"? They're not proofs.' I was happy to agree with her. 'They're circular arguments, at best. I could help you write your essay.'

She put down her pen and stood up. 'It's time for the walk of shame.'

'Oh, go on then.' I anticipated a morning-after purifying ritual as prescribed by Bhagwan.

'Not me. You. You have to sneak out and hope nobody sees you. Isn't that what happens on a university campus?'

'Why don't I want anyone to see me?'

'Because they'll know you've slept out.'

'Oh. I'd better stay where I am, then.'

Diana tilted her head, puckered her cheeks and put hands to hips, prompting me to get up and dress as though obeying orders.

'Are you going to be around later?' I asked as I reached for the door.

'I should think so. Hey, aren't you forgetting something?' She stopped me in my tracks for a long, lingering kiss.

'Hell-ohhhhh...' Sally thought I was stoned. 'What about your stuff?' She nodded at my bag of groceries.

'I haven't got any cash. If I'd known I was coming...'

'Why didn't you say? How much is it?' Sally reached for her purse and handed Jimmy a fiver.

'One pound, ninety-four,' said Jimmy.

'That's very kind of you,' I said.

'You remember where we live, don't you? Flat 4, 17 Cornwallis Terrace. Come by anytime and we'll cook you a meal. Bring Diana.'

Jimmy opened the door for me, his smile expressing a new friendliness. 'Bye, Jake,' he said.

I couldn't wait to tell Skunk about Jimmy, and Sally, and Diana, and the pyramid of enlightenment and Nietzsche's master-slave dialectic. And how wrong he was about love.

A blanket hung over Skunk's window. His room was stale and stuffy. Kitty was passed out, her arm dangling overboard. Skunk lay corpse-like under a speaker. A syringe needle glinted in the gloom.

Letter 13

A tiny pyramid of brown powder melted on a square of silver foil. A burning tear rolled down a crease. I inhaled the tear's smoke through a Biro tube and... Wham! A collage of memories and movie scenes, dreams and thoughts passed serenely through my mind as I relaxed in Gordon's groovy pad. Only in my mind did the world exist. That made me an idealist. Were I to put the world before my mind, I would be a materialist.

I opened my eyes to find a desk dedicated to chess, albums arranged in alphabetical order and Fysh's psychedelic artwork, posters of obscure hippy bands and photos of clouds over Arundel on the walls. Through an open door I heard natter and laughter and a song about a man at a station. He was catching the next train home.

Then Skunk appeared. 'Your texture's changed,' he said.

'I'm just a bit itchy.' Invisible mites were crawling all over me. They had probably come with the pet rat that Gordon looked after for a friend, until Boney sat on it.

'What I mean is, you're overcooking the soppy side.'

Skunk disapproved of my fawning over Diana. I would gaze into her eyes, hold her hand and insist on a kiss whenever we parted company, after which I counted the minutes of her absence.

'What are you doing for Christmas?' she asked. 'I haven't been back to London since I came down here. I really ought to make an effort over Christmas to know George, my new stepdad. Plus, I've got a stepbrother and stepsister to meet. Guy is in and out of lunatic asylums, and Giselle's an actress, which you can put in inverted commas according to Verity. Then there's George's gay brother, Willie, who Verity says is a hoot. And of course Hector and Tarquin will be there, along with Hector's girlfriend Laetitia, who's a banker in Hong Kong, and whoever happens to be Tarquin's latest young lady. Verity reckons Laetitia will relocate to London so they can get married, though she won't let them live at her place. She's going to sell it next year because George has a cottage in the countryside and she's tired of owning a big townhouse. I think she'll like being retired in Dorset, tending the garden, taking walks in the woods...'

'I love you.'

My execution fell flat, for all my rehearsals in front of a mirror. (My first attempt was too desperate and sounded like a plea for affection. I tried to be more casual and it sounded like an afterthought. So I applied more passion, and it could have been an audition for amateur-dramatics night.) The plan was to seize a romantic moment, not blurt it out while she was talking about something else.

Diana rested her eyes on Greta Garbo. 'We are passing strangers. It's all we can ever be. Love doesn't last. Love is transient.'

'Is that what Bhagwan says?'

'To be in love is like standing on a sandy beach on a beautiful day. You think the tide will never turn. You are so sure, you want to stay there forever. Then the tide turns and you're stranded.' She reached for my hand, which didn't respond. 'You should never become so close that parting is unbearable. Because parting is inevitable. We are ships passing in the night. As soon as you get used to someone, it is time to move on. Hello, good luck, goodbye.'

'But...'

'Take Anna Karenina. Why does she kill herself? Is it because she can't bear the guilt after abandoning her adoring child? No. Is it because a hypocritical society shuns her? No. Is it because she's become an opium addict? No, it's not that either. She kills herself because her love of Vronksy, that love she thought was eternal, has curdled.'

'That's just a novel.'

'The most important thing is to be friends. Friendship is the highest form of love.'

Skunk reappeared just as I sat up and was reaching for the foil.

'Why don't you jack it up?' he asked.

'I'm not going to jack it up.'

'Chasing the dragon, you use five times as much smack, *my* smack I might add, for a fraction of the effect. You don't know what you're missing. Jacking up produces the same chemical reaction in your brain as an orgasm. I'll do it for you if you like.' Skunk wanted to demonstrate his nursing skills.

'Thank you so much. Then I'll come to you when I get gangrene.'

'You won't get gangrene. Oh, well. It's your funeral.'

On Skunk's exit, I chased a dragon and my sweat turned feverish. I vomited on the floor and felt better. Serene once again, I lay back down and listened to the chatter in central space.

'The Madwoman of Caledonia was looking for you, Skunk,' said Faye.

'Yeah, you're in trouble there,' said Gordon.

'Why?' asked Skunk. 'What have *I* done?'

'She said she'll be back, with an axe,' said Faye.

'An axe?' Skunk sounded incredulous. 'When was all this?'

'The other day, at about three.' Gordon would have made a good secretary. 'She reckons you're responsible for all the noise.'

'She thinks people come round here to see *you*,' said Boney.

'Must be your engaging personality,' said Kitty.

'I don't even know most of the people who come round here. Who is this Madwoman of Caledonia anyway?'

'Big ruddy Scottish chick,' said Faye. 'Looks like she's been busy tossing cabers.'

'She *said* she lives next door.' Gordon sounded sceptical, though I couldn't think why she would lie about living next door. 'She said she has exams, and she's sick of being woken up by opera music at five in the morning. She wanted to smash your hi-fi.'

'Gordon barred her way.' Faye sounded proud of Gordon's unlikely heroics. 'He held her off, getting a scratched face for his trouble. It was savage, man.'

'It wasn't "opera music,"' tutted Skunk. 'It was the Resurrection Symphony.' For Mahler especially, Skunk wheeled his speakers into the corridor to give everyone on Lumumba Slope that concert-hall experience.

'I asked her if she prefers the Bee Gees,' said Gordon. 'And she nearly took my eye out.'

'She really has it in for you,' laughed Skunk.

'I respectfully told her, "If you have a complaint, you should take it up with the authorities".'

'We should have told her to fuck off.' Faye's hindsight was tinged by regret.

'And she agreed,' Gordon continued. 'She said she'd bring someone from admin round. I asked if she was threatening us and she said, no, it would just be a discussion.'

'Fine.' Skunk liked a good discussion.

'Obviously nobody wants any trouble,' added Gordon.

'What's wrong with trouble?' Skunk wanted to know.

A draught blew in, along with the sound of Casey's swishing waterproofs.

'Casey!' exclaimed Diana. 'What brings you here?'

'So when are we having this discussion?' Skunk was still looking forward to it.

'I thought Jake might want to borrow my Harley,' said Casey, to a chorus of laughter.

'You ride a Harley-Davidson?' Diana was apparently into motorbikes. 'I used to ride a Yamaha 500.'

'*Doo-doo, doo-doo, doooo....,*' went the Doors as I faded into some sort of sleep.

Gordon was crashed out on the floor. He must have chased a dragon and fallen where he stood. I pocketed a foil of smack, stepped over a puddle of vomit and left quietly, taking care not to wake my host.

'We were staying at St Catherine's Monastery in the Sinai,' Kitty was telling Skunk in the kitchen. Down below, there was nobody left in central space. 'A priest in long black robes came to our hostel with a chillum. After we'd smoked it, he sat there staring at a mirror, said he was talking to John the Baptist.'

Skunk nodded knowingly, as though talking to his mirror's image of John the Baptist was one of his own hobbies.

'I took a foil of smack,' I said. 'You don't mind.'

'Are you asking me or telling me?'

'Telling.'

'Well that's alright then.'

'It's for my other half,' I said, though deep down, I knew I was lying.

Letter 14

'I could see him through the net curtains, brandishing a carving knife.' Skunk was telling Diana about the time he first met Vincent. 'I rang the bell and he said, "What do you want?" through a crack in the door. You could feel the prickles of his paranoia. "Is Jake in?" I asked, and he let me in, even though Jake wasn't there. He was covered in plaster dust.'

'Must have been when the kitchen ceiling fell in,' I said. 'That place is so damp, my books' pages got stuck together.'

'Basement flat near the sea.' Skunk reckoned dampness was inevitable.

'He sounds like a psycho,' said Diana.

'He is a psycho. He sleeps with a meat cleaver under his pillow.' Gordon always brought up Vincent's meat cleaver. 'He's a real boots-and-braces bovver-boy.'

'He likes the sense of danger,' Skunk told Diana, to whom danger was an old friend.

Skunk was one of the few people Vincent liked. Junkie Simon was 'a bust waiting to happen,' Lush Liz was 'a fat slapper' and Sally and Tim were 'cock-sucking toffs'. Even his best mates he called 'the obligatory wogs' though technically Samir was an Arab and Royston a Sikh. When I told him that 'the cunt outside the launderette going "feesh" to passers-by' was a friend of ours, he said it would soon be me if I kept dropping acid. So I wasn't confident about his reaction to Diana's code of colour.

'Ehhhh areet, Jake.'

Samir's gigantic figure filled the doorway of Vincent's basement hovel. He clasped me to his midriff, where I remained until he let go. On seeing Diana, his broad smile widened further.

A vestibule the size of a phone box led to a kitchen with half a ceiling, a grease-stained window and bubbly linoleum. Beyond the kitchen, a dank hallway led to two bedrooms and a bathroom door whose frosted glass had been replaced by a cardboard screen after one of Vincent's Bruce Lee impersonations. My old room was kept locked by my successor, Lemonade Steve, who was wary of Vincent's meat cleaver.

The front room faced street-level railings, though the outside world was barely visible through yellowing net curtains. A pair of shabby armchairs flanked a defunct fireplace opposite an old-fashioned television propped up by four piles of books. Album covers and empty beer cans littered a threadbare carpet.

Royston was sprawled across a bare mattress in the corner. His bloodshot eyes and trim beard, his tie at half-mast and crumpled suit were all present and correct but his waist-length ponytail was missing.

'What happened to your hair?'

'Now it is someone else's hair, hee hee hee.'

'He sold it, for ten quid. It is forbidden for Sikhs to cut their hair.' Samir beamed at this happy confluence of profit and transgression.

'Where's Vincent?'

'At his granny's funeral, hee hee hee.'

'Oh, shit. Any idea when he'll be back?'

'Sometimes we have to wait for the last train.' Royston was being mystical.

I introduced Diana and we took off our coats to wait, for the last train if necessary.

'Can I write him a cheque?' whispered Diana.

'You can't score hash with a cheque.'

'Why not? Does he not have a bank account?'

'He has a bank account,' said Royston. 'That's the problem. When you've got debts like Vincent's, you can't pay money into your account.'

'Why is that?' Diana didn't get the iniquities of capitalism.

'The bank takes it and you never see it again, hee hee hee.'

'You want to roll one?' Samir pushed a rolling deck across the floor.

It was Exodus underneath the Rothmans, Rizlas, lighter and hash. Which is to say, Bob Marley's album on the movement of Jah people, not Leon Uris's novel on the movement of Jew people.

'What's this?' Diana dug a thumbnail into Samir's lump of hash.

'Temple ball,' beamed Samir. 'Laced with opium.'

'That's not temple ball.' Diana put a flame to the hash and sniffed. 'Uh-uh.'

'Once upon a time, in the mountains of Nepal, a pure little temple ball embarked on a journey,' said Royston. 'It started out fresh as a daisy but in the course of its travels it ran into profiteers who mixed it with boot polish. By the time it reaches us, our temple ball has lost much of its original goodness.'

'Is the same in Lebanon,' said Samir. 'Their good shit they smoke. Their low-grade shit they send to Europe.'

Diana filled a pipe. '*Boomshanka, boumboulay.*'

The pipe went round a couple of times and we were still standing, or lying around at any rate.

'It's not temple ball,' Diana insisted. 'Are you from Lebanon?'

'I am Palestinian.' Stoned though he was, Samir tried to be serious. 'I have a brother who sells pizza in Venice, a brother who operates tanning machines in Florida and an uncle in Canada.'

'So how come you're in Westbourne?'

'It is a long story.'

'What do you do?'

'I study economics.'

'You don't have to do that anymore,' said Royston. 'Samir's a married man, hee hee hee.'

Samir's wedding day was easily remembered.

'Samir's getting hitched today,' said Evie, who was all spruced up in a frock and high-heeled shoes. 'I specifically brought it up last night. "Have an early night," I said.'

Skunk and I had been up all night helping Gordon navigate an Oedipus crisis. 'You don't want to kill your father,' Skunk assured him. 'You want to fuck your mother.'

'Is it going to be in a church?' asked Boney.

'Of course it's not going to be in a fucking church,' said Evie. 'Samir's a Muslim. It's a civil service at Westbourne town hall followed by drinks and grub at the Belvedere. Is Samir your friend or not?' Evie appealed to me in particular, because we used to sleep together. Me and Evie, that is. Which seemed a bit unfair given her previous flings with Fysh and Skunk.

'I thought marriage is a pillar of the patriarchy,' I said.

'We're not going to support the institution of marriage. We're going to support Samir and Mandy. It's not as if he'll have any family present. Her neither from what I've heard.'

'A wedding is like a funeral,' said Skunk. 'Without the hope.'

'You're such a bunch of miseries. Honestly! It's going to be a really good bash.'

'Why doesn't Gordon have to go?' asked Skunk.

Boney fell about laughing at the idea of Gordon doing anything, let alone attending Samir's wedding. To be fair, Boney had just had his first hot knife of the morning.

'Gor-don!' Evie stormed off to add a fresh harangue to Gordon's nightmares. A minute later she was back, with a new argument. 'Do any of you even know Mandy?'

'Who's Mandy?' Fysh was reeling from a hot knife but could still respond to a girl's name.

'I don't know her,' said Boney. 'What does she study, like?'

'See?' said Evie. 'That's exactly my point. This is our chance to get to know her.'

'I don't want to get to know her,' said Skunk.

As it turned out, nobody got to know her, and Evie wished she'd let sleeping Gordons lie.

'I'm not going to speak,' Gordon told Evie when they reached Stancombe station. 'A slip of the tongue might expose a guilty truth that's hiding in my subconscious.'

Gordon honoured his vow of silence throughout the wedding, until he fell asleep over his crème brûlée. After the meal, Evie went off to congratulate the happy couple but Samir and Mandy were nowhere to be found, and Mandy was never seen again. Samir's wedding was, we belatedly realised, not for love so much as a British passport.

'It was a sham,' said Evie. 'Which makes it much the same as any other wedding.'

'I'm a secretary,' said Royston.

'Oh.' Diana was surprised. 'Where do you work?'

'The LCC.'

'London County Council?'

'The London County Council doesn't exist anymore,' giggled Royston. 'I'm talking about the Legalise Cannabis Campaign.'

'For what does the Legalise Cannabis Campaign need a secretary?' I sounded like Papa, though Papa didn't know about the LCC. 'It's twelve blokes sitting in a circle passing each other joints till it's time to go someplace else. What do you do, take minutes?'

'You should come along,' Royston advised Diana, whose face suggested there was nothing she would rather do less. 'When was the last time you came to a meeting, Jake?'

'Last year?'

'Do you know how many people in this country smoke ganja?' he asked Diana.

Diana didn't know.

'Millions. Legalisation is the only solution, for the police, the prisons, the taxman... It's going to happen real soon, I can feel it in my water.'

'You're talking through your hat.' We'd had this argument before. Then we forgot all about it and had it again. 'The Tories don't want to be soft on drugs, socialists think drugs are counter-revolutionary and the Liberals are about as enlightened as...'

'Who is enlightened?' Royston asked Diana.

'Everyone has the capacity for enlightenment.' Diana straightened her back.

'So nobody's going to vote for it,' I continued. 'Nobody wants to rock the boat.'

'You think like a true Buddhist,' Royston told Diana.

'Bhagwan says we are all Buddhists.'

My stomach groaned.

'I see you are a Sannyasin.' Royston looked admiringly at Diana's colour scheme. 'I have known a number of Sannyasins...'

'Did they go to Poona?' Diana wanted to know.

'Does anyone fancy a burger?' I asked.

Nobody fancied a burger. Diana was vegetarian, Samir never ate in public and Royston called Time to Fry 'Time to Die'. I put on my coat and stooped to kiss Diana, who was holding forth on Bhagwan's eternal verities.

Time to Fry's frontman took my order and returned to his *Daily Mirror*. Waiting for my cheeseburger in premises bereft of tables, chairs and a floor that didn't stick to your shoes, I watched raindrops trickle down a large window. Mizzle and exhaust fumes blurred a view of flashing orange lights, a chemist's green cross and stationary traffic. A man in a trilby emerged from Foodmart, where we used to shop. (Which is to say, I shopped while Vincent nicked bread rolls or a bottle of wine destined to remain unopened on his mantelpiece because Vincent didn't like wine.) A woman was grappling with an umbrella while her dog urinated on a lamppost. Four lads were piling into an offie. Townspeople going through the motions, watched by an alien.

'*We're already dead, just not yet in the ground.*'

The sound of John Cale meant Vincent was home. He greeted me at the door, can of Special Brew in hand. 'Forgot your keys again?' he said, like I still lived there.

In the front room, Samir was offering to crash Diana's car as an insurance scam but Diana didn't get it. I would have stopped to explain but for an urgent appointment, courtesy of Time to Fry, with the toilet.

In a previous life, Vincent was surely a pirate. So said his roguish swagger, gold-cross earring and scarred cheek. Stuck in the life of a sociology student, he was ill-suited to domesticity. He was stacking his wardrobe with T-shirts ironed and folded by his mum when he beckoned me into his room.

'Who's the bird?'

'Diana. She's a first-year.'

'Why is she dressed all in red? Is she trying to attract attention?'

'She was at an ashram in India and that's how they dress there.'

'Don't tell me. Philosophy student, right? What do you do with them? Stay up all night debating the categorical imperative?' Vincent bobbed his head to the lah-de-dah pretentiousness of the categorical imperative.

'I have been out with girls who don't do philosophy, you know.'

'Not very often. What happened to Fran Mullens?'

'When was the last time *you* went out with a girl? One who wasn't Karen, I mean.'

'Karen won't let me go out with anyone else.'

'Like they'd be beating a path to your door if she did.'

Vincent roared with laughter, like he laughed at Percy Sugden on Coronation Street. Like he laughed at first-years he'd hustled at pool. Like he laughed at holders of IOUs he'd signed after an all-night poker session.

'How was the funeral?'

'Fucking awful.' Vincent crinkled his can of Special Brew and lobbed it into a pile of near misses by the bin. 'Some cousin I've never met comes up to me, right when they're lowering the coffin into the grave. And he starts hassling me, in front of my mum and everyone. "Where were you when she was alive? Where were you when she was in hospital?" Fucking cunt. I should have decked him.' Vincent punched the wardrobe door.

'It was your grandmother, right?'

'Nah, a great aunt. It's quite sad when you stop to think about it. Though not in New Orleans, where funerals are celebrations, right? I know that from your fucking jazz albums.' Vincent didn't like jazz. 'How's Skunk?'

'Smacked out, I expect.'

'Hitting the aitch is he?'

'Yeah, with Kitty.'

'Who's Kitty? Is that his new squeeze?'

'Friend of Diana's.'

'What a bastard, eh? So are you serious about her, or what?'

'Could be. I really like her.'

'She's even more off her head than you.' Vincent used to say I'd wind up in a lunatic asylum, Skunk too. Now Diana made three. 'She'll do your head in, Jake, I'm telling you. She's dangerous.'

'Have you got a quarterweight or what?' It was time to focus on what was important, as Dad would say.

'*Bien sûr, monsieur.* Tried and tested Leb,' he added, in pointed contrast to Samir's 'temple ball'. He counted my cash and gave me a joint's worth to smoke with the others while he cut up a quarterweight. When Vincent was cutting up hash, even Karen had to leave the room.

'We fought the Phalange,' Samir was telling Diana. 'The Phalangists are Christian, they belong in France, not Lebanon. They are not friends of Muslims. They are friends of the Israyelis...'

Our eyes met. My heartbeat quickened. A self-conscious heat rose to my face. If we lived by predetermined loyalties, we would be mortal enemies. Samir looked through me, like I wasn't there.

'Do you fast for Ramadan?' asked Diana.

'Always.' Samir raised a forefinger. On this his word was final, for all Royston's giggles.

Vincent came in and sat so close to me, you'd think *he* was my girlfriend. Vincent was always next in line for a joint. I had intended to pass it to Diana but now I had a dilemma that became more urgent with every toke. It was Vincent's hash, Vincent's home and Vincent's psychological pressure. Yet surely a girlfriend trumped all. You could ignore a casual sleeping partner but a girlfriend you had to put first. Besides, I wanted to show Diana that I wasn't intimidated by Vincent. There again, I didn't want Vincent thinking I was pussy-whipped. Skunk would have held the joint halfway between them on Darwinian grounds.

Diana leaned across my lap, took a long drag of the joint then passed it to Vincent. Problem solved.

Driving back to campus, Diana stayed in her lane, at a legal speed, and gave way to other vehicles. I had to keep adjusting my bollocks because the family-sized bar of hash I had stashed in my underpants was poking my pelvis, but I did my best at small talk to keep Diana focused on the here and now. Were the police to stop us, we would pass for a regular couple going home after a dinner party.

'Samir was on good form,' I said.

'He gave me the creeps. Didn't you see him undressing me with his eyes?'

'That's what men do, Diana. You're a very pretty girl. Anyway, you probably have more in common with Royston. Royston's from India.'

'He's never been to India. And he laughed at the pyramid of enlightenment.'

'Royston laughs at everything. Doesn't mean it's funny. Did you talk to Vincent while I was getting a burger?'

'He looked like he wanted to kill me.'

It wasn't Diana he wanted to kill so much as the Sannyasin.

'At least we got a quarterweight.' Soon enough we'd be back in Flat 22, celebrating our success. Or so I thought.

Evie and Smiley Dave were standing in the kitchen, fuming. Skunk was sitting alone at the table down below.

'Junkie Simon raped Liz,' Evie informed us.

'We're gonna go find the bastard. We're gonna do him.' Smiley Dave put an awkward arm around Evie's shoulder.

'He should be castrated,' said Evie. 'I'd cut his balls off myself.'

'We need a posse.' Smiley Dave had given the matter some thought. 'Are you coming?'

I assumed he was talking to me. I took out my quarterweight of hash, put it down on the kitchen counter and readjusted my underpants. 'Don't be ridiculous.'

'What do you mean?' Smiley Dave withdrew his arm from Evie's shoulder.

'We're not cowboys. It's not a Western.'

'Do we look like vigilantes?' Skunk asked Diana.

'If there's going to be a witch-hunt, we're on the witch's side,' I said, to Diana in particular.

'Someone's gotta teach that bastard a lesson.' Smiley Dave wanted to be someone.

'Simon couldn't rape Lush Liz,' said Skunk, dismissively.

'Why not?' demanded Evie.

'You saw him yesterday. He was too smacked out to move, let alone get it up, let alone force himself on Lush Liz.'

'Don't call her that!'

'How do you know he raped her?' I asked.

'She said so. And I think she'd know.' Evie's glare caught Diana, her fellow sister.

'Where is she now?' asked Diana.

'In Flat 7. She's safe there. My flatmates are looking after her.'

'Did she actually use the word "rape"?' Skunk wanted to know.

'What are you getting at?' Smiley Dave scrunched up his face.

'Well did she?'

'Don't start being pedantic, or semantic, or whatever the fuck you are,' said Evie. 'Now's not the time, Skunk.'

'She didn't, did she?'

'She said he attacked her!' screamed Evie. 'Isn't that enough?'

'She would have said "raped" but she was too traumatised,' explained Smiley Dave.

'What does Simon say?' We had yet to hear from the accused.

'We'll let you know when we find him,' sneered Smiley Dave.

Diana pouted. She didn't like the cut of Smiley Dave's jib.

'It doesn't matter what that bastard says,' said Evie.

'He'll just deny it.' Smiley Dave knew what to expect. 'They always do.'

'He might be telling the truth,' I said.

'Who would believe that junkie?' Smiley Dave thought it a question of credibility.

'We would, actually,' said Skunk.

'Who would believe Lush Liz?' I countered.

'We would, actually.' Evie contorted her face into a hyperbolic approximation of Skunk's casual nonchalance.

'They were probably sitting on the sofa and he touched her breast,' said Skunk, in a spirit of compromise.

'That's not how Liz described it.' Evie was in no mood to compromise.

'How did she describe it?' This was like a do-it-yourself trial, without the protagonists.

'She said he was all over her,' said Evie. 'He wouldn't get off her. What? You think she's making it up?'

'Not making it up. Just exaggerating.' I tried another compromise.

'Why would she exaggerate? It takes courage to say anything. Especially to a maaan.'

'You know Liz. She wants to be the centre of attention.' In other circumstances, Evie would have agreed with me.

'Liz isn't going to let the truth stand in the way of a good story,' argued Skunk.

'It's not "a good story".' Evie exaggerated another impersonation. 'It's fucking horrible.'

'Liz is much bigger than Simon,' I pointed out. 'It's not like she can't defend herself.'

'A woman shouldn't have to defend herself.' Smiley Dave was an unlikely mouthpiece for women's rights, or anyone else's for that matter.

'She was probably drunk.' On this at least, Skunk thought we could all agree.

Evie gasped at the depths to which Skunk would sink. 'So now you're blaming the victim?'

'Nohhh. There's nothing wrong with being drunk.'

'He's just saying that alcohol might have impaired her perceptions, or her memory,' I said.

'Isn't it typical of men to stick together?' Evie asked Diana.

'Smiley Dave's not sticking together,' I said, and Skunk laughed for both of us.

Smiley Dave stepped forward. Thinking better of it, he stepped back. Smiley Dave was his own man.

'Men think they can get away with anything,' said Evie.

Diana was unmoved by Evie's feminism. Diana felt as little allegiance to her gender as she did to her class, or her nationality or her civilisation. Diana had enough trouble with allegiance to herself.

'Well I say we go get the bastard.' Smiley Dave's return to square one cued more laughter from Skunk.

'You don't know where he lives,' I pointed out. 'You don't even know where he goes. So how are you going to "get" him?'

'Junkie Simon's a man of mystery,' said Skunk. 'Like the Saint.'

'We'll find him, don't you worry.' Smiley Dave cracked his knuckles.

'Where *does* he live?' Evie's tone of voice registered a tactical shift. If she was nice, we would divulge Simon's whereabouts.

'We don't know.' I shrugged both shoulders to emphasise our ignorance. 'Honest, guv.'

'You make me sick.' Evie stormed off, Smiley Dave in tow.

Moments later, we were making tracks for Diana's room in Guevara House, arms linked against a wet, windy night.

'Do you really think your friend is innocent?'

'Simon wouldn't force himself on a woman.'

'How can you be so sure?'

'Oh, I know him.'

Letter 16

It was a mild winter's day in Stancombe Woods. Surfing a current over tall trees and fallow fields, steering clear of a seagull, I approached grey clouds. A celestial choir whistled. I swooped down between creaking branches and perched on a sturdy bough amid a flutter of leaves. Down below, two tiny toy soldiers were pacing around in a clearing.

'I'm a bird! I can fly!'

'You're not a bird,' said God. 'You're a human being.'

I looked down and recognised Skunk and Gordon. Then the tree swayed and my body started to tremble, except for my hands and feet, which were stuck rigid. First I could fly; now I couldn't move. Frigid in terror, I dared not look down. I had climbed too high and at any moment might fall, accidentally or on purpose, to my death.

'Your job is to live,' said God. 'One day you will know why. This is My blessing.'

God's blessing rang in my ears. My job was to carry on, and not to reason why. Now I could move quite freely and climbing down was easy.

'Someone's missing,' said Gordon.

'God brought me down,' I said.

'He has that effect on me,' said Skunk.

Some things were best kept to yourself.

'Not that anyone listens to me.' Gordon pulled up his duffle-coat hood.

'It must be nearly teatime,' I said.

Campus was almost deserted. Everyone had gone home for Christmas, or to the Outer Hebrides in Boney's case. Four Korean students were playing men's doubles on the Luxembourg Village tennis courts where, just days ago, Diana had looked so splendid in a white Fred Perry top, pleated navy-blue skirt and

Adidas trainers, an outfit that put my dancing-bears T-shirt and black socks to shame, to say nothing of violating Bhagwan's colour scheme. Tossing back her hair, swivelling her hips, swinging her arms, Diana played not to win points but on the contrary, to keep our rallies going. We barely bothered to acknowledge the score and, on changing ends between games, we would stop to kiss at the net. The Koreans, who evidently put tennis before romance, played baseline rallies that seemed to go on forever.

'Fucking hell! It's only twenty to ten,' I said, after seeing a clock in a Guevara House kitchen. I could have sworn we'd been out all day. 'Time must have stopped moving.'

Gordon broke into a trot, as though you can run away when time stops moving. Skunk ran after him and I ran after Skunk. By the time I caught up, Skunk was in Flat 22's top corridor, eavesdropping on central space.

'Why didn't you come with to Stancombe Woods?' Gordon was asking Evie.

'I was looking after this one,' said Evie.

'Someone whispered "paranoia" in my ear,' said Gordon. 'I spun round to see Skunk scuttling off, pretending it wasn't him. But I knew it was him. And he knew that I knew. And I knew that he knew that I knew...'

Skunk's laughter gave us away and we came out of hiding to find Evie stroking a black cat and Gordon still in his duffel coat.

'How's the outside world?' asked Evie.

'No bone-rattling chill as yet,' reported Skunk as he set about making tea. 'Winter's waging a phoney war. I'd give it another week.'

'I found God up a tree,' I said as I took off my coat and shoes. I was putting on my Nepalese-style slipper socks when I noticed a new piece of furniture. Someone had placed a television on the ledge. I could just see Boney knocking it off, onto whoever's head was directly below in central space. Meanwhile it was broadcasting my reflection. 'But you know what's really weird? Fucking time has stopped moving.'

'That is weird,' agreed Evie. 'Have you met Felix?'

'Who's Felix?' asked Gordon, who was in no mood to meet anyone.

'Felix the cat.' Evie looked down at the cat in her lap.

'Hello, Felix,' said Skunk.

'I'm going to visit my brother,' said Gordon.

'You can't visit your brother,' scoffed Skunk. 'You can't visit anyone. It's Christmas Day. You forgot about that, didn't you?'

'Who cares about Christmas?' asked Gordon.

'Not me,' said Felix.

'There won't be any trains or buses,' said Evie. 'We're here for the duration. Why don't you take off your coat and have a nice cup of tea?'

'Since when do you have a brother?' I'd never heard of him.

'He's schizophrenic,' whispered Skunk.

'Oh, it's an imaginary brother.'

'Nohhh. It's the brother who's schizophrenic. Lives in Westbourne, in a state-approved seaside accommodation.'

'Come on, Gordon,' I said. 'What about our game?' The game we had adjourned the previous night, on Christmas Eve, was waiting on the table.

Gordon's queen was pinned to his king. Gordon's queen represented his mother, the mother to whom, according to Freud, he had pledged undying love in his infancy. Now he was responsible for her imminent demise. Gordon took his position to heart because chess was his religion. Rather than resign a losing position, he would always carry on, prolonging his agony, putting off his inevitable end in hope of a miracle. But on this occasion, overwhelmed by guilt, Gordon sought refuge in his room.

Evie followed him with a nice cup of tea. Then Skunk went to the bog, leaving me to my own devices.

'So here it is, Merry Christmas, everybody's having fun.'

While everybody was having fun in Lumumba Slope bar, I was saying goodbye to Diana in the car park. When she wasn't looking, I slipped a letter into her rucksack. She'd think it was a love letter, a passionate poem lamenting our separation and yearning for her return, not an ultimatum. How I wished I hadn't written it.

Diana had gone to Pentagrams, the campus book shop, to buy Christmas presents. 'I was just browsing when, whoops, Euripides falls into my bag,' she told me on her return. 'Then Sophocles. And Aeschylus. I walked out pretending I hadn't found the book I was after.'

'The anarchists used to liberate books.'

'I don't even want them,' she said.

'That's possession for you. As soon as you have something, you don't want it anymore.'

'I don't know what came over me. Bloody hell!'

'I'm sure Pentagrams can withstand the loss of a few Greek classics. They're a chain store.'

'If they caught me, I'd be expelled. I could get sent to prison.'

We made love as though purging our guilt. Diana couldn't understand her bout of kleptomania while I felt bad about my planned ultimatum. It was stupid and cowardly and still I went ahead. Now I felt even more guilty.

'Not again,' said Evie. Steve McQueen was revving up a motorbike in a field. 'Every Christmas, it's The Great Escape.'

'When's the Queen's speech?' Perhaps the Queen would take my mind off Diana.

'We are not watching the Queen's speech.' Evie switched off the television, lest the Queen suddenly start her speech.

If I were an artist or novelist, I could express my longing in a meaningful way. Creative types were inspired by infatuation, not daunted. I picked up Fysh's sketch pad and a Biro from the mess beside the chess board.

'I love Diana... I love Diana... I love Diana...' I wrote. When my Biro ran out of ink, I continued with a pencil. 'I love Diana... I love Diana... I love Diana...'

'I love Diana.' Skunk too was saying it. 'You're like a schoolboy writing lines for a sadistic prefect.'

'Love is like the sun,' said Evie.

'Why?' asked Skunk. 'Because it doesn't come out?'

Evie ignored him. 'It lights up the world but you can't look at it. All you can do is feel its warmth.'

'If you're capable of love, then you're capable of hate,' said Skunk. 'If you're not armed with hate, you're naked in the chamber.'

'Oh that's riiiight. Hate the one you're with. Dada, dada, dah dah da dah,' sang Evie.

'"I too was created by eternal hate,"' said Skunk. 'That's Freddie. After Dante.'

'I thought love and hate were the same difference,' said Evie.

'I gave her an ultimatum.'

'What, for Christmas?' said Skunk. 'What did you say?'

'I said, "I'm not putting up with your ridiculous 'religion' anymore. It's your choice: Bhagwan or me." I wrote it in a letter that I put in her bag as she was leaving.'

'Good for you,' said Evie. 'Standing up for truth, whatever the cost.'

Skunk smiled. 'She's going to hate you. You know that, don't you?'

'She's not going to hate him.' Evie turned to me. 'I've seen the way she looks at you. I bet she's thinking about you right now. I bet she's replied to your letter loads of times, and thrown all her efforts in the bin. That's what girls, I mean women, do. Deep down she knows you're right. Don't worry, Jake. She's not going to choose Baggy over you.'

'I'm going to call her.' I had almost stopped at the phone boxes outside Lumumba Slope bar when chasing Skunk and Gordon.

'Don't do that,' said Evie.

'I miss her. I want to hear her voice.'

'She won't talk to you,' warned Skunk. 'And then you'll feel even worse.'

'It's too soon,' said Evie. 'Let sleeping feesh lie.'

'I want to apologise.'

Skunk rolled his eyes. 'You've got nothing to apologise for.'

'Not bad.' Evie was looking over my shoulder. While we had been talking, my pencil had been sketching. 'What do you think?' she asked Skunk.

Skunk got up to have a look. 'The perspective's not right.'

Her wavy blonde hair, delicate nose, close-set eyes and pouting lips were instantly recognisable. But the harder I tried to capture her essence, the more elusive it became. In a fit of frustration, I scoured the page with a rubber. Smudged lines revealed the glow of Diana's radiance.

Down came my gallery of Hollywood stars. Up went a real goddess. Then I lay on the bed, to listen to Beethoven's Pastoral Symphony, for which Skunk had moved his giant speakers into the upstairs corridor. On Beethoven's cuckoo calls, I rolled over and communed with Diana.

'Grub's ready!' shouted Skunk.

A homely aroma of cooking wafted through the flat. Skunk had made spaghetti carbonara. I opened a window between curtains half drawn on a darkening sky and Skunk served up dinner while Evie poured drinks.

'Do you like Irish coffee, Jake?' Evie handed me a liqueur glass full of treacly brown liquid. 'I got the recipe from my mum. Cheers. Merry Christmas.'

'To our swansong,' said Skunk.

'Next year in Jerusalem,' I heard myself say. I twisted my fork in a creamy nest of slithering worms and bacon bits but couldn't bring myself to eat any more than I could drink Evie's Irish coffee.

'Good Christmas dinner, Skunk,' said Evie as she shook salt over her carbonara. 'I wonder where Felix went. And where's Gordon?'

'He left during The Great Escape,' laughed Skunk.

'We could do with some mince pies,' said Evie. 'I wonder whether the co-op's open.'

'Oh, God.' Now I had something else to worry about. 'I think I invited Jimmy over for Christmas dinner.' It was the type of misunderstanding which, in great literature, leads to tragedy. In reality it led to the sorry scenario of Jimmy celebrating Christmas Day on his own, for want of confirmation of my invitation.

My guilt was misplaced. In the course of his rounds, Jimmy found Jethro washing his smalls at the laundrette and Gordon looking for his brother. Like three musketeers, they raided the co-op, drank at an officially closed bar then decamped for some exclusive festivities at Nightline.

Duck Soup was about to begin when Gordon rolled in with unexpected provisions. The four of us huddled on the sofa under Evie's knitted blanket, sharing munchies from the co-op and drinks from Guevara House bar. We laughed so hard at Groucho and Harpo's mirror dance, we fell in a heap on the floor.

Letter 17

The start of term was marked by rambunctious reunions and reorientations in residences and faculty alike. Tucked away in a remote corner of the philosophy department, undisturbed by the fuss, Prof Cricklemore was marking papers. A tonsured head and academic gown lent him an old-fashioned gravitas.

'Hello, Professor Cricklemore. Do you remember me? I did Metaphysics with you a couple of years ago.'

Prof Cricklemore either didn't recognise me and didn't want to admit it, or he did recognise me and didn't want to admit it.

'You'll never guess what happened in Stanmore Woods,' I said.

Prof Cricklemore looked up but rather than guess what happened in Stanmore Woods, he waited for me to tell him.

'God spoke to me,' I said.

Prof Cricklemore was unmoved. 'And why, exactly, are you sharing this news with me?'

'You know God. You used to be a monk.'

Prof Cricklemore straightened up. 'If you had bothered to attend tutorials or lectures, or read my book, Cartesian Metaphysics: A Beginner's Guide, or indeed any of my essays in Radical Philosophy, you would know that I am a neo-Platonist. As such, I'm hardly likely to give credence to any notion of a God who speaks to people on an individual basis. The very idea of God as an external entity strikes me as a fundamental misunderstanding of the theology that underpins Western civilisation.'

'He gave me His blessing.'

'Did He really?' Prof Cricklemore sounded unconvinced, if not sarcastic. 'I must say, I find the Judeo-Christian concept of God the Creator a little primitive.'

'I'm not talking about God the Creator.'

'And the idea of having to account for ourselves before an Almighty tribunal in a life to come is somewhat superstitious, don't you think?'

'I'm not talking about a life to come. I'm talking about staying alive. Didn't Descartes say God's existence is less about the cause of my being than about conserving me at any given time?'

'Yes, that's a close enough approximation. But Descartes wouldn't be the only philosopher to misrepresent the nature of God. Take Spinoza.'

'When I was up my tree on Christmas Day...'

'"God" is merely a name we give the divine. And the route to this divinity is through love.'

'How does that work?' It sounded like a neo-Platonist pyramid of enlightenment.

'Do you understand what Plato meant by "love"?'

'The sovereignty of friendship, right?'

'Wrong. To Plato, the love of another person is a means to an end, that end being love of the divine. Say you're in love with a beautiful girl.'

'I am in love with a beautiful girl.'

'Don't be funny. The point is, her beauty inspires you. Beauty is the virtue that touches your soul like no other. It unlocks your awareness of a spiritual transcendence. Your recognition of beauty in a girl facilitates an appreciation of beauty in itself. Everywhere you look, in nature, in art, in life, you will find examples of beauty. "How can it be?" you ask yourself. "What can be the source of so much beauty?" The answer, of course, is God. So you see, the love of an individual is merely a stepping stone to love of God.'

Prof Cricklemore had it the wrong way round. I wasn't talking about my love of God. I was talking about God's love of me.

Letter 18

Diana returned to campus wearing a navy-blue shawl, regulation jeans and black Doc Martens.

Overjoyed, I stood up for a kiss. 'I'm so happy you came to your senses!'

'Don't touch me, you bastard! How could you write a letter like that? It ruined my whole Christmas.'

She had ditched Bhagwan and was ditching me, too. She was visiting Flat 22 only to kick me into touch. She was about to leave when she noticed her portrait on the wall. Her jaw dropped, she turned round and conceded a glimmer of eye contact.

'Verity sends her regards,' she said, before sitting at my desk and taking out her rolling gear. 'So do Hector and Tarquin.'

'That's nice. Send my regards back to them.' We laughed at our stilted voices and rose for a conciliatory embrace.

The door opened. A bright light flashed. Kitty was taking our picture.

A week later we moved into a couple's room in Flat 59 at the top of Lumumba Slope and our photograph, which Kitty had inserted into a Charles & Diana royal-wedding souvenir frame, found a home on Diana's desk. Facing the photo at the other end of her desk was a golden Buddha. The Buddha played several roles, including religious icon, spiritual ornament and useful paperweight. Whatever he was, the Buddha beamed. Above her desk, Diana had covered the wall in silk scarves, each featuring a mystical motif. But whereas motes of dust danced and Buddha gleamed when morning sunlight shone through our window, the scarves' intricate mandala, yin and yang and doe-eyed goddess all became invisible.

The sun caught us making love on our futon. It caught us breakfasting in bed on buttered croissants and strawberry jam, fresh orange juice and real coffee, it caught the Sunday papers and a burning joint. It caught the morning of our lives.

Diana handed me a parchment scroll inscribed in her beautiful calligraphic handwriting.

'"*The privilege of a lifetime is to become who you truly are.*" *– Jung*'

I thanked her with a kiss and sellotaped it to the wall above my desk. To be honest, I didn't want to become who I truly was, not then. For all that we had moved in together, we were travelling in opposite directions.

Diana's influences had gone west. Now she found enlightenment in Montaigne's Essays and Yeats's poetry and in Rilke's Duino Elegies, which she carried in her bag 'in case of emergencies'. Bhagwan's Book of Wisdom (volume one) disappeared, as did Abstinence Tuesdays. She continued to attend Hare Krishna events at the Meeting House (wearing a navy-blue shawl), but only out of habit or custom.

Meanwhile I was seduced by Kitty's tales of Kibbutz Galuyot, of young volunteers who came from all over the world, forsaking home and possessions, escaping everyday ennui to experience an intimate, communal life. Nothing, Kitty said, could compare with the volunteers' camaraderie. But at some point, Kitty's memories of this ideal society would invariably turn to Yoni, the kibbutznik in her heart.

'Shall I wash your hair?' asked Diana as she ran her fingers through my shoulder-length locks.

'I did have a shampoo the other day,' I said.

We stepped out of our room and hadn't advanced beyond the corridor when we sensed an air of menace. I was naked under Diana's fluffy pink robe and, equipped with only a bottle of Badedas and a folded towel, ill-prepared for a confrontation with our flatmates. Diana was fully dressed but had her hands full with an incense candle, a soap dish and a bottle of Timotei in case I changed my mind.

Our three flatmates, who were on a year's secondment from the Royal Navy, regarded Flat 59 as a battleship of their own. In respect for their military traditions and our status as newcomers, we left the bathroom and toilet shipshape at all times, we didn't smoke hash in communal areas and we washed-up, dried-up and put away our stuff after meals, though Diana did drink their milk, and re-mark the plimsoll line they had drawn on their milk bottle. If we saw one of them alone, he would grunt an acknowledgement. Together, they were less friendly.

Ginger Cadet was leaning on the wall, barring our way to the bathroom. He ogled Diana then cast a less amorous look at my fluffy pink robe.

Rodent Cadet was perched on the ledge, holding a teaspoon. 'Is this anything to do with you?'

'It's a teaspoon.' Diana curled her lip.

'I know what it is,' snapped Rodent. 'I found it in the sink.'

'Are you the petty officer?' I couldn't resist a touch of levity, wasted though it was.

'A spoon does not belong in the sink,' said Rodent. 'It belongs in a drawer, with its mates.'

'Well if you know where it belongs...,' I began.

Sssss.

A sizzling iron made me jump. Down below, in an area designated for lounging and dining, Prop-Forward Cadet was standing over a pile of shirts, red-hot iron in hand.

'Put that man on a charge of impertinence,' said Rodent.

'And her.' Ginger wanted to include Diana.

'You're not in the navy now,' said Diana.

Ginger's eye twitched. How dare she defy him, in front of his peers? Ginger took Diana's insolence personally.

'I think it's time to put hippy boy through an initiation ceremony,' smirked Rodent.

'What do you mean?' Diana thrust out her chin.

'You'll see,' said Rodent. 'You're invited to watch.'

Diana pursed her lips and looked to me.

They were going to tie me to a chair and shave my head. Or force me to eat some disgusting shit. Or flush my head down the bog, Ginger restraining Diana all the while. Prop-Forward's iron induced a new fear. Surely they weren't going to brand me. That would be grievous bodily harm, they'd go to prison. A dreadful thought sent a chill down my spine: could Her Majesty's armed forces be exempt from civilian laws?

Vincent would know what to do. Whether it was torturing rival dealers, knocking policemen off their motorbikes or kidnapping squaddies, Vincent dreamed of tackling his enemies. On campus he had to make do with words. Whether it was political activists, trendy posers or public-school toffs in his line of fire, Vincent applied the same invective. Shoulders back, jaw clenched, he'd look them in the eye and snarl, 'Fuck off, you fascist cunts!'

'Fuck off, you fascist cunts!' I said. A bit belatedly, I pulled back my shoulders, clenched my jaw and snarled. I looked each of them in the eye, and felt a pressing need to pee. Our trip to the bathroom had suddenly become more urgent.

'Oh yeah?' Rodent jumped to the floor. 'Bring it on, hippy boy.'

'You really are asking for it,' brayed Ginger.

Down below, Prop-Forward drew the curtain and limbered up his neck.

I swayed to and fro to placate my bladder while cursing my bravado. I had only made a bad situation worse. What the hell was I thinking? How now was I going to come up with a diplomatic solution? I was scrambling for an answer when my big mouth struck again.

'If you *ever* threaten me again, you'll be sorry,' I warned them.

Prop-Forward laughed, like I'd just told a joke.

'Do you know how we punish insubordination?' Ginger advanced a step.

'Wait a minute, Bob.' Rodent stuck out an arm. 'Initiation first. Punishment second.'

'*Then* you can make us sorry,' promised Prop-Forward.

I remembered Mary and my special power. I should have asked her what it was. I wished it was indifference to pain, or a cloak of invisibility, or a secret weapon. Then I remembered God's blessing. And you'll never guess what happened next. Just when I needed it most, lo! A flash of inspiration. I *did* have a secret weapon!

I set aside my towel and bottle of Badedas and tightened my belt. The cadets didn't scare me. On the contrary, they amused me. Quite unaware of their impotence as they stood poised to pounce, they grinned like a troop of monkeys.

'I'm warning you,' I said. 'You had better back off.'

'Or what?' asked Rodent.

'With every word, you're earning another lash,' said Ginger.

'If you don't leave us alone, I'll spike your tea with LSD.'

Their smiles disappeared, their faces fell and their postures flopped.

'Do you know what LSD is? It's lysergic acid di-ethel... something. You'll be out of your fucking heads for a very long time. Possibly forever.'

The cadets looked at each other in despair and, without need of words, they surrendered unconditionally. 'We just want to keep the place tidy,' muttered Rodent as he made himself busy with a dishcloth. Prop-Forward returned to his ironing board and Ginger gave way as though ready to salute a pair of rear admirals.

'What's this dry land?'

'What happened to the sea?'

'Who's the commanding officer?'

'Is it you or is it me?'

After we'd finished laughing at the cadets, and I'd had a pee, Diana lit an incense candle and turned on the bath taps. She rolled up her sleeves and poured Badedas into the water, which she tested with her elbow. Green foam rose as the room steamed up.

I pressed Diana from behind. We were celebrating victory.

'No, Jake.'

'Come on, Di.'

'Get in!' She wrangled me into the tub.

Immersion in water subdued my erection. I flicked suds at Diana, who shied away in irritation. I chucked a handful of water, then another. Diana was drenched, the floor flooded.

Her screams turned to laughter as she undressed. Then she joined me, though the bath was barely big enough for one. The taps got in our way and the porcelain was slippery but we moaned loudly for our flatmates' benefit and kept going for mine. As our lovemaking reached a climax, Diana regarded me with pity. Desire had enslaved me.

Letter 19

'There will be outbreaks of rain in the east and scattered showers in the south.'

I switched off the radio, put on a Grateful Dead tape and rolled a number. Having set out to beat the rush of Saturday-morning shoppers, we were going to arrive too early. Then roadworks brought us to a standstill. At this rate we would be late.

A Rolls-Royce heading in the opposite direction drew up beside us, white ribbons trailing its silver lady. The chauffeur offered a packet of cigarettes over his shoulder. A lone passenger raised her white veil to light up. Then she blew us a kiss and I wished her good luck.

'I hate weddings,' said Diana. 'I had to go all the way to India to avoid the Verity-and-George pantomime.' She honked her horn to nudge the car in front. 'Isn't there an alternative route? What does the map say?'

'What good's an alternative route when we can't move?'

'Well if we could move, we wouldn't need an alternative route.'

A church spire rose above a field of sheep wearing sprayed red 'K's. The sun flashed in a catherine-wheel window and lit up a graveyard's crooked tombstones. Beyond the church lay a patchwork of allotments and a white, blossoming orchard. The scarlet gash of a post office added a flash of colour to a row of thatched cottages that wound down towards a pub sign for The Bird & Bush. On the motorway's other side, workers in yellow helmets and high-vis jackets dotted a slate quarry. A rearing white horse on a crested sign welcomed us to Kent. I passed the joint to Diana and closed my eyes.

'How's school, young man?' Cedric eyed me through the rear-view mirror.

I was in a back seat with my holdall, which contained my autograph book, a paperback in case of rain delays, a cricket bat for a game after stumps and a tupperware lunch box that Mum had filled with sandwiches, an apple and a packet of crisps.

'Your schooldays are the best days of your life,' said Cedric, a stockbroker pal of Dad's who was correct as ever in his navy-blue blazer and maroon club tie.

'There goes Eddie Merckx,' said Alf, from the passenger seat, on spotting a cyclist. He cleaned his glasses on a chunky knit jumper and looked out the window again. 'John Shepherd's cousin,' he said, on seeing a black man. Then his thoughts turned to the game ahead. 'Who do you think's gonna win the toss, eh, Cedric?'

'What you got in your sandwiches today?' asked Bernie, who was sitting beside me. 'Cor, you're lucky,' he'd say, whatever was in my sandwiches. 'We used to get bread and jam. And if we misbehaved, we were sent to bed without any tea at all.'

'Youngsters today,' said Cedric. 'They don't know they're alive.'

Bernie pulled out a rolled-up newspaper and we lingered over the Page 3 girl while pretending to read an adjacent news story. Bernie wore a wide-lapelled jacket and kipper tie, flared trousers and cowboy boots, a silver bracelet and Brut aftershave like a hip young dude, but a receding hairline, greying sideburns and the onset of liver spots told their own story.

'Show Bernie your autograph book,' said Cedric, who solicited autographs on my behalf at benevolent-fund dinners. Collecting autographs was an honourable tradition enjoyed by schoolboys down the ages, he said. Today's scribbled signatures were tomorrow's cultural artefacts.

'Danny La Rue. Henry Cooper. Babs from Pan's People...,' read Bernie, from the names Cedric had printed under their squiggles. 'Is Babs the blonde one?'

'Let's have a look,' said Alf. 'Mike Smith, John Edrich, Jackie Bond,' he read. 'You remember that catch, Cedric? Cor blimey, eh?'

The St Lawrence Ground was a rhapsody in green and white. Mature yew trees looked down on a rustic wooden sightscreen, a lime tree watched from midwicket. Marquees billowed gently either side of a pavilion in need of fresh paint. All was set fair for a lazy day of soporific rhythms and the bucolic harmonies of olde England. Here sang the spirits of Alfred the Great, burning cakes as he pondered, good Queen Bess making no windows into men's souls and brave Spitfire pilots engaged in mortal combat in skies of cornflower blue. Their ancestors sat around a boundary rope in deck chairs or tiered stands, from callow schoolboys marking scorebooks to genteel pensioners warmed by tartan blankets and thermos flasks of tea.

To me the cricket was riveting, whether it was Asif Iqbal driving half-volleys for four, 'Deadly' Derek Underwood bamboozling batsmen with his left-arm spin or Knotty in a sun hat leaping for a catch behind the wicket. Cedric was less attentive. Awoken by a bowler's 'Howzaaaat?' or a ripple of applause, Cedric appealed or applauded too. His binoculars he trained on the members' stand. 'I see JC's been let off the leash,' he'd say. Or 'there goes Bunny from the Rotary Club.' When Alf reminisced over players whose like we'd never see again, Cedric corrected him or told him to watch the cricket. During intervals for lunch and tea, we strolled around the ground, stopping to chat with fellow regulars. There was Colin Jenks, his face the colour of a lobster, handkerchief knotted around his head, beer gut seeping out of a paisley shirt, carrying pints from the bar or heading back with the empties; lanky Steve Chippenhurst taking bookings for the supporters' coach or soliciting contributions to a retiring player's testimonial fund; and Dawn and Cherie, glamorous blonde sisters who hung out at the players' car park. Dawn and Cherie didn't say much to us, for all Bernie's banter, though he had better luck with the corporate dolly birds who stood, in their sponsor's livery, outside tents that reeked of warm beer and white-bread sandwiches. After stumps, Cedric, Alf and Bernie retired to a members' bar while out on the greensward, our shadows lengthening, we schoolboys played cricket on the boundary.

Now I was returning, a long-haired student with a beautiful girl on my arm, ready to revisit the old regulars. They were going to see me as a prodigal son, though I wasn't quite sure what that meant. Anyway, as fate would have it, we wound up revisiting another set of old regulars altogether.

Hexleigh had changed. The second-hand record shop had become a beauty salon, the library a Comet warehouse. Apartment blocks had replaced my primary school, a new multistorey car park rose above the municipal swimming pool. In Hexleigh Park, where we used to play three-and-in using jumpers for goalposts, adult footballers in real kits were playing on a marked pitch with real goals and nets.

We strolled hand in hand, exchanging self-conscious smiles with other loved-up couples, past an old landowner's mansion that was hidden by scaffolding, a Victorian bandstand on a hill and a park-keeper's shed. We ambled through a garden of waterfalls and rock pools crossed by stepping stones and paused to look at the budgies, finches and canaries in a timbered aviary. We swung on playground swings, slid down a slide and dizzied ourselves on a roundabout. On seeing an island in the lake, Diana wanted to swim 'there and back' and I had to smother her in a hug to keep her clothes on. I would have suggested a round of pitch and putt but I was getting hungry and it was getting dark.

'Good heffens!' Mum came out to greet us before we had even parked up. 'Why have you come home?'

'We were going to watch cricket in Canterbury but the car broke down.'

'Heffens alive! You should haff told us you were coming. You must be Diana. I haff heard so much about you.'

'No you haven't.'

'You said you haff a beautiful girlfriend who studies philosophy.'

'When did I say that?'

'I don't know. When we spoke on the phone. Oh, what is the point of arguing?'

She ushered us into the kitchen, where she listened to The Archers at a volume so low you couldn't hear what anyone was saying. 'This is my domain,' she said, and I half-expected her to tell Diana she could eat off the floor, not as a punishment so much as a demonstration of Mum's high standards of hygiene.

'Would you like a cup of tea, Diana?'

'You haven't got herbal tea, have you, Mrs Green?'

'"Cynthia," please.' I thought she was talking to herself. 'There is no need to stand on ceremony here. We do not have herbal tea but I can offer you lemon tea.' She pulled out a stepladder that she climbed to reach her best china.

'That would be lovely. Thank you.' Diana half-sat on a table stool.

I filled the kettle and plugged it in, though Mum regarded help in the kitchen as an intrusion, if not evidence of a plot to undermine her authority.

'If I had known you were coming, I would haff cooked a proper meal and laid the dining-room table. Now you will haff to haff homemade vegetable soup and sandwiches, here in the kitchen with Dad and me.'

'Thank you,' said Diana. 'That sounds delicious.'

'Diana's vegetarian.'

'Is that so?' Mum nodded in understanding. Youngsters today joined all sorts of cults.

'Where's Dad?'

Dad was usually at home on Saturday afternoons, or in the garden shed at any rate. On weekday evenings, when I was doing homework in my room, I'd hear a hammering of nails or a buzzing saw, a plane going whoosh or an angry curse as Dad laboured away in the shed.

'He's at the timber yard. He *will* be surprised…'

'Why, what's he making now?'

'A magazine rack, if you don't mind.'

'I'd like to be a carpenter,' said Diana.

'Stanley is not a carpenter.' We weren't tradespeople. 'Stanley is a stockbroker. Woodwork is his hobby.'

'You have a slight accent,' said Diana.

'That's right. Did Jacob tell you where I am from?'

'Germany?'

'Vienna.'

'What made you leave?'

Mum sighed. 'In the 1930s, Vienna was the most beautiful city. Charming, elegant, sophisticated…'

Mum never talked about the family she lost, not that she had anyone to talk to. Dad saw no point in dwelling on the past, Great-Aunt Flora had Alzheimers and I was too young to count. She wasn't going to confide in Mrs Godsmark, our long-serving cleaning lady, nor our neighbours, for all their shared pleasantries over a garden fence. Though Papa came over for Friday night dinner, sometimes with Dad's cousins from Finchley, their conversations steered well clear of intimacies.

'Mum was on a Kindertransport. Her family all perished in the Holocaust, except Great-Aunt Flora.'

'Damn it all!' Mum had spilled tealeaves on her pristine kitchen counter. At the same time we heard Dad's Ford Capri in the drive. Mum took a paper towel to the tealeaves then hurried out to apprise Dad of our visit.

Diana smoothed her skirt, scratched at a stain on my Grateful Dead T-shirt then readied herself to curtsy.

'Hullo.' Dad lingered for a moment on Diana before frowning at me, like I'd done something stupid. 'Mum says you were going to Gravesend but came home instead.'

'It was Canterbury. We were going to Canterbury.'

'We were going on a pilgrimage,' said Diana. '"Whan that aprill with his shoures soote, the droghte of march hath perced to roote, thanne longen folk to go on pilgrimaaarge."'

Dad narrowed his eyes as if assessing Diana's mental health.

Mum shook her head. She didn't know what the world was coming to.

'We were going to watch cricket, or visit the cathedral if it rained,' I said.

'Canterbury Cathedral, woooh...' Diana's ghoulish tone suggested a Chamber of Horrors rather than the seat of Anglican power. 'They murdered Thomas à Becket in the nave, you know. While the monks were chanting vespers.'

'Did they really?' said Mum.

'Have you seen Powell and Pressburger's A Canterbury Tale?' I asked.

Dad shook his head, though not in answer to my question.

'It was made in your day, in 1944, during the war. We thought we'd follow in the footsteps of its characters, and those of Chaucer's pilgrims. A Canterbury Tale is my second-favourite movie.'

'What's your first favourite?' asked Diana.

'Oh, The Passenger, directed by Michelangelo Antonioni. It's about a journalist played by Jack Nicholson who changes his identity and becomes someone else, in a desert. I always thought something like that would happen to me.'

Diana smiled indulgently while Mum pursed her lips and Dad furrowed his brow.

'It's an existential parable,' I told them. 'You've never seen Jack Nicholson give such an understated performance, and Maria Schneider is a completely different person to The Girl in Last Tango in Paris. It's like she's not even acting. Mind you, she was addicted to heroin.'

Not only were Mum and Dad not listening, they were having a wordless conversation between themselves. When I stopped talking, they stopped too.

'Anyway, we didn't get to Canterbury because Diana's car broke down. By the time we found a garage and got it fixed, it wasn't worth carrying on to Canterbury.'

'And it was such a nice day,' said Diana.

'What a shame,' said Mum.

'What was wrong with the car?' asked Dad.

'I dunno.'

'How can you not know?'

'I didn't watch them fix it. And even if I was watching...'

'Didn't they tell you?'

'Was it the fan belt?' suggested Diana. 'I had a Yamaha 500 and there were always problems with the fan belt. And when it wasn't the fan belt, it was...'

'How much did it cost?' asked Dad.

'Diana put it on her credit card.' In other words, we didn't know that either.

'*She* does the driving, *she* pays the mechanic, *she* has the pretty face. What do *you* contribute?' Dad's thoughts didn't need words, though they were a bit unfair. It was *my* idea to go to Canterbury in the first place.

'Do you like cricket?' Mum asked Diana.

'Not really. Verity used to drag me along to watch Tarquin play at Harrow. It was all very civilised. Chaps in boaters saying "jolly good show" when someone hit the ball, or "hard cheese" when they were out. I read a book in the sunshine.'

'You will stay the night, won't you?'

'That was the idea,' I said. 'Not the original idea, obviously.'

'Did they bring overnight bags?' Dad asked Mum.

'We can get by without a change of clothes for one day,' I told him.

Dad didn't doubt it. Or understand it. You'd think I'd want to smarten myself up, if only to impress Diana.

'I will change the linen in the spare room,' said Mum.

'You really needn't bother, Mum. Diana can sleep with me.'

'Certainly not.'

'Why not?'

'This is our house, and when you stay here you liff by our conventions.'

I hadn't heard of a convention on celibacy, though I recalled plenty of others. Meals for instance were eaten in silence, notwithstanding my parents' hushed exchanges 'about someone you don't know'. You couldn't eat in silence or talk about someone you don't know in front of a dinner guest, so Mum went to the other extreme, firing so many questions at Diana that by the time we had finished our soup she knew all about Verity and George and their three-storey house in South Kensington, Diana's father Maurice, his gold-digging wife and their mansion in Holland Park, and her brothers Hector, whose imminent takeover of their father's business empire was going to make him 'rich as Croesus,' and Tarquin, who was coming into his own in The Tatler's society pages.

'Take two or three.' Mum set down a platter of sandwiches cut into triangles. 'There's egg mayonnaise, cheese and pickle, and salami.'

'Oooh, I don't think I could manage more than one.' Diana took an egg mayonnaise and I helped myself to one of each.

'Yummy scrummy,' said Dad. 'What sort of business does your father own?'

'He's a publisher,' said Diana.

Dad's eyes narrowed. 'Diana's father could be a good contact, Jacob. It's about time you started thinking about your future.'

'He's not going to give me a job just because I'm going out with Diana.'

'Probably the opposite,' laughed Diana.

'He might, if he had a haircut.' He meant me. 'If you play your cards right, you could be onto a good thing. You never know.'

'Publishing would suit you,' said Mum. 'With a degree in philosophy you will know which books to publish.'

Dad wasn't so sure. 'A philosophy degree isn't a ticket to a top job with a big salary, you know, especially in today's economic climate. You have to have ambition.'

'Do you have ambition, Jake?' Diana stifled a laugh.

'Ambition is the last refuge of the scoundrel,' I would have said, were it time for one of my sayings.

'When you meet Diana's father, you want to make a good impression,' said Dad. 'You want to show your willingness to provide for his daughter. And then, if you're lucky, he might let you start at the bottom.'

'It is the same for everyone,' said Mum. 'You haff to start somewhere.'

'Then it'll be up to you to show you can do the job,' Dad continued. 'You'll have to show your mettle, take responsibility. That's the way to get ahead, to get promoted. You want Diana's father to see you as a future partner.'

'What sort of books does he publish?' Mum pointed the platter at Diana. 'Are you sure you won't haff another sandwich?'

'No, thank you. *He* doesn't publish anything. He's more of a businessman really.'

'What's his company called?' If it was listed on the stock exchange, Dad would probably know about it.

'He has several.' Diana wasn't sure of their names. 'There's one that buys and sells the rights to dead authors, another that prints technical books in foreign languages... or something like that. He's transferring the business to Hector at the moment. Tarquin too I shouldn't wonder.'

Dad nodded. Her brothers' inheritance represented the natural order of things.

'What about you?' asked Mum. 'Surely you are entitled to a share also?'

'I don't want it. Hector and Tarquin can keep it.'

'You might want it one day,' said Dad.

'Why don't you write a book about philosophy, Jacob? I haff always said what a good writer you are. Haffn't I always said that, Stanley?'

'I don't make it to lectures or tutorials, I don't read things I don't like and when I do get down to studying, I'm distracted by visions of Diana. So how am I going to write a book about philosophy?' I wanted to say.

'Diana's father could publish it,' Mum added.

'Sure,' said Dad. 'I expect Jacob's philosophy book is just what Diana's father is waiting for.'

'You could put your beliefs in a book,' said Mum, as though that would keep the place tidy.

'No, he couldn't,' said Diana.

'Why not?' Mum wondered what was wrong with my beliefs, as though Dad hadn't told her, numerous times. 'Are they too extreme?'

'He hasn't got any beliefs.'

'Yes I do. I believe in God. Or, should I say, God believes in me.'

'That's schizophrenic,' said Dad. 'I grew up acquainted with people who were obsessed by God. They thought they were married to Him.'

'Take some fruit,' said Mum and she offered us a bowl filled by red and green apples, a pair of wrinkly oranges and a long-suffering banana.

'This orange might have come from Kitty's kibbutz.' I held up an orange which, following Diana's example, I peeled with my fingers, until it squirted juice at Dad, who was excising V-shaped cores from an apple he'd cut into quarters. Dad paused for a moment's indignation, Mum fussed to no purpose and Diana bit her lip. I told Mum and Dad about Kibbutz Galuyot and asked after Papa's kibbutz, but Dad was still smarting from my orange and in any case he claimed to know nothing about Papa's part in redeeming the land of Israel.

We drank lemon tea served in special-occasion china cups then Mum got up to stack the dishwasher. Diana offered to help but Mum wouldn't hear of it so I invited her outside to smoke a joint. Diana, that is.

'We don't want to be stoned in front of your parents,' said Diana as we clambered up a climbing frame in the back garden. It was true, we didn't want to be stoned in front of my parents. There again, I had already rolled a joint. After smoking it all myself, I couldn't go inside for quite a while, so we sat atop the climbing frame, looking at Hexleigh Park in one direction and the spire of St Mary's in the other.

Dad poured drinks in the lounge and Diana accepted a Harveys Bristol Cream, which was my parents' tipple. I took a can of Heineken and we all said 'cheers' before settling into the sofa and armchairs. Mum checked her watch and when it was time, she got up to switch on the television.

Mum and Dad watched the News in silence. The idea was to sit and listen, like tribespeople gathered at the feet of a prophet. If you interrupted the News, Dad gnashed his teeth and Mum raised a hand like a policeman stopping traffic.

'Who's that?' asked Diana. Eyes magnified by a pair of round glasses, face flushed by sherry, Diana looked like a tipsy granny. 'I didn't know they have women newscasters.'

'Have you never seen Angela Rippon?' Diana was so unworldly. 'What about Anna Ford? And Jan Leeming?'

'What happened to Robert Dougall?'

'I think he's on the other side.'

'He died?'

'Nohhhh. ITV. We only watch the BBC.'

Dad fumed in silence. He didn't work all day broking stocks or making things with wood only to have his hard-earned rest ruined by mindless chatter. I made a tamping-down gesture at Diana and resolved to keep quiet.

Lights flashed. Jewellery sparkled. A ballgown swept a red carpet. A shy and awkward ingenue lowered her cobalt eyes at a line of men in tuxedos.

'That's Lady Diana,' I told Diana.

'*Princess* Diana,' said Mum, before leaning over to share a confidence with our guest. 'Jacob used to wear a badge that said, "The Queen Mother: eighty years a scrounger".'

Diana laughed politely.

'That was during our school election,' I said.

'Jacob was the communist candidate.' Now, years later, Mum could talk about my communist days without shame, not least to Diana, who clearly had mental issues of her own. At the time, Mum told Dad's cousins it was just a phase, lest they think my communism congenital.

'How many votes did you get?' Diana sensed a bigger laugh coming.

'I quintupled the communist vote, if you don't mind.'

'From one to five?'

'From twenty to nearly a hundred, seeing as you ask.'

'He promised to abolish school uniform,' said Mum.

'I should think Marx would approve of school uniforms.' Diana looked at me over the rim of her glasses. 'Not that I've read any of his books.'

'He was appealing to yobs who support the National Front.' Dad couldn't resist a tale of filial idiocy. 'They're fascists,' he added, for Diana's benefit.

'I was upholding a long-standing tradition.'

'What tradition?' scoffed Dad.

'Selling your soul for votes. Isn't that how democracy works?'

'The National Front have their headquarters near here,' said Mum. 'On Hexleigh Lane, by the roundabout.'

'The Tories won, of course. Mr Downer fixed it.'

'Mr Down-ing,' said Mum.

'How did Mr Downer fix it?' Dad's scepticism had lost nothing to age.

'He gave the teachers a vote. And not one of them voted for me.'

'How do you know that?' Dad didn't believe me, though he could believe it.

'He told me. He was my history teacher.'

'History teachers will stop at nothing in their quest for power,' said Diana. 'Nothing, I tell you!'

'In the week leading up to election day, opinion polls pointed to a communist victory. It would have been like Paris in 1968.'

'You're talking out of your hat,' said Dad.

'It's true. Mr Downer said if I won, he would declare the results null and void on a technicality.'

'That's history teachers all over,' said Diana.

My experience with Mr Downer validated Diana's theory on history teachers. This, I thought, exemplified our synchronicity. Mum and Dad reached a different conclusion, which they kept to themselves.

Women in bright kagoules and Wellington boots were linking arms or holding hands, '*to form a human chain. The demonstration stretched for fourteen miles along the southern ridge of the valley. It was doubled up for much of its length, and three or four deep in places.*'

'And what do you think of them, Diana?' Mum crossed her legs and clasped her fingers.

'What are they protesting against?' asked Diana.

'Oh, don't tell me...' Mum tried to think.

'*Coaches brought supporters from all over the country and formed a snail's-pace procession of their own. In the air, nine helicopters and two light aircraft added to the general clutter.'* There was footage of a Mrs Joan Ruddock claiming *'an unprecedented success. It is a great victory, and especially a victory over the government's propaganda. We have defeated the government today.'*

'It will come to me when I am thinking about something else.' Mum shook her head. 'I am just not with it today.'

'It's Greenham Common,' I said. 'They're protesting against nuclear weapons.'

'Nuclear weapons, of course.' Mum watched the protestors for a bit then asked Diana, 'And what do you think of Mrs Thatcher?'

Diana didn't think of Mrs Thatcher. 'She's an imperialist fascist warmonger!' Diana's impersonation of a radical student elicited a smile from Dad.

'That is so interesting.' Mum took people at their word. 'What makes you say that?'

'Mrs Thatcher is the only man in the government.' Dad's refrain found new ears in Diana, who found it most amusing.

A man standing under an umbrella was talking about the fiscal deficit. Then it was back to Angela Rippon in the studio for a roundup of the sports news. Diana took off her glasses and excused herself from our company.

'Well? Do you like her?'

'She is beautiful,' said Mum. 'You should cherish her, Jacob.'

'She seems a bit mixed-up,' said Dad. 'Like the Youngers' boy.'

'Didn't he join the Hare Krishnas and shave his head off?' I asked, quoting Mum.

Mum raised a hand to forestall further conversation. It was time for the weather forecast with Michael Fish, who was standing by a map of the United Kingdom and Ireland. Diana returned just in time to catch a low front over Cornwall and Devon.

'Heigh-ho. I'm ready to hit the sack,' said Dad.

Mum gathered sherry glasses and shook my can of Heineken to check it wasn't empty. 'Don't forget to pull out the plug and switch off the lights before you go upstairs,' she said. We didn't want an electrical fire, nor was there any need to waste electricity. 'And remember to lock the doors.' We didn't want to be burgled either. 'Haff you got everything you need, Diana? Then I'll say goodnight. God bless. Sleep well.'

Ordinarily I would have been looking forward to Match of the Day, followed by a late-night movie, but Diana said she too was turning in. So I switched off the TV and pulled out the plug, switched off the lights and locked the doors then showed Diana upstairs.

My bedroom enshrined my schooldays. There was a vase of plastic tulips, from my girlfriend, Penny Bracewell, a little transistor radio and old textbooks, exercise books and sixth-form folders on my desk. A bookshelf was filled by Jennings stories, Agatha Christie whodunnits and Alistair MacLean thrillers. Captain Fantastic loomed over a single bed made up by an old-fashioned bedspread.

'Did your dad make the wardrobe?' asked Diana. 'And the desk?'

'The desk, yeah. But I put up the Captain Fantastic poster.'

The artist needed his head examined, said Dad. Captain Fantastic represented Elton John, and the Brown Dirt Cowboy was Bernie Taupin, I told him. They needed their heads examined too.

'He's funny, your dad. And Cynthia's so warm and friendly. They're not what I expected at all. Now I've met them I see you quite differently.'

A sliver of light appeared beneath the door. A floorboard in the hallway creaked. A toilet flushed and the floorboard creaked again.

'I don't mind sleeping in the spare room,' said Diana.

'What for? They won't be on night patrol.'

'I'm not going to disobey your mum. And even if I did sleep here, we couldn't make love.'

'Why not?'

'Not in your parents' house. Not with your parents here.' Having waited on the bed's edge while I rolled a number, and taken a toke to be polite, Diana got up to go.

'No, stay.'

'I'm tired, Jake. I need a good night's sleep. I'll see you in the morning.' We kissed, then I showed Diana to the spare room. I finished the joint in bed and went to sleep, single-handed.

'Woo woo, woo woo. Woo woo, woo woo.'

A woodpigeon was calling from a birch tree in the garden. It was a Sunday morning, when the bells of St Mary's lamented the passage of time every hour. On this particular Sunday morning, the chimes were fast and festive. They were celebrating a wedding.

I could just see a beautiful blonde bride, sparkling in a tiara and long white gown, holding hands with a dark, handsome groom who's uncomfortable in his morning suit and giddied by the fuss. And there, peering over their shoulders, stands Skunk, as best man, ready to hand me a wedding ring on the happiest day of my life.

Letter 20

'I say!' said Hector, whose pouty lips and chubby cheeks, thinning hair and supercilious air recalled Robert Morley at his most pompous. Likewise his country gentleman's corduroys and brown Oxford shoes, his spotted bow-tie and a canary-yellow waistcoat that bulged between its buttons. He mwah-mwah kissed Diana and shot me a look that said, 'Get up, dammit. And don't you dare fail in your responsibilities to my sister or I'll have your guts for garters.' He ran a finger through a layer of dust and sniffed at the scent of incense, no doubt logging examples of our decadence to report to their father.

'Don't get up.' Tarquin didn't mind me reclining on our futon. Dressed in a double-breasted suit, with a tie-clip that matched his signet ring, Tarquin exuded the charm of easy privilege. Tall and handsome, he had Diana's blue eyes and resolute jawline. 'You must be Jake,' he said as he leaned down, arm outstretched, and crushed my fingers. 'The rum cove who's fallen for Diana. I would never have imagined anyone brave enough, hiargh.' He placed my chair mid-room and sat on it backwards, one arm dangling, the other curled over his head.

'What tawdry lodgings,' said Hector.

I got up to kiss Diana, to show that we lived in a love nest, though in Hector and Tarquin's presence it seemed more like a doll's house. Diana took my place on the futon and sat cross-legged, low to the ground, to show off her humility. I sat at Diana's desk and Hector remained standing, above such childish games of musical chairs.

'To what do we owe the honour?' asked Diana.

'We've got a christening in Chichester.' Tarquin arched an eyebrow. 'Mummy says it's a three-line whip. You remember the Turtledoves. Friends of Grandma Prudence. Well, it's Celia's great-granddaughter who's being christened. We thought you might care to join us. Jake can come too. Do you have something to wear?'

'Why would we want to go to a christening?' Diana spoke my mind.

'Answering a question with a question, eh?' Hector gripped his lapels and raised his nose. 'That must be Jake's influence.' He cast a sly glance at me.

'What do you mean?' Diana detected an undercurrent.

'It's a Jewish thing.' Hector tapped his nose. Noses too were a Jewish thing.

'Mummy calls you "Diana's mystery man".' Tarquin rotated his chair towards mine. 'She says she can't get anything out of Diana so she's hoping you'll come to the christening. If you don't show, we'll get a thorough grilling. "Is he presentable? Is he well-mannered? Is he a strapping young man?" What it boils down to is this: do you cut the mustard?'

'I'd say he's a long-haired hippy,' said Hector.

'If this were the eighteenth century, you'd also have long hair,' Diana informed him. 'With ringlets.'

'If I'm a hippy, you're a Sloane Ranger.'

'Don't be impertinent.' Hector put on a cross face.

'What's a Sloane Ranger?' asked Diana.

'You know, the hooray Henrys and Henriettas you see going to private parties in the Crypt. Rugger buggers and debutantes.'

'Tell me more,' said Tarquin.

'What about Kitty?' asked Hector. 'Does Kitty go to parties in the Crypt?'

'Yes, Kitty!' exclaimed Tarquin. 'How is the dear girl getting on? We haven't seen Kitty for, oooh, since before she went to... Where was it? It was somewhere beginning with "J".'

'Israel,' said Diana.

'One letter out!' Tarquin clicked his fingers.

'*Kitty* is a hippy,' said Diana. 'Her whole philosophy revolves round peace and love.'

'What about you, Jake?' asked Hector. 'What's *your* philosophy?'

'Hector!' Now Diana looked cross. 'You're not the Spanish Inquisition.'

'Nobody expects the Spanish Inquisition, hiargh.' Tarquin roared at his joke.

'Let him answer,' said Hector. 'Surely you have *something* to show for all those hours dedicated to the elevated thoughts of, of...'

'Isn't it Karl Marx?' Tarquin arched an eyebrow. 'Isn't that what you study? Mummy says you students are unwashed Marxists. Though I must say, we haven't seen any yet. I once knew an undergraduate in sociological studies. When I say "knew," I mean...'

'Come on,' pressed Hector. 'You do study philosophy, don't you? So what's *your* philosophy?'

'Yes, what's it all about?' wondered Tarquin.

'*Fati amor.*' Diana answered for me.

'Are you calling me names?' Hector was sensitive about his girth.

'I'm only telling you what Nietzsche says,' said Diana. 'Did you not do Latin at school? "*Fati amor*" means "Love your fate".'

'I've never heard such nonsense. To think that Father, whom you never deign to visit, pays good money just for you to waste your time talking such balderdash.' Hector turned his ruddy face to me. 'Come on! What have you got to say for yourself?'

'Act only in accordance with that maxim through which you can at the same time will that it become a universal law,' said Kant. That was the essence of Western morality. 'Consciousness determines social existence,' said Hegel. That was the essence of dialectical idealism. 'The higher we soar, the smaller we appear to those who cannot fly,' said Nietzsche. I couldn't choose between these jewels of our syllabus, none of which seemed appropriate to a man of Hector's standing.

Hector consulted his watch. Tarquin followed suit, if less to check on time than admire his jewellery.

'Alright then,' I said. 'You want to know what's the most important thing I've learned in three years of studying philosophy? It's this. Be cheerful.'

'That's not much of a philosophy.' Tarquin expected something more profound.

'That's also Nietzsche,' Diana told them. 'It's in The Gay Science.'

'"The Gay Science,"' echoed Hector. 'Says it all.'

'He says it in Ecce Homo, too.'

Hector harrumphed anew. 'We hoped that going to university would make you grow up,' he told Diana. 'Regrettably it appears to have had the opposite effect.'

'Mummy says Wessex will be the making of Di,' countered Tarquin. 'And, what's more, she says we should be grateful to Jake for putting an end to Di's Bhagwan nonsense. Mummy says...'

'Don't be such a mummy's boy,' said Hector.

'Don't say that!'

'Very well. Don't be such a baby.'

'If you don't pipe down, I'll tell Jake about the time you wet yourself in Corfu and tried to frame me up. Or what about the time...'

'La, la, la...' Hector put his hands over his ears and stomped around in circles. 'La, la, la...'

'What time's your christening?' Diana rose to her feet. 'You don't want to be late.'

'Right you are.' Tarquin too stood up, erect as a guardsman. 'Come on Hector, let's leave the lovebirds to it.'

'Won't you stay for a cup of tea?' It was, I thought, the least we could offer. 'I'm sure we have some herbal.'

Hector snorted. If I thought I could tempt them with some herbal, I was more stupid than I looked.

'Time to burn rubber,' said Tarquin. 'Can't be late on a three-line whip.'

'You must come up to town for dinner, Di.' Hector assumed the convivial tone of one wrapping up a successful family gathering. He pulled on a pair of driving gloves and extended his arms for a farewell embrace.

'It's been jolly nice meeting you, Jake,' said Tarquin as he crushed my hand. 'Best of British luck, old boy.'

'I'm driving,' said Hector.

'Now just one moment...'

'You can drive back tonight.'

'You know I'll be riding with the Ponsonby-Smythes.'

'Lover boy here thinks he has a chance with Pru Ponsonby-Smythe,' said Hector.

'It's not a *chance*.' Tarquin blushed at his good fortune. 'It's a dead cert.'

'Spoken like a man who sells second-hand vehicles for a living,' said Hector.

'Take that back! Just because Mummy...'

'Mustn't be late for the christening,' Diana reminded them.

'How primitive,' said Hector as they exited past our kitchen and dining quarters.

'Positively barbaric,' agreed Tarquin.

I thought we'd have a debriefing following her brothers' departure, but Diana wasn't in a mood for idle chat. She said she was going to work on her dissertation, which meant she didn't want to be disturbed. So I went out on my own.

And I never came back.

Letter 21

'Dear all. Please fuck off,' read a sign on Flat 22's front door. The message was aimed at first-years looking to score hash, even though I'd moved out, and at administrators looking for trouble. The previous week a pair of jobsworths from the University of Wessex administration department had arrived, unannounced, to discuss the Madwoman of Caledonia case, which gave Skunk a platform to air his grievances. These included their neighbour's aggression, Lumumba Slope's thin walls and alienation in modern society. The administrators took notes, and several days later they moved a mature student into my old room to keep an eye on the inmates.

I would have thought the message a good one, were I not waiting in the rain for someone to let me in.

Only Kitty, parched and sallow like a veteran junkie, was home. A couple of sleeping bags were unfurled in a corner of central space despite admin's ban on 'squatters'. The TV was nowhere to be seen.

'Where's the telly?'

'Boney knocked it over. I was sitting where you used to sit and it just missed my head.'

'Karma, right?' I sat where I used to sit and played a finger rhythm on the table.

'You could say that.' Kitty returned to her armchair and her book. Kitty had been reading The Master and Margarita for weeks. Everywhere she went, she took her big red book.

'How's my replacement?'

'He moved out after one night.'

'I don't blame him. It's like a morgue in here. Where's the party? Oh well. You don't know what you've got till it's gone. They've paved paradise, put up a parking lot.'

'You're babbling, Jake.'

'That's Joni Mitchell. I get to hear a lot of Joni Mitchell.'
'Jolly good.'
'Guess who I saw in the library earlier.'
Kitty sighed so deeply I thought she was holding her breath. Her exasperation was no doubt well exercised by Skunk.

'Casey, that's who. He gave Andy Ox and Nutty John and me a line of coke.' I waited for Kitty's response. 'Don't you want to know if it was any good?'

'Well if it's the same as he had the other day, I'd say it was mediocre.'

'Must have been a different one. This one's good shit. I ran outside and climbed a lamppost. Almost got stuck, actually. Then Casey rode off on his Harley and Andy Ox, Nutty John and me went to the coffee shop for some chips. Now I've got indigestion.'

'Here. Why don't you roll one with this.' Kitty chucked over a lump of red-seal to be hospitable, or to shut me up. 'How's Diana?'

'Diana' made me gulp. She had been disappearing again, and I didn't want to question her for fear of seeming possessive. 'She's fine, as far as I know. How's The Master and Margarita? What's it about, anyway?'

'Shouldn't you be revising for finals?'

'Finals' made me gulp. The closer they loomed, the more frequent were my nightmares. Everyone in the exam hall was scribbling away while I just sat there, naked from the waist down. Or I was fully dressed and looking at questions about logical positivism. Finals meant our ivory-tower idyll was over and I would have to make my way in the outside world. It didn't bear thinking about.

'Where is everyone?'
'Gone to see Tron at the Odeon.'
'What's Tron?'
'It's a new movie. Some sort of science fiction, I believe.'
'You're all such space cadets.'

'And what are you?'

'I'm about time. In time you're just a link in a chain that goes back to your ancestors and forwards to your descendants. It's dialectical, isn't it? Your fate is determined by your ancestry.'

'What happened to being free? What happened to creating yourself?'

'You're such an existentialist, Kitty. I can just see you as a wise old professor with long grey hair and half-moon glasses addressing a lecture hall full of philosophy students. Maybe you'll sound the first trumpet blast against the monstrous regiment of...'

'Will you shut up! Skunk will be back soon,' she added apologetically.

'Where's he gone?'

'For a walk.'

'At this time of night? In the rain?'

Kitty shrugged a shoulder; both shoulders would have compromised her indifference.

'Where's he walking to? Don't tell me, it's not the destination, it's the journey, right?'

'I wouldn't be surprised if he went to the Red Duck.'

'Nah. We got banned.'

'Apparently it's under new ownership.'

'Really? Do you think they rescinded our ban?'

'Most probably.'

'They should take it upmarket, rename it, "The Red Pheasant". Geddit? Oh, never mind. Well if he has gone to the pub, he won't be back till after closing time. Unless he picked up a bird and went back to her place.'

Kitty closed her book. She'd had enough of The Master and Margarita.

A key clicked in a lock. The front door creaked open. A gust of wind slammed it shut behind a dripping, bedraggled Skunk. His eyes, dilated as ever, fixed on mine. Something was amiss.

'What's up?'

'I just saw Casey.'

'Did he give you some coke?' No wonder Skunk was off his head.

'I've got some bad news.'

Something had happened to Casey. He had probably come off his Harley on a wet, treacherous surface and was being rushed to an intensive-care unit as we spoke. His movie-star looks would never be the same. At least he had friends...

'It's Casey and Diana. They're... I don't know how to say this...'

I can't continue.
They have changed my medication and I tend to forget where I was.
Twice a day they give me drugs that loosen my grasp of reality.
God willing, I'll be back shortly.

Letter 22

'Aaaaaaargh!'

Silence.

I slashed a root, squirted petrol into the wound and moved on. Crouch, slash, squirt, advance. Crouch, slash, squirt, advance. Columns of green banana trees extended in every direction beneath fronds the size of elephants' ears. Early morning sunshine flashed through cracks in a canopy of leaves. Crouch, slash, squirt, advance. Crouch, slash, squirt, advance. Unfamiliar birdsong accompanied a tractor's rumble. My back was already aching. Crouch, slash, squirt, advance. Crouch, slash, squirt, advance. I took a step back and developed a new rhythm. Slash, squirt, waddle on haunches. Slash, squirt, waddle on haunches. Now my hips ached. I carved a 'D' into a healthy green tree. White juice bled through every cut.

'What are you doing, English?'

I looked up to find Abdullah wielding a knife three times the size of mine. His muscular limbs seemed to flow from his torso.

'You must bend your knees. Like this.' He showed me how to crouch, slash and squirt in a fluent combination. '*Chick-chack.* See? I know you, English. You are an old man spraying petrol in the air. Where is your hat? Soon the sun will be too hot for your soft skin. Where is your water?'

'Aaaaaaargh!'

Three obese figures in a neighbouring grove were locked in a standoff. Their guttural voices peaked in demented screams. Sunlight flashed in their sickles' blades.

'Who are they?'

'They weed the plantation while you sleep in bed,' said Abdullah as he led the way to investigate. 'Always they are fighting. Last week we took Zubeida to hospital in Rehovot. They stitched her together then she went back to work. You or me would be dead; they are protected by their fat.

'Why are they so fat?'

'Their men like them that way. And their heavy clothes are thanks to the prophets of Allah, who say... *koos emek*!' Abdullah interrupted himself to yell at Zubeida and friends, who yelled right back.

Then we all returned to work.

Crouch, slash, squirt, advance. Crouch, slash, squirt, advance. A rising sun glared through the cracks. Crouch, slash, squirt, advance. Crouch, slash, squirt, advance. A pleasant warmth had given way to an ever more ferocious heat. Crouch, slash, squirt, advance. Crouch, slash, squirt, advance. This was my new life, labouring in a plantation.

'*Lai* lai, la-la-la *lai* lai, la-la-la *lai* lai, la-la-la *lai* la-la lai.*'*

The singer was sitting under a banana tree, a bongo drum between his thighs. A tight thatch of curls, thick black stubble and hairy limbs recalled the simian provenance of our species. His hooked nose, dark eyes and obsequious smile recalled an old-fashioned caricature of the Jew.

'*Hola* Jacob.'

'How do you know my name?'

'You are the new volunteer, no? Everyone knows when a new volunteer comes. I am Danny. I make *aliyah*.' He steepled his fingers and raised his arms above his head. 'Whoosh,' he said, in imitation of a skybound rocket. 'In September I go to *Yerushalyim*, to study.'

'What are you going to study?'

'*Electromagnetismo*. But first I must learn Hebrew.'

'Where are you from?'

'I come from a village in Bolivia, is too small to see on maps. Seems like end of the world. My father says, "Danny, you must go to North America. Is best place to live." I say, "North America, he rapes South America. I will go to our forefathers' land in *eretz*

Yisrael." Is long journey, three days by land and air. Hey, are you *Americano?*'

'No, I'm British, but that's just by chance. I would have been *Americano*, had my Lithuanian grandmother sailed to New York, as per the ticket. But she was swindled by the ship's captain, who said Cardiff was New York. So Granny became Welsh instead of American and I was born a Brit.'

'*Lai* lai, la-la-la *lai* lai, la-la-la *lai* lai, la-la-la *lai* la-la lai.'

Crouch, slash, squirt, advance. Crouch, slash, squirt, advance. I wasn't cut out to be a fruit farmer. Perhaps I could do something else. There was also turkey farming, cotton picking and construction work, though Dudu, the volunteer leader, said you had to do the job you were designated. Crouch, slash, squirt, advance. Crouch, slash, squirt, advance. I mopped my brow and looked ahead, in hope of seeing a finishing line through the endless vista of banana trees. Crouch, slash, squirt, advance. Crouch, slash, squirt, advance. 'Ai-na!' A blister at the base of my left thumb sent a pain through my hand on every squirt. Crouch, slash, squirt, 'ouch'. Crouch, slash, squirt, 'ouch'. And so it continued until Moshe's whistle called us to breakfast.

Moshe drove the tractor. In his aviator sunglasses, red baseball cap and padded headphones, he was oblivious to his passengers on the trailer behind. Three gum-chewing Swedish girls were dangling their legs over the side while Herbie, a plump American with a mop of grey hair and varicose veins in his legs, lay on his back to sunbathe. I was dodging low-hanging fronds after one smacked me in the face.

Abdullah swooped down like Tarzan. He leaped aboard the trailer and sat leaning against a broad Swedish back. As we bumped along a muddy track, Abdullah sharpened his blade on a stone block.

We turned onto a deserted highway that gave rise to a hazy shimmer. On one side were groves of bushy trees from which oranges hung like baubles. On the other, a line of cypress trees, through which Kibbutz Galuyot resembled a model village.

A flagpole on a water tower raised the Israeli flag above a row of white stucco bungalows, all with slanting solar panels on red-tile roofs. Low-level palm trees flanked neat, paved paths, water sprinklers sprayed lawns and flowerbeds. The sun glistened in a swimming pool. It illuminated a giant mural of Bob Marley on a clubhouse wall, a Swedish flag painted on a stone pavilion and the pastel shades of a children's enclosure. A worker's silhouette cast sparks in a metalworks yard.

Moshe turned left at a pair of rusty cow-gates. 'Kibbutz Galuyot,' announced a signpost under a pine tree, in Hebrew, English and Arabic. Three wooden arrows were nailed to the tree. The top one said, 'Members,' the middle one, 'Volunteers,' the bottom one, 'Turkeys' as though listing us in hierarchical order. All pointed to the same dirt-track that led into the interior.

Letter 23

A beautiful young soldier with a submachine-gun slung over her shoulder waited for me to alight before boarding the bus. She exchanged a few words with the driver and made her way up the aisle. Then the bus set off, in a cloud of dust, towards a pink and mauve sunset.

I had arrived later than expected after a couple of rides, from Ben Gurion airport to Rehovot and from that town's bus terminal to Kibbutz Galuyot, had taken longer than expected. I hauled a heavy rucksack onto my back and headed towards a light that shone through a cluster of willowy trees. Walking that dirt-track, I had a vague sense of being watched. As a matter of habit, I put it down to paranoia. But I wasn't paranoid so I attributed it to a combination of tiredness, dislocation and culture shock.

The door to a ramshackle office was held open by a stack of Jerusalem Posts. A black-and-tan Alsatian dozed in front of a filing cabinet while an Arab chanteuse wailed on the radio. A rotund, black-bearded figure in a blue boilersuit was seated behind a desk in front of a wall dominated by an enlarged, framed photograph.

Tribespeople were lugging holdalls and rolled-up rugs. Men in jellabiyas held hands with little children. Women in headscarves carried babies. A trail of refugees extended back across a sandy desert towards a long, flat horizon. 'Operation Magic Carpet rescues 47,000 Jews from Yemen,' read a mounted caption.

'Good evening, Jacob Green.' Dudu switched off the radio, introduced himself and shook hands. 'We have been waiting for you.'

'Sorry to keep you waiting. I didn't know the way and got a bit lost.'

'Give me your passport.'

Dudu checked my stoned-hippy photo against my new face before stashing the passport in a safe. Then he handed me a contract, which I signed once I had read it. Volunteers were paid one American dollar per day, in return for which we were to work as required, refrain from drugs and behave like guests in a commune that was the kibbutzniks' permanent home. We were entitled to use Galuyot's facilities and amenities, which included a laundrette, a swimming pool and an infirmary, though a subclause under 'infirmary' noted Galuyot's inability to treat medical cases of a mental nature that would require hospitalisation. We were also entitled to a day's holiday after every four weeks.

I was going to reside in Roman's room in the brown barrack, said Dudu. There I'd have Lottie, and also Jim and Wolfgang, who shared a room, as neighbours. I was to start work at six in the morning, after coffee in the *cheder ochel* and a workers' rendezvous at the banana bar outside, where the tractors and trailers were parked. Dudu opened a cabinet from which I found my size in baggy blue shirts, long cotton trousers, khaki shorts and mud-caked boots. He told me to add a floppy hat then he and his Alsatian led me down a whitewashed path to my new home.

'Did you know Kitty, an English volunteer who was here last year?' Kitty hadn't mentioned Dudu.

The burly kibbutznik stopped in his tracks. 'Is Kitty a friend of yours?'

'Oh yes. We were at university together.'

'Your friend Kitty grew marijuana plants in the orange groves. Every day she was getting high. And she was giving it to our young members. When Avraham found out he wanted to inform the police and have her put in jail or deported back to England. "That girl will ruin the reputation of Kibbutz Galuyot," he said. But Rivka overruled him because Kitty was pregnant.'

'Pregnant?' She hadn't mentioned that, either. 'What about her kibbutznik friend, Yoni? Is he around?'

'Yoni is in the army. I hope you are not another crazy.'

'Oh, you needn't worry about me,' I said. My crazy days were behind me.

The brown barrack was situated beyond a hardscrabble lawn that served as a yard and a patio furnished by an antiquated fridge. Three adjoining rooms each had a window protected by a mosquito screen that curled away at the corners. My neighbours' rooms were dark. Everyone seemed to be at a twin barrack a little further into the interior, where patio lights shone on what looked like a party outside a Swiss chalet.

Inside my room, an unshaded bulb dangled just above head height. 'Love Your Enemy,' read a needlepoint tapestry over a bed made with military precision. That was Roman's side of the room. A pile of sheets, a pillowcase and a blanket were folded on the other bed's naked mattress. A previous inmate had marked time, a line for each day in crossed-out rows of four, forming a fence that stretched halfway across the wall. A kerosene heater stood unused on a tatty rug, empty bottles lined a precarious shelf held up by twine at both ends. Two chairs were tucked under a table in front of a wardrobe without doors. The beds shared a bedside table, or rather an upturned beer crate draped in a scarf.

I unpacked my rucksack, pausing over a dog-eared paperback that was Skunk's parting gift. *La Bête Humaine*, whose cover pictured a steam train hurtling towards the reader, reminded me of you. I was making my bed when the barrack turned orange. A campfire was burning outside, attended by faces that looked like gargoyles.

A tall, colonial type with a pronounced Adam's apple stepped out to greet me. He introduced himself – 'Roger, from Weston-super-Mare' – and the others, who were sitting on benches or standing around the fire. He gave me a bottle of Nesher beer and I mingled with my new *compadres*.

'How long have you been here?' I asked one called Caitlin.

'Long enough to be sick of crazy volunteers,' she said, in an Ulster accent. She was wearing work fatigues even at this late hour, and a tightly tied hair-bun that pulled at her face, making jug handles of her ears. 'Watch out for Jackson, that's all I'm saying. He's a psychopath. Where I come from, we know the type, believe me. And stay away from Wolfgang, our one-man Baader-Meinhof gang. And Roman, who is totally...' Caitlin circled a finger round her temple.

'I am a Viking.' Olaf's goatee beard curled up towards a squashed, gnomish face. 'I don't know why you came to this shithole. There is nothing to do except drink. You can get booze from the *kolbo* on Tuesday and Thursday afternoons, when they're open to volunteers, four till six. And you don't need money because they only take vouchers, which are subsidised by the kibbutz. They have ciggies too: Noblesse, which are disgusting; Nelson, which are worse; and Time. Most people smoke Time.'

Jim prodded the fire. A branch snapped in two, the fire crackled and spat. Back home, Jim's shaved head, potato face and black tattoos would cast him as a football hooligan. Here he had the air of a Mediaeval yeoman.

I sat on a bench beside Lottie and Rudi, 'our Swiss siblings,' as Roger called them. Rudi wore his blondness in a moustache and a quiff, Lottie in wavy tresses that tumbled over a cheesecloth shirt onto tight, faded jeans. Rudi rolled a cigarette one-handed, his ear-stud glinting. Popeye winked from his bicep. Lottie budged-up to make space for me and I couldn't help but notice how pretty she was.

'We're neighbours,' I told Lottie.

'I know,' she said. 'Welcome to Galuyot. I arrived last week so I am also new. Rudi was already here and he said I must come because it will be better for me here than at home. Where are you working?'

'Banana plantation. Starting at six in the morning. I don't remember ever getting up that early.'

'I work in the kitchen, starting at seven. I make salads. Today we had a power failure. I plugged in a slicer and bang! All the electrics go off because of me. Mira, our boss, had to find Modi the electrician to fix it.'

'We're not very big on health and safety,' admitted Roger.

'Health and safety has nothing to do with it,' sniffed Caitlin. 'It was most likely Jackson fucking around with a fuse box. You know he killed the cats?'

'Feral strays round the Stone House,' explained Roger. 'It was like a plague.'

Lottie's face darkened, inasmuch as her face could darken. 'Jackson is horrible. I will not talk to him.' She leaned into me conspiratorially. 'Can you keep a secret?'

'Of course,' I lied.

'I should not be here.'

'Me neither,' I said, thinking of the finals exams I was missing at Wessex. 'Why shouldn't you be here?'

'I am not yet sixteen.'

'Thank God for that,' I thought. Here was another reason to stay this side of a fall.

'Roman will be surprised to find *you* in his room,' predicted Olaf. 'Where is the wodka?'

'Where is Roman?' I was impatient, and nervous, to meet my roommate.

'Roman went to Jerusalem,' Roger blurted out, as if parroting an official line.

'When's he coming back?'

'Nobody knows.' Rudi shrugged, as did Popeye. 'But Dudu, our beloved leader, says Roman will return.'

Back in my room, our room, I set the alarm on my clock to 5:40 and hoped I would fall asleep soon, given my early start in the morning. On that blissful cusp of sleep, I remembered that my clock was still on British Summer Time.

I put it forward an hour and the clock said, '00:00'.

Letter 24

Mechanics in boilersuits and laundrywomen in aprons, elders driving mobility buggies and volunteers trudging forth in work fatigues converged on the *cheder ochel,* a modern, grey, L-shaped building that was Galuyot's social centre. Some lingered in the surrounding square on shaded benches, some queued, loosely, at a water fountain. I couldn't wait, not only for breakfast but to cool down in Galuyot's air-conditioned dining hall.

A violinist played on a roof. A man levitated in a night sky. A bride in red awaited her groom.

Beneath the Chagalls, Suzette was in command of several stainless-steel food trolleys. Speaking in an Afrikaans accent, she ordered a young subordinate to take an empty vat to the kitchen and return with a vat full of cream cheese. Suzette inspected the remaining vats then regarded her profile in a window. She held in her stomach, flexed her bosoms and nodded approvingly.

At the self-service trolleys, you had to know what you liked. Did you want your eggs boiled or fried, poached or scrambled, in a mushroom omelette or a flan with sausage? Did you want white bread or brown, rye or wholemeal or pastries better suited to a party? If you liked cereal, you could have cornflakes, muesli or porridge. In shallower vats that had an island to themselves, there were soft and hard cheeses, yoghurts and fruits plus spreads, dips and dressings. And that was before you reached the salads, mixed and in component parts. On another table there were refrigerated juice dispensers and urns of tea and coffee. Diana would have opted for muesli, mauve yoghurt and a cup of herbal tea that she wouldn't drink until it was cold. I loaded my tray with a portion of flan, two slices of rye bread, a couple of knobs of butter, a glass of grapefruit juice and a white coffee then picked up cutlery from a rack of grey plastic containers. There was no cashier. Everything was free.

Lottie was smoking a cigarette while basking in golden sunshine at the volunteers' long table. She was wearing an apron and her hair was clasped in a loose bun. At the other end, two of my Swedish colleagues from the plantation were hunkered down over bowls of steaming porridge. In between, seated facing the hall, Roger and Caitlin had finished eating and pushed aside their trays. Caitlin was smoking while Roger twiddled a Biro over a blank postcard.

On seeing me and my breakfast, Lottie stubbed her cigarette in an ashtray. 'Hi, Jacob, my *harzige schatz*,' she said in a voice so sweet, even Germanic words sounded tender.

'Your what?'

'In English you say, "darling". But why you don't like my salad?' Lottie looked askance at my plate. 'My Israeli salad is Galuyot's favourite: tomato, cucumber, lettuce, onion, red and green peppers and parsley, all diced into tiny pieces.'

'Who has salad for breakfast? This is egg and sausage, even if it's in a flan. A proper worker's breakfast.'

'Aha!' said Roger. 'I *do* have some news. We're inseminating the turkeys tomorrow.'

'Do you mind?' Caitlin pulled a face. 'Just because we're stuck in the back of beyond, we don't have to forget our manners.'

Danny arrived on bare feet arced at ten to two. His face lit up by a crescent smile, he bowed a salutation to all present then set down his tray beside me. 'Always I am fixing broken things, and collecting garbages.'

'How did you get into that line of work?' I asked.

'Modi is my uncle.'

'Nepotism, eh?'

'*Nepotismo.*' Danny beamed at the felicitous commonality of our native languages. 'This morning we clean flytraps at the pool. Is all dead flies. Dirty work, no? Modi holds a ladder for me to climb. Then Suzette arrives to sunbathe and Modi forgets my ladder. I scream and fall into the water. Splash! Is like the movies, no?'

'What's the movie this week?' asked Caitlin.

'Who cares about movies?' Rudi put down a tray laden with a large helping of Israeli salad, half a loaf of unsliced bread and two bowls of purple yoghurt. 'Why watch somebody else's life on a screen?'

Danny mixed mayonnaise and chilli powder into a dressing that he poured over his salad. Before tucking in, he offered a forkful to me, as though aiming for the wrong head.

I crunched a mouthful and immediately felt a buzz. 'Wow!' Having seen how it was made, I resolved to have pink salad for breakfast every day.

Olaf arrived with a bowl of yoghurt big enough to serve the whole table. He sat opposite Roger and bowed as though acknowledging a fellow warrior. 'Come on, Roger. You don't must refuse me.'

'Alright.' Roger put down his Biro and plonked an elbow on the table in readiness.

'I will put one arm behind my back, to make it easier for you.' Olaf winked at Lottie, whom he was sure to impress with his arm-wrestling prowess. But in setting himself up he lost his balance and upended his bowl of yoghurt.

Sticky white liquid flowed down the table, expanding as it went. Like a sudden ocean wave it carried abandoned trays of leftovers, stainless-steel paper-napkin dispensers and Roger's unfinished postcard, all flotsam surfing towards the Swedish girls.

'You fucking eejit!' Caitlin jumped to her feet.

Olaf tried wiping the table, scared as he was of Caitlin and shamed by a chorus of 'tsk tsk's, but his little napkins were instantly drenched. He ran off to get help, returning with a bucket and mop, and Suzette, who came to supervise, by which time Roger and Caitlin had gone, the Swedes had decamped to another table and Lottie had noticed me wince at my blistered thumb.

'Let me see,' she said. 'Urgh! Eat up and I will fix you up with a Swiss plaster. I have a first-aid box in my room.'

After meals you had to take your cutlery, crockery and tray to the dishwasher. A triangular conveyor belt carried plastic pallets of dirty items a clanking mechanical maw from which everything emerged hot and clean. A half-naked worker toiled to unload pallets inside the automaton's conveyor belt. Bandana wound round his head, ponytail swishing between his shoulder blades, hunting knife gleaming at his hip, Jackson disappeared in the steam, a ghost in the machine.

I arrived at the banana bar with my hat, a bottle I'd refilled at a water fountain and a plastered thumb. Moshe was waiting in the tractor seat, the others were on the trailer.

'Thanks for waiting.' I didn't fancy walking, not in that heat.

'Say, limey, I saw you leaving breakfast with Lottie,' said Herbie as we headed back to work. 'Have you got to first base yet?'

'She's my neighbour. We're friends.'

'Gee, she sure looks sweet. What's her story? She got a boyfriend?'

'She's only fifteen.'

'She has Rudi, her brother,' said Abdullah. 'If you try something with Lottie, Rudi will kill you.'

'*Neuken in der keuken*,' said Herbie. 'Tell her that. That's what they say in Holland. *Neuken in der keuken.*'

'She's not Dutch, she's Swiss.'

'A Swiss miss, huh? How do you say, "Let's go back to my place" in Swiss?' he asked the Swedish girls. 'When I was your age, there was no holding me back. These days I have to wait until my wife's visiting her mother in Petah Tikva.'

'What you say, Heebie-Djeebie?' Abdullah put down his knife and block. 'What you do when your wife visits her mother? You watch volunteer girls at the disco, then you go home alone.'

'Sometimes I get lucky, Abdullah. You know what... Hey!'

Abdullah was on top of him, pinning down his wrists. 'What you do when your wife is away? Eh? What you do Heebie-Djeebie?'

'Stop it! That tickles.' Herbie turned to me, insofar as he could manoeuvre his neck at all. 'Abdullah's a married man. At last count he had three wives. Or was it four?'

'What you say, Heebie-Djeebie?' Abdullah gave Herbie's cheek a quick slap.

'When he's tired of one wife, he moves on to another,' squealed Herbie. 'Good system, huh? And when he's tired of them all, he *shtups* a volunteer. Isn't that right, Marietta?'

Abdullah slapped the other cheek. Herbie squirmed and giggled. Marietta gazed over her shoulder and turned back to face the plantation.

Crouch, slash, squirt, advance. Crouch, slash, squirt, advance. Beads of sweat dripped down my face. Crouch, slash, squirt, advance. Crouch, slash, squirt, advance. A tantalising breeze offered a moment's relief then withdrew. Crouch, slash, squirt, advance. Crouch, slash, squirt, advance. Surely it was time for a break. Crouch, slash, squirt, advance. Crouch, slash, squirt, advance. I downed tools and went back to my starting point for a drink of water, a pee and a cigarette. Crouch, slash, squirt, advance. Crouch, slash, squirt, advance. Go through the alphabet naming a band beginning with each letter. Crouch, slash, squirt, advance. Crouch, slash, squirt, advance. Same thing with footballers, difficult letters excluded. Crouch, slash, squirt, advance. Crouch, slash, squirt, advance.

'Dada *dah*, dada *dah*, dada dum dum; dada dah, dada dah, dada *dahhhh*. Dada *dah*, dada *dah*, dada dum dum... Hey, you!'

Wolfgang could have been a patient taking his morning constitutional in the gardens of an Alpine sanatorium. He had the pale, moustached face, wire glasses and round shoulders of an intellectual and the walking boots, knee-length long socks and *lederhosen* of a Bavarian rambler.

'Why are you hiding down there?'

'I'm not hiding. I'm killing roots.'

Wolfgang laughed mirthlessly. 'How pointless.'

'If you let them grow, they steal water from the main plant. Every plant has several superfluous roots, which... why, what's it to you?'

'I am curious. But I must say, it looks like a tedious exercise. Not an activity to engage one's mind at all.'

'Well that's work for you, isn't it? Why aren't *you* working?'

'They put me in the kitchen. Such a stupid mistake. Only women are working in the kitchen.'

'You don't get to choose where you work. Unless you have a special skill. Do you have a special skill?'

Before he could answer, Abdullah arrived, his blade flashing beside him. 'You are late,' he said.

'Ah, *guten morgen*. I am Wolfgang. I am sorry, but I am not knowing your name.'

'*Koos emek!*

'I thought so. If I am not mistaken, you are a Palestinian.'

'What you say?'

'I said... you... are Palestinian,' Wolfgang shouted, as though Abdullah were a simpleton or hard of hearing. 'I admire you. Revolutionaries throughout the world place their hopes on you. Wherever the oppressed rise up against the oppressor, they are inspired by your example.'

'I am not *Philastin*.' Abdullah glared at the German volunteer. 'I am not sitting in refugee camp in Gaza or Jordan dreaming of my grandparents' home in Jaffa. I am Arab Israeli.'

'This I do not understand. You should be fighting the Zionists, not working for them. Like you fought in '67.'

'In the Six-Day War I was five years old. My family hid in a cave.'

'This is what I am saying. You had to hide in caves while the Israelis stole your homes.'

'The Israelis gave us water and food, and sweets for the children. "Go home," they said. "The fighting is over." This is what I remember.'

'Your memory is historically inaccurate.'

'You say I lie?' A swipe of Abdullah's mighty blade left half a banana tree horizontal in the dirt.

'It is the Israelis who lie,' said Wolfgang. 'Only when the Palestinian flag flies over al-Quds will you live in dignity. Only when...'

'You know what happens when my wife is sick? She sees the same doctor who treats the president of Israel's wife. You know what happens when the government makes an election? I vote in the *cheder ochel,* with the Jews. Then I go to a barbecue at the swimming pool, with the Jews.'

'That is all very nice. However...'

'You know what happens when I say the government is *kaka?* Nothing happens. No policeman knocks on my door or throws me in prison like the British threw my father, like the Turkish threw his father, like they throw my cousins in Lebanon.'

'The Palestinians are fighting for their land.'

'*This* is my land.' Abdullah gestured at the plantation. 'So what you say?'

'I say, who owns it? The kibbutz, that's who owns it. They exploit you. To them you're nothing but cheap labour.'

Abdullah's frown deepened. 'Before the Jews built here, there was no banana plantation, there was no work, there was no nothing.'

'There was Palestine.'

'You think I am stupid Arab?' Abdullah's eyes blazed. 'You think I do not know history? Never was there a Palestine. Before Israel the land was ruled by invaders. The British...,' he spat at the earth. 'The Turkish...,' he spat again. 'Then Romans and Mamelukes and Assyrians...'

'Now you are ruled by Zionists.'

'You can say "Jews,"' I said.

'I do not speak of Jews in black hats,' Wolfgang assured me. 'I speak of Israeli imperialists.'

'Israelis aren't imperialists, you pillock. Jews have lived in Israel, and yearned for Israel, since biblical times. Everywhere else, the Jews have been subjected to one round of murderous persecution after another. It happened quite recently, in Germany, if you remember. Now we have reclaimed our nation.'

'We' slipped out, just like that. Almost by accident, I had rejoined my tribe.

Letter 25

We sat around a bonfire, telling stories, making plans and drinking alcohol to pass the time. Dudu announced a volunteers' trip to Nuweiba for three nights in September, which elicited whoops, cheers and groans. September used to mean the end of summer holidays and a return to school. Now it meant a vacation in Nuweiba.

'Where is Nuweiba?' Kitty said she had been there with Yoni.

'Is the Sinai desert,' said Danny.

'We went to Nuweiba last year,' moaned Caitlin.

'Isn't it rather uncivilised down there?' Roger, too, had reservations.

'In the Sinai it is too hot to move,' said Rudi. 'And there is nowhere to move to. At night, when it is cool, you barbecue lamb and smoke hashish with the Bedouin. You swim in a warm sea and sleep under a sky full of stars. One night I had a strange hallucination. I was on a fishing boat, which sailed into a great storm. Thunder roared, great waves fell from black skies, the storm threatened to drown us all. The fishermen needed a sacrifice to throw overboard and they chose me. The gods were pleased, the storm blew over and I washed up on a sandy shore. There I lay, watching a big round moon rise over calm waters.'

'Seems like Jonah,' said Danny.

'Seems like good hashish,' I said, and everyone laughed, Lottie most of all. After a few more swigs of vodka, I was ready to tell them my story.

'I was in love with a beautiful girl,' I said, to a wolf whistle from Olaf and a 'woargh' from Roger. 'We did everything together: cooking Indian dinners in our little kitchen, walking in the woods, going to bed at ten o'clock...'

'Ahh, that is sweet.' Rudi smiled tipsily.

'I was mad about her.'

'Then something went wrong,' Lottie predicted.

'Well, I got sick of Indian food, I didn't want to walk in the woods and I couldn't fall asleep at ten o'clock. So Diana walked alone and I ate at a coffee shop then stayed up all night with friends. By the time I went to bed, it was already light and Diana was getting up. And when I got up, she was going to bed. Then I heard she was two-timing me with Casey, our American friend.'

Lottie gasped.

'I wished we'd never met. "You whore!" I screamed when I happened to see her the following day. "I wish you were dead. You never really loved me. Well, I don't love you either. I was just putting on an act."

'"It wasn't like that," she sobbed. "I will always love you. And if you really loved me, you would let me go."

'I moved in with my mate Vincent, who got rid of well-wishers bearing condolences while I moped. "You've got to get over her, or you'll drive us both mad," he said.

'My mum suggested I come home for a break. My dad told me to focus on my finals. "Give it time," said the doctor. "A broken heart triggers the same response as a bereavement." In other words, love becomes death.'

'That is so silly.' Olaf didn't think much of my story.

'My girl was abducted, probably raped and killed,' Jackson told the fire. 'She was buying vegetables in a market in Managua, fooling around with friends, when Sandinista bandits grabbed her. They kidnapped people at random, for a ransom, or information, or the sheer fun of torture and rape. Juanita was just a kid.'

'What were you doing in Nicaragua?' asked Wolfgang. 'Working for Uncle Sam?'

'I was a special operative.'

'You mean a secret agent,' said Olaf. 'CIA, was that it?'

'I was freelance. Before Nicaragua I served in Matabeleland, searching and destroying guerrillas in the bush. I was paid one hundred US dollars for every dead guerrilla, paid on receipt of enemy scalps. One time I had Joshua Nkomo in my crosshairs. And I blew my chance to make history. Well that was another war we couldn't win. The white man was in retreat, again.'

'We are the white men!' Olaf belched extravagantly. 'Who has the wodka?'

'I hate white men,' said Lottie.

'How about Red Indians?' Jackson asked her.

'"Red Indians,"' said Wolfgang, '...are not red or Indians. And they lived in North America long before you white Europeans arrived.'

'My mother was Cherokee Nation,' said Jackson. 'Until she married Scottie Vanburgh, all-American quarterback and wounded hero of Monte Cassino. I was a half-breed, too Cherokee for white folks, too white for the Nation.'

'Tell them about Vietnam,' said Olaf.

'Let's have a fancy-dress party,' said Lottie.

'I killed three US Marines in Vietnam,' said Jackson. 'You know why? Because our mortars were dated 1952, and the shells didn't reach their target. The most lethal military capability the world has ever seen and we're using twenty-year-old leftovers from the fucking Korean War. I got sent down, dishonourably discharged.'

I stood up under a spinning sky and had to sit back down.

'I will be Jeanne D'Arc,' said Lottie.

'John Dark?' echoed Olaf.

'The Maid of Orleans,' said Lottie. 'She heard a voice telling her what to do. It was the voice of God.'

'Vikings do not believe in God, my dear.'

'I wanted to go visit the dead Marines' parents, to tell them it should have been me who got killed, not their boys, but I couldn't do it,' said Jackson. 'So I headed west, to Oregon. "The man of resentment lives underground."'

'I haven't got a costume,' I said. 'And I gotta go lie down.'

It wasn't far to go, from bonfire to barrack. But I needed Lottie's help, and she stayed to rub my back when I threw up in the outhouse.

Letter 26

Wispy clouds float round Alpine peaks, craggy boulders break through pristine snow. A lush green forest descends a vertiginous valley. Mountains reflect in a placid lake. A short-haired woman in a black dress and white pinny strides across a grassy plateau then pirouettes in joy.

'The hills are aliiive...'

A spine-tingling soprano cuts through the murmurs of a dark auditorium. Some sing along, some chat in low voices. Some snaffle sunflower seeds, some walk out. We're watching my dad's favourite film, a staple of childhood bank holidays.

A group of nuns frets over a wayward sister in a courtyard.

'How do you solve a problem like Maria?'

Heads in the audience bob along.

'Which one is Maria?' whispers Olaf.

'Shhh!'

Maria finds herself alone in the outside world carrying a valise and a guitar. Her situation is much like mine, though I don't sing and dance or bring good cheer with my sunny disposition.

'This is not good cinema,' says Wolfgang.

'Shhhhh!'

In the sumptuous hall of a palatial residence, a Captain's whistle summons seven blond children. Captain Von Trapp is supposed to be a martinet, but his handsome face is too kind, his gestures are too gentle. The children are too American, the dance sequences too stagey. And Julie Andrews simpers.

Or so I thought in my student days. Now I was free from such opinions, positions and postures. Now I had a life to lead.

A storm frightens the children and they climb into bed with Maria, who breaks into an oompah version of My Favorite Things.

The children's harmonies captivate their father.

'*I go to the hills, when my heart is lowwwwnely...*' Von Trapp takes up their song in his masculine tenor. It's a moving new development. Von Trapp has succumbed to the sound of music.

'Dudu!'

A cry from the rear breaks the spell. We are sitting in rows in the *cheder ochel,* kibbutzniks and volunteers together, facing a makeshift screen. Dudu waddles down the central aisle to the public phone booth, waving like a celebrity, to answer his call.

Maria and Von Trapp have fallen in love. I should have seen it coming. Maria runs away, to resume holy orders in her original abbey.

'If you love this man, it doesn't mean you love God less,' says her Mother Superior. And that is the heart of the story. A long, lingering close-up captures Maria and Von Trapp's first kiss.

'That's sohhh romantic, yaah,' sniffles Suzette.

A red drape unfurls over a wall facing the town square. A black swastika prompts mutterings of disquiet in the *cheder ochel.* Under cover of night, Von Trapp and Uncle Max push their car across a courtyard. Holding hands beneath their capes, Maria and the children take refuge in her old abbey, where they hide in gloomy catacombs.

'I'm scared,' says one child.

'Me, too,' says another.

'And me,' says Olaf.

'Nohhhh!' screams Caitlin when the postboy betrays them.

The family escapes. The Nazis' cars won't start. The nuns have sabotaged their engines. Von Trapp, Maria and their seven children hike across the mountains.

Credits roll. Electric lights illuminate the *cheder ochel.* We stretch and yawn and reacquaint ourselves with the reality of our daily lives.

Letter 27

'Shall I wake him up, tell him you're here?'

'No, let him sleep. Does he have any hash, do you know?'

'I expect so.'

'Don't worry. I'll come back later.'

'Stay. He'll be up in a minute.'

'Hey, limey!' Someone was knocking on my door. 'Yaassi needs you in the turkeys.'

It was dark. I was sleeping. It was 4:55. 'Go away, Herbie.'

He knocked on another door. 'Wolfman! Get up! Yaassi needs vaalunteers in the turkeys.'

The moon was so low, so big and so clear I thought I was on another planet. A familiar farmyard stench, and Wolfgang's latest grievances, brought me down to earth. Searchlights mounted on towers shone on twin coops, their bright rays clouded by steam that billowed from a corrugated-iron Portakabin.

'What do you need us for?' I asked Roger, who had appeared behind a high mesh fence like a captured airman sent to brief newly arrived PoWs.

'I am not a turkey man,' Wolfgang told him.

'We were expecting you half an hour ago. We haven't got time for explanations so take a shower and find some work clothes in the changing hut. I'll see you in coop *aleph*. Chop, chop!'

Coop *aleph* stank to high heaven. It was the length of an aircraft hanger, with striplights dangling from makeshift horizontal rafters over a sawdust-covered floor. I thought turkeys were oversized chickens but these creatures were more like shrunken dinosaurs.

'These are the males,' said Roger, whose protruding Adam's apple helped him blend in. 'We have six hundred of them.' He lifted a turkey from a squawking mass of birds and held it upside down to inspect its armpits. 'It's all hands to the pump today.

We're doing a special project. Phase one: transfer these chaps to coop *bet* before daylight.'

'Why before daylight?' Wolfgang wanted to know. 'They are turkeys, not vampires.'

A cockerel crowed and a muezzin's faint drone wafted over from Ramle as we exited coop *aleph*. Orange streaks coloured a purple sky. A wispy corona formed a halo around the flag. Resplendent in a still, quiet morning, the high-flying Star of David inspired a sense of pride, in God, His people and His land. It was going to be another hot day.

We assembled a causeway with interlocking plastic barriers between coops *aleph* and *bet* then Roger let the turkeys out. Captives transported on a mob's momentum, they squawked, flapped and collided with each other as they tumbled down the causeway.

'Can you two manage while I make breakfast?' asked Roger.

'What are we supposed to be doing?' I wasn't cut out to be a turkey farmer.

Roger shook his head in despair. 'Just make sure they get into coop *bet*,' he said, like they had to take entrance exams, before heading off to the Portakabin.

Wolfgang waved a small red flag.

'Where did you get that?' If Wolfgang had a flag, I should have one too.

'Roger gave it to me.' He leaned over the barrier and poked his flag into a turkey while hissing like an electric current.

'Don't do that.' I lunged at his flag.

'Hey! It's mine.' Wolfgang pulled away. 'Get off!'

I lunged again, got a grip and ripped the cloth from its stick. Now neither of us had a flag.

'You are such a child.' Wolfgang pocketed the red cloth then turned on a gaggle of stragglers. 'Hey, you! There is no chance of escape. The sooner you understand this, the better it will be for everyone. If you try to fly away, you will be shot before you reach the highway.'

'Turkeys can't fly.'

'No? What sort of bird can't... *Guten morgen*, Herr Schnitzel,' he said to a turkey that had escaped the causeway and was running around free, like a lunatic.

'Catch it!' I shouted.

Wolfgang bent his knees, straightened his back and chased the fugitive turkey like Groucho Marx in pursuit of a fat lady. I chased it too, and trapped it in a corner, but the big, scary bird slipped through my grasp. Suddenly it was joined by its mates, hordes of them breaking out and running in all directions.

The ninth cavalry arrived in the form of Yossi, our boss. Wearing a blue-and-white crocheted *kippa* and a faded Rolling Stones vest that exposed his hairy back and shoulders, he herded the escapees into coop *bet* and dismantled the causeway, with Wolfgang and me right behind him.

Job done, we retired to the Portakabin, where we washed our hands and sat down for breakfast. Roger dished up an industrial-sized omelette and we helped ourselves to bread, assorted cheeses and a rough version of Lottie's Israeli salad.

'Are these eggs from coop *bet*?' asked Wolfgang.

'The turkeys in coop *bet* are males.' Roger shook his head at Wolfgang's ignorance. 'Don't they teach you biology in German schools?'

'Biology is for girls,' muttered Wolfgang.

'After breakfast, we move on to stage two.' Yossi briefed us while we ate, until he was interrupted by a short, tubby newcomer whose toupée clashed with his sideburns. He was wearing an AC Milan football shirt whose red and black vertical stripes added a rare dash of colour to our work fatigues.

'Shalom, *haverim*.' He measured us up through dolly-blue eyes. 'I am Boris. In Leningrad I am clerk in bank. On kibbutz I am farmer in turkey compound.'

I had seen him in the *cheder ochel,* where he could have been tourist on cruise ship. Dressed in sandals, socks and a shirt too tight for his paunch, he wore the fascinated expression of one who had just arrived from a very different place. His wife and young daughter seemed less well-disposed.

'*Slicha, adoni.*' Yossi politely reclaimed the floor.

'Ah, you are making speech. Okay.'

Boris put on an apron and a pair of rubber gloves that he found under the sink. He turned on the taps and proceeded to wash the dirty dishes while singing a Russian melody. Yossi's briefing didn't stand a chance.

After breakfast, we regrouped in coop *bet,* where the smell was too much for Wolfgang. We had only been there for a couple of minutes when he headed for the exit, retching into a cloth. The red flag had a use after all.

'*Yalla! Yalla!*' barked a kibbutznik whose crew-cut would have suited a full-time sergeant major. Sitting on a low stool surrounded by turkeys, she ground her cigarette stub under her heel and pulled a huge syringe from a bucket.

'This is Noga,' said Roger.

'Noga is sweet,' said Boris, who was trying to befriend the turkeys. He clucked and flapped his arms to show solidarity but the birds turned away as though offended by his impersonation.

'That's *nougat,*' said Roger. '"Noga" means "Venus".'

'*Yalla! Yalla!*' barked Noga.

Boris spat on his hands and rubbed them together. 'Are you with me, my brave English comrade?' Boris was determined to acquit himself with honour. 'We will succeed where our German friend ran away. I call you, "Winston Churchill".'

'And I call you "Josef Stalin".' We were going to shake hands when Boris changed his mind.

'I am Franco Baresi.' He thrust out his chest as though projecting a resemblance to AC Milan's hard-man centre back.

Yossi, Roger and Noga formed a well-organised team that moved in fast rotation. Yossi and Roger took it in turns to hand turkeys to Noga, who jabbed them with a syringe then tossed them over her shoulder. The turkeys, that is.

I bent down to catch an uncooperative turkey and *Bash!* My head collided with Boris's head. Stars circled.

Boris, too, was staggering. 'We are wounded in turkey campaign,' he said, as we retreated to the sidelines to tend our heads. 'In Soviet Union my wife, Svetlana, worked as nurse in hospital after years of training. In Israel, they have plenty of nurses, therefore my wife, she now works in kitchen. Where you work in Great Britain?'

'I was a student.'

'My wife, Svetlana, she not want to leave Russia. I tell her, I will not stay and be sent to Afghanistan to fight *mujahedeen*, even if that makes me refusenik and enemy of the people. So we come to Israel. Now, says Svetlana, you will be sent to Lebanon to fight *mujahedeen*. Is funny world.'

The world was about to become funnier. We were in the showers, shivering under trickles of tepid water when Noga sauntered in, breasts and bush exposed for all to see.

'*Slicha, giveret,*' said Boris. 'I am married man.' He covered his loins with one hand and slapped the other on his head to hold his toupée in place. Swaying to keep his balance, he looked like a man praying naked in the rain. While Noga went about her ablutions quite indifferent to Boris's embarrassment, Boris reached out to the wall, slipped and fell onto all fours. He stayed that way to depart, dripping soapsuds and crawling on his knees like a dog in disgrace.

'What is so funny?' Noga was not amused. 'You are useless. Tomorrow you return to the plantation.'

'Hurray!'

'What are you so happy about?' Noga glared at my button mushroom of a penis.

You will no doubt be shocked by the crude realities of communal life and our cheek-to-arse living standards. Or perhaps you will think, 'What can you expect from a secular, decadent kibbutz?' Yet at Galuyot there was also transcendence.

On tranquil, balmy evenings, as the day's oppressive heat gave way to a heavenly warmth, as the sun bowed out, the sky faded and shadows grew, Marietta played sonatas, nocturnes and rags on the clubhouse piano. Volunteers played table tennis outside the Stone House or football with young and older kibbutzniks, neighbours shared refreshments al fresco and elders passed by on mobility scooters. I sat under an acacia tree, reading *La Bête Humaine* for news of the human condition, or a Jerusalem Post for updates. Lottie sat with me, writing long letters home. While faraway hills yawned at their own eternity, the desert bloomed on our kibbutz. Wherever you looked, there were palm trees or cherry blossoms, colourful flowers or green lawns, fertile soil or virgin rocks, all God's furniture celebrating Israel's renewal.

'You belong here,' said the land. 'At last, you have come home.'

It seemed like a dream. I was playing a part in God's dream.

Letter 28

I showered in the Stone House and shaved off a week's growth of stubble. I sprayed my armpits, brushed my hair and dressed in a polo shirt, jeans and a pair of leather shoes that I'd thought I wouldn't need. The mirror showed a face so brown I could have been a native.

Danny was talking to a wildflower as the sun went down behind him. He was wearing a proper shirt, long trousers and Gandhi sandals and his own clean-shaven face enhanced his smile. '*Shabbat shalom*, my friend,' he said as I joined him on the path to the *cheder ochel*.

Spruced-up members, associates and volunteers congregated outside the *cheder ochel*, where little children cycled in circles and tethered dogs slept. '*Shabbat shalom*,' they all said. Shabbat sanctified bonhomie. Shabbat was God's most precious gift.

That's what Papa used to say when he came round for Friday-night dinner, exclaiming 'Good *Shabbos!* Good *Shabbos!* before touch-kissing the *mezuzah* that he himself had affixed to our doorpost 'to honour God's everlasting presence'. He would give a large, colourful bouquet to 'my favourite daughter-in-law' with a kiss and Mum would remind him that she was his only daughter-in-law. He'd give me a tube of Smarties, which Mum said I wasn't to eat before dinner and he'd shake hands with Dad. Dad poured drinks in the lounge and Papa bounced me on his knee. 'Next year in Jerusalem,' he'd say as he clunked his glass of sherry to my beaker of orange squash. Dad could be talking to him and Papa would suddenly roar like a lion. Then he'd cuddle me tight, to protect me from the lion. 'How's tricks?' he'd ask Dad, after Dad, now hidden behind his pink Financial Times, had just given a full account of his tricks. On Mum's call to dinner, Papa went to the toilet to perform a washing-hands ritual as prescribed by religious law or his own eccentricity. In the dining room he recited *kiddush*, prayer book in hand. He knew the blessing by heart but loved to read its Hebrew words from a prayer book. He actually liked *kiddush* wine and he never failed to compliment Mum on her traditional '*heimische*' meal of chopped liver on *matzoh,* chicken soup and *kneidlach,* roast chicken and vegetables, followed by homemade strawberry sorbet. Leftovers were bagged for Papa to take home. While the grown-ups drank lemon tea, Papa sang Grace After Meals in a reverie so joyous I thought he must be drunk. After dinner, his stories segued from Yiddish folktales to family lore to his own memories. 'Drunken Cossacks raided the shtetls, committing unspeakable atrocities,' he said. 'Which isn't to say the *yidden* were angels. Any shtetl had its fair share of *shlemiels, schnorrers* and *ganefs.* It was well-known,' he added, as though the knavery of our ancestors were a universally acknowledged truth. 'Papa has a good imagination,' Dad said. When Papa died, Friday night's blessings and graces went with him.

At Galuyot, Suzette was Shabbat dinner's *maître d'.* Stationed outside the *cheder ochel* doors in a figure-clinging dress and stilettoes that raised her to an unnerving height, she greeted diners with an enthusiasm appropriate to their status. Danny and me she ignored, for all our fine grooming.

'What is this?' Danny pinched Suzette's powdered cheek.

Suzette swatted the air in annoyance.

Danny beamed. 'This morning I am covered in tractor oil. Now I have a taste of something much sweeter.'

'*Ich-sa!*' said Suzette.

'Ach.' Danny swatted the air, Suzette-style.

On Friday nights, kitchen staff served us at the food trolleys. Seeing Lottie dispensing a vegetarian option to a longer than usual queue, I hoped she would call me '*harzige schatz*' in front of everyone. But Lottie was focusing on her customers and I was queueing for a *heimische* Friday night dinner.

Shabbat candles and freshly baked *challah*, bottles of red Gamla wine and flowers in vases adorned dining tables dressed in white linen cloth, rolled serviettes, and sparkling silver cutlery. A solitary elder was slurping chicken soup through toothless gums. Sarah always ate at the same table, smiling weakly, rheumy eyes blinking, knowing she was never alone.

'*Shabbat shalom*, Sarah,' we said.

The volunteers' long table was a picture of dissolution. Olaf was groping Anki, his compatriot, who was playfully fending him off with a fork. Jim was flicking bread balls at Wolfgang, who was making notes in an exercise book. 'Wake me up again and you'll ge' a bucke' of cold wa'er over your 'ead,' Jim warned him. Caitlin was pouring wine for Rudi and flirting with Popeye.

Danny and I sat at a table for two. 'People behave in ways we do not understand,' he said, as he unfolded a serviette. 'Seems like they are stupid. Everywhere they touch without feeling. They listen without hearing. They sense and think but do not know what is happening.'

'What *is* happening?' I asked, between spoonfuls of chicken soup.

'We are waiting.'

'What are we waiting for?'

'We wait for the messiah. We have nine months in our mother's womb with a view to harmony. After we are born, life's false views destroy our harmony and we become full of prejudice. Our mind is in a labyrinth. Seems like chaos. The messiah will show us who we were. He will restore our harmony.'

'I had a previous life, before I was born.'

'This is *reencarnación*.' Danny dunked a wedge of *challah* in his soup. 'It is a big mystery. Our kabbalists in Safed say we know our leaders because we recognise their souls from before. It is the same with Buddhists in Tibet. They know, by supernatural things, when a lama is reborn. And Druse people in Ramat Ha-Golan, and in Syria and Lebanon, they have *reencarnación.* Even little children recognise people from before.'

I told him about you and our night in Stancombe Woods.

'*Se busca un extraterrestre, para un amor infinito.* You look for an alien for infinite love.'

'I suppose I do.'

'You are like a man with two heads. In one head you are dust and ashes. In the other, this world was created for you.'

Danny understood me better than I did. Or we did.

*

Bob Marley's mural turned green then yellow then red. Inside the clubhouse, a dancefloor of beautiful young bodies heaved to a booming beat. Lights flashed. Strobes flickered. The whole kibbutz shook.

'*Ah, ah, ah, ah, stayin' alive, stayin' alive...*'

On Friday nights, everyone went to the disco. There were elders such as Rivka, who wiggled her hips and coiled her wrists, couples who became such if they weren't beforehand and teenagers looking out for hot volunteers. Even Jackson lurked outside in the foliage. Herbie bumped and ground, his wife twisted and twirled. Jim thrashed up and down, Olaf stomped mechanically. Rudi skanked in slow motion, with Caitlin acting as his mirror. Suzette led with her bosom, drifting between dancers in search of a suitable partner.

I watched from the margins with Wolfgang, who looked as happy as he did in coop *bet,* and Danny, who kept talking in my ear even though I couldn't hear him and wouldn't understand what he was saying if I could. I had drunk a few Neshers and was about to head off to bed when the DJ's patter gave way to 'Hotter Than July'.

Cheers! Shrieks! Screams!

A bouncy bass tattoo drew everyone in.

'Everyone's feelin' pretty...'

We tore the place up, souls reunited, sharing each other in dance. Funking, grooving, faces clenched in rapture, we collided and coalesced. Individual selves dissolved, every dancer was your closest friend. Touched by Lottie's swirling hair, moved by Rudi's smile, delighted by Danny's ecstatic syncopations, I wished the moment would last forever. Only after daybreak, after a slow last number and the DJ's valedictions did we diehards depart, into a serene Shabbat morning.

*

An explosion rattled my window. The earth rumbled. I dashed out in my shorts and espadrilles, expecting a frantic scramble for the air-raid shelter before another blast. There was no panic, no scramble, just a thump, thump, thump. Jim's big feet were descending a ladder from the roof. Red paint dripped from his paintbrush.

'What was that explosion?'

'Sonic boom, ma'e.' Jim came at me head first, stopping inches short of a Glasgae kiss. He took a Nesher from the fridge, opened it with his teeth and knocked it back in one. Then he returned to the ladder, sunburnt skin and block tattoos merging in scarlet and black under a merciless sun.

'Why are you painting the roof?'

'I'm pain'ing the whole fuckin' barrack.'

'Why?'

'Cos it's brown.'

'What's wrong with that?'

'It should be red.'

'But it's Shabbat.'

'You know the trouble with doing nothing?' he asked, in pointed reference to my lifestyle.

'No, what's the trouble with doing nothing?'

'You can't stop and rest.'

'I wouldn't be doing nothing if you hadn't woken me up.'

Summer's furnace burned hotter than ever. I wiped my brow, scratched a mosquito bite behind my knee and looked through Lottie's window. She wasn't home.

'It is too hot, no?' Danny appeared out of nowhere. 'This is a *hamsin*, a hot wind from Sinai. We live in a desert, my friend.'

'I don't feel any wind. In England, wind means a pleasant breeze that blows clouds and flickers in trees, and gets blustery in autumn. This is a hot breath. It saps your energy. I can't do anything in this heat. I can't even think.'

'The *hamsin* can make you crazy. Look.' Danny shielded his eyes. 'There is a man on your roof.'

*

Water splashed, children shrieked, motionless bodies absorbed the sun. Toddlers floated in inflatable rings, parents paddled in the shallows. Boisterous lads ducked their mates and jeered a lifeguard's objections. Up on a grassy bank, elders played backgammon under parasols. A beach ball levitated against a deep blue sky.

Suzette was lying on a poolside lounger, reading a Harold Robbins paperback. A tiny black bikini exhibited her ample cleavage and bronzed, glistening body. She lowered her book and there I was, in her sunglasses, one of me in each lens.

'Where's Lottie today?' she asked, her voice laden with intrigue.

'How would I know?'

'Ah, shame. Rub some cream on my back, will you?' Suzette rolled onto her stomach and unclasped her bikini top.

'Do what?'

'Don't be such a sissy, man.'

I put down my towel, bottle of water and *Bête Humaine* and squeezed a dollop of suncream into my hand. I knelt at her side, sticky white liquid oozing through my fingers, and kneaded her shoulder blades. On every press of warm flesh, her breast squished out. My hand's descent towards her bottom's cotton triangle stirred my loins. I didn't fancy Suzette, I didn't even like her, but that didn't bother lust. 'Turn her over, massage her breasts, tear down that skimpy cloth,' said the erection straining my swimming trunks. 'Mount her from behind. Go on. What are you waiting for?'

I was being watched. Suddenly inhibited, my erection cringed. I rearranged my indiscretion and wiped my oily hands on the hot stone ground.

'You're in my sun,' said Suzette. 'Come over this side.'

I took a running jump into the swimming pool.

*

'*Shabbat shalom*, Rivka. *Hakol beseider?*'

'*Shabbat shalom*, Jacob.' Galuyot's small, wizened matriarch smiled through owlish spectacles. '*Beseider gamoor.* Come in, come in.' She ushered me through a gate in her white picket fence.

Rivka lived on an avenue lined by verdant trees. Whereas young members were issued a new stucco bungalow with a red tiled roof and water tank on top, veterans stayed in their original homes, residences that conformed to no single style. On Rivka's avenue there was a concrete Bauhaus building with a semi-circular balcony, an Arab-style villa with ornate arches and intricate mosaic floors, and a wooden shack surrounded by a scrapyard. A crazy-paving path wound through Rivka's unkempt garden to a fairytale cottage clad in climbing wisteria.

Drawn blinds pitched a musty lounge into semi-darkness. A ceiling fan whirred too slowly to ruffle a pair of rubber plants or a pile of yellowing newspapers. A thin shaft of daylight caught an antique gramophone whose brass horn curled over a stack of vintage records. 'Anthems of the Red Army' read the top record sleeve above a crude picture of a muscular blond soldier planting the blood-red flag of a glorious new dawn. In a museum, Anthems of the Red Army would be a cultural artefact; in Rivka's home it was a melancholy personal relic.

'It is so nice to be visited by a volunteer,' said Rivka.

I was actually strolling aimlessly, exploring Galuyot, but was too polite to say so.

Rivka extended a bony arm towards a rattan armchair. She laid out a bowl of peanuts and a matching bowl of sunflower seeds, then offered me a larger bowl of apples, oranges, pomegranates and bananas. Each fruit possessed a hidden peril. Apples made a noisy crunch, oranges were sticky, pomegranates stained your clothes and bananas weighed on your stomach – I didn't want to unpeel a banana then give up half-way, leaving half a banana in a half-floppy peel.

'No, thanks.'

'You English are too polite.'

'I'm still full from last night.'

She held out a dish of dates. 'One of the seven species referred to in the Bible. Endorsed by God, as it were.'

The dates' gnarled brown carapace spoke of a hot, parched patrimony. Their caramel scent evoked a feminine earthiness. A rich, honeyed wodge melted on my tongue and buzzed in my head. I spat the pit into a spittoon and took another date. I was still eating dates when Rivka came up with a loaded tea tray. Not wanting to be too polite, I uttered a dismissive 'tch' at her little jug of milk and sprinkled *nana* leaves into my tea instead.

'Just like a *sabra*,' said Rivka of my taste in tea as she lowered herself into a rattan chair, her cup rattling in its saucer. 'You must forgive me for not meeting you sooner. Usually I welcome volunteers officially, which gives me a chance to answer your questions and tell you our history. Do you know when we founded Kibbutz Galuyot? It was in 1933, when a Zionist youth movement bought the land from a local Arab. Those pioneers were quite extreme by our standards. You weren't allowed possessions and you couldn't marry without permission from a central committee. Families were regarded as a bourgeois construct so the children were put in a children's house. Then came war against the British.' Rivka wagged a finger at my Britishness. 'Your soldiers came to Galuyot looking for rifles and ammunition, which we had buried in the banana plantation. They could not make anyone talk so they took Avraham hostage and threatened to execute him. In the end, we gave them their weapons and they released Avraham. Much has changed since those days, of course. Today we aren't so socialist, but we still have our ideals. You know there is a national election coming up? For thirty years we had Labour governments, then six or seven years ago... *Shabbat shalom*, Yuval.'

A young kibbutznik had sauntered in after a perfunctory knock on Rivka's door. Yuval was a familiar figure who often hung out with the volunteers, especially if Lottie was there.

'*Ma nishma?*' I asked him. I cracked a sunflower seed between my teeth, spat its husk into the spittoon and chewed its tiny pulse. And again. One seed was no good, you had to keep going.

Yuval nodded sulkily and sat on a chair's edge as though unsure whether to stay.

'Yuval won a year-twelve English-recital poetry prize in Jerusalem,' said Rivka. 'What did you recite, remind me?'

'Rachel,' mumbled Yuval.

'Oh, yes, Song of Sorrow.' Rivka clasped her hands to her chest. 'Rachel is the mother of modern Hebrew poetry. She was born in Russia, like so many of us, in 1890, and made *aliyah* while still a teenager. She actually lived not far from here, in Rehovot, with her sister. Recite Song of Sorrow for Jacob, Yuval.'

'*Ma pitom?*' Yuval had come to talk to Rivka in confidence, not recite poetry to his rival for Lottie's hand.

'*Kadima!*'

Yuval stood up. 'Song of Sorrow, by Rachel.'

'Louder! And more clearly.'

'Song of Sorrow by Rachel,' he shouted.

'*"Will you hear my voice, my distant one?*
Will you hear my voice, wherever you are?
A voice calling strongly, a voice filled with tears
Blessing you forever and ever.

"This world is great and its many paths
Meet for a moment, part for ever
Man seeks, but his feet stumble
He cannot find what he has lost.

"Perhaps my last days are close
The day of parting tears is nigh
I shall wait for you till the end of my life
As Rachel awaited her beloved."'

'Very good,' said Rivka, as Yuval sat back down. 'At Galuyot we regard Rachel as...'

'Why are you here?' Yuval asked me, and not in a spirit of ontological debate. 'To work in a plantation? To live in a barracks? To find a pretty blonde girlfriend?'

'That would be ironic.'

'Jacob is Jewish,' said Rivka.

'I know.' Yuval turned to me. 'Every year you diaspora Jews say, "Next year in Jerusalem". But instead of coming to Jerusalem, you marry out and raise non-Jewish children. You think you are American, or British, or a citizen of the world, just like Jews in the

1930s. You come to Israel for a holiday then return to your secure, comfortable life.'

'I'm not returning to my secure, comfortable life,' I said, not only to give him an argument but to hear how it would sound.

Rivka chuckled then turned serious. 'Do you have family in Israel, Jacob?'

'Not that I know of.' Not unless Papa's Sephardi girlfriend in Haifa gave birth to his baby. In which case I could have a whole family here. 'Can I apply for membership of Galuyot?'

'You can if you really want to.' Rivka sounded doubtful.

'Why not?' Yuval viewed me with a new respect. 'Zionism means Jews making *aliyah*. And "Kibbutz Galuyot" means "Ingathering of Exiles". You are doing the right thing.'

Rivka sighed. 'In the old days we had many volunteers like you. They stayed, got married and had families here. They were idealistic, they loved our land and our people. But things are very different today. Youngsters put themselves before the collective, they put rights before duty. It is understandable. We can't compete with Western standards of living, or offer much prospect of peace.'

'To be honest, I never thought I'd be a kibbutznik,' I said, as a future of physical labour, communal meals and seclusion from the outside world unfolded before my eyes.

'Nobody is a banana farmer when they arrive,' said Rivka. 'You think I knew anything about bananas, coming from Russia? You learn, you adapt. But life on kibbutz can be claustrophobic. Our work can be monotonous, whatever it is, especially if you are used to a world of the mind. And it is not easy to change from volunteer to member. It's never easy when the temporary becomes permanent. Take Herbie, for example. He was a volunteer then a candidate for years before he became a member. It is not something to decide on an impulse.'

'Hmm. Maybe I should think about it. In the meantime I could explore the world, see what's out there. I've always thought that one day I would travel.'

'Are you a wandering Jew?' asked Yuval. 'Or a wondering Jew?'

'Well I haven't wandered very far so far. I've hardly even been abroad. This is my first time in Israel and I haven't been off the kibbutz.'

'You are never in Israel for the first time,' said Rivka. 'Israel you can only revisit.'

'In other words, we were here in a previous life?' I thought of you and was struck by a realisation. You and I were originally together in *eretz Yisrael*, at some point in the past few thousand years. 'It must be easy to fall in love here,' I said, and I must admit, my mind strayed to the soldier I saw at the bus stop.

Rivka smiled. Her eyes twinkled. 'Have you heard the story of Pinchas, the traveller?'

Yuval rolled his eyes at the story of Pinchas, the traveller. He made a noise of getting up, threw a peanut in the air, which he caught in his mouth, and sauntered out without another word.

'It was a dark and stormy night in Vishtinetz and Pinchas was looking for shelter in the shtetl,' Rivka began. 'He made enquiries at a respectable house, where a modest young woman invited him in. Her husband, Rabbi Simcha, was out on his rounds, she said, but Pinchas should warm himself by the fire and sit in Rabbi Simcha's armchair. The *rebbetzin* was shy and demure but something about the stranger encouraged her to confide in him. God had given her an assignment, she said. While her young, married peers were busy producing babies, her job was to tend the poor parishioners of Vishtinetz. Unfortunately the townsfolk had long since abandoned piety – Rabbi Simcha had to bribe them to attend synagogue, paying double for their prayers – and they rebuffed and ridiculed the *rebbetzin* even as she brought God's light into their lives.

'"You should leave Vishtinetz and find a God-fearing parish," said Pinchas.

'The *rebbetzin* disagreed, saying, "A God-fearing parish has less need of a good rabbi and his wife."

'"But what of *your* needs?" asked Pinchas. "Surely you owe yourself a better life."

'Again the *rebbetzin* disagreed. "To search for something better is a fool's errand. It is not we who should leave but you who should stay."

'"I can't stay," said Pinchas. "I am a traveller."

'The rabbi came home and after dinner, he started to teach him Torah, a lesson that went on late into the night. So Pinchas stayed the night. And he stayed the next night and the next, because there aren't enough hours in the day to study Torah. Pinchas was an outstanding student and before long Rabbi Simcha took him on as his apprentice, showing by his own example the virtues of humility, frugality, dignity and tact while emphasising the cardinal importance of honesty before God. Pinchas learned so fast, it wasn't long before Rabbi Simcha could visit distant parishioners confident in the knowledge that Pinchas was fulfilling his rabbinical duties in his absence. But of course there was a monkey in the works.'

'A monkey?'

Rivka smiled and took a sip of tea. 'It was love. Pinchas was in love with the *rebbetzin*. Can you imagine? Living in a house with the woman he secretly loved but couldn't touch or even look at without betraying Rabbi Simcha. What could he do? One morning he rose early, packed his bag and set out on the road once more.'

'Did the *rebbetzin* know he loved her?'

'Oh, I'm sure she suspected. But what could she do? She was married. Their love was doomed.'

'Did she love him, too?'

Yuval bound in carrying a book the size of an encyclopaedia. He squatted at my side and opened its well-illustrated pages. 'That's the Kinneret, where Christians say Jesus walked on water,' he said at a picture of a lake. 'That's the Dead Sea, where people float on water,' he said, a few pages on. 'Masada,' he announced at a desert fortress. 'That's where we committed suicide rather than surrender to Roman invaders.' He stopped again at snowy mountain peaks in the Golan Heights then at waterfalls in Ein Gedi then at partygoers in Tel Aviv and a golden, secluded beach before lingering over worshippers in Jerusalem.

'The question...,' he said, on closing his book, '...is where to begin?'

Letter 29

Lawns were freshly mown, hedges neatly trimmed. The loungers and parasols had gone and the mound was rigged up as a bandstand. Floodlights illuminated pristine paths, Chinese lanterns swayed over the pool. Lines of Israeli flags hung from the sky. A ceremonial *chupa* awaited its bride and groom beneath the high diving board.

Suzette was wearing a white gardenia in her hair, a strapless mini-dress and a celebratory smile. 'We're so glad you could make it,' she told arriving guests.

'I had a letter from home today.' Caitlin gestured to the barman for another. Neshers were on the house at a drinks table at the shallow end.

'Good news?' I lit a Time and reached for my bottle.

'Nobody writes to me,' pouted Lottie. 'Let's write to each other.'

'It was from me mam,' said Caitlin. 'Sometimes I really miss me mam. And me stepdad. Know what I mean?'

'Not really.'

'I was talking to Roger.'

'You're not thinking of going back to Blighty, are you?' Roger was aghast.

'Letting the bloody team down,' said Jim, in Roger's middle-class accent.

'I can see it now.' Caitlin ignored them. 'Rashers of bacon sizzling in a pan, coals burning in the hearth, Archie polishing his shoes on an old newspaper, football results coming through on the radio...'

'The grass is always greener on the other side,' I said. Homesickness wasn't to be trusted.

'This is so true,' agreed Lottie.

'Grass is greener when it is longer,' beamed Danny. 'Then you must be careful. You cannot see what hides in long grass.'

'There is nothing to do but drink,' said Olaf.

'There's loads to do,' countered Roger. 'Yossi is starting up a folk-dancing group. I'm going to request Morris dancing. I like a good Morris dance.'

'It's Israeli dancing,' snorted Caitlin. 'Not that hankies-on-the-head shit.'

'You do realise,' Roger warned, '...if you go home, you can't come back?'

'Why not?' I'd never heard of that rule.

'It's never the same when you go back.'

'Doesn't mean she *can't* come back,' I argued. If Caitlin left and came back, I would be the veteran and she the newcomer.

'My point is, she will be disappointed if she does come back,' said Roger. 'There'll be a whole new volunteers' corps by then.'

'I'm already disappointed,' said Olaf.

'*Ahat, shteim, shlosh.*' The best man, Nissim, tapped a microphone at the *chupa*, his gold medallion flashing in a hairy gap in his open Hawaiian shirt.

Someone moved behind a tree. It was Wolfgang, returning from Ramle, where he had attended a meeting with the PLO. 'It's top-secret,' he had told me while folding a keffiyeh into his sports bag, his excitement grounded by a serious sense of purpose. His was a mission of historical, revolutionary destiny. Approaching the bar, he looked like a child whose dream had not come true.

'Hey, Wolfgang! How was the meeting?'

'What meeting?' Caitlin forgot about being homesick.

'He had a meeting with the PLO.'

'That's radical,' said Rudi. 'Now we can expect a visit from Shin Bet.'

'Oh, that's just grand. Well you listen to me, Mr P-L-O,' said Caitlin, prodding Wolfgang's chest on each initial. 'I've lived with the Troubles since I was a wee bairn. I came here to get away from that shit. And I'm warning you, when we get raided by Sinn Fein, I mean Shin Bet, I'm going to point them directly to your room.'

'And when they bust in,' Jim warned his roommate, 'I'm gonna tell 'em 'oo you are.'

'Why she calls him Mr P-L-O?' Olaf asked Jim.

'Silly fucker 'ad a mee'ing wiff terrorists.'

Olaf was thrilled. 'Did they teach you how to make a bomb?' he asked Wolfgang.

Wolfgang twirled his moustache. 'They invited me into a basketball hall full of Palestinian flags and pictures of al-Aqsa and Chairman Arafat. As word of my visit spread, more and more people, mostly elderly men, lined up to shake my hand. "*Shukran, shukran*," they said. There is no denying they were honoured to meet me. But I think I was in the wrong basketball hall. Nobody spoke German, or English, and there was no political meeting. They gave me mint tea and sweet pastries, and showed me how to dance the debka.'

'Show us,' said Roger, amid hoots of exaggerated laughter.

'Show, show, show,' chanted Olaf.

'*Vive la révolution!*' Rudi raised a bottle.

There was no sign of the wedding ceremony starting, so I took the opportunity to fetch a cardigan from my room. After long hot days, nights could be chilly. A soldier in uniform stood out among a throng at the compound gate. I recognised his equine face.

'Excuse me.' Old habits died hard. 'Are you Yoni? I'm Jacob Green.'

He looked at me quizzically then broke into a buck-toothed smile. 'Heeeeey! *Ma nishma?* Kitty's friend, right? You don't match her description at all.' He stepped aside and we embraced like long-lost cousins. 'How long have you been in Israel?'

'Almost a month.'

'And you like our kibbutz?'

'Yes, I was thinking of starting a new life here.'

'Kitty said I must show you around because this is your first time in Israel. But as you can see, I have been away. And tomorrow I return to my unit.'

'Then I'll see you when you get back.'

'Have you been to Jerusalem?'

'No, I haven't.'

'You're kidding.' Yoni's buck-toothed smile turned incredulous. 'Then you must go.'

'Why? I'm not religious.'

'You can't come to Israel and not visit Jerusalem. Zehava!'

A slender gossamer figure stepped out of the darkness and directed some Hebrew words at Yoni. It was the soldier I had seen on my arrival. She was even more beautiful out of uniform.

'This is Jake. He has never been to *Yerushalyim.*'

'*Be'emet?*' Zehava looked me in the eye all too briefly. 'A Jerusalem virgin?'

'I'm due a day off next week. I could go then.' I felt strangely inspired. 'Can you recommend a hostel?'

'There are lots of hostels for tourists in the Old City.' Her voice sounded like a cello. 'But do us a favour: don't follow Roman's example.'

Yoni shook his head. 'I thought he was a normal guy. What's normal, right? What is it with tourists and Jerusalem syndrome?'

'What's Jerusalem syndrome?' I asked.

'Jerusalem can make you think you are someone else,' said Zehava. 'You can be Napoleon or a white rabbit, though the favourite is Jesus, especially for Christians. I don't know who Roman thinks he is. Now he is in a mental hospital.'

'Does the bus to Galuyot go there?'

'Of course,' said Yoni. '*Yerushalyim* is only about twenty kilometers away.'

'And twenty centuries.' Zehava turned to Yoni and her low cadences reverted to Hebrew.

Yoni put his arm round her and whispered in her ear. Then he turned to face me. '*Tov.* I will see you soon.' He bowed over namaste hands then placed an arm round Zehava's waist and led her to the pool just as a loud cheer said the wedding was underway.

A shiver ran down my spine. Maybe it was wishing the arm round Zehava's waist was mine. Maybe it was Papa, whose dream was to visit Jerusalem. Or God was giving me a nudge. I shivered again and made my way to the barrack to get my cardigan.

Back at the wedding party, everyone was either heading to the buffet or eating at tables configured corner to corner like a giant necklace around the swimming pool.

'*Nu?*' asked Rivka when I joined her in the queue for the buffet. 'What did you think of Michal and Doron?'

'The bride and groom? I haven't actually seen them. I missed the ceremony.'

'They are the most beautiful couple. Yaah.' Suzette didn't miss anything. 'They are made for one another. It's a marriage made in heaven.'

'You *will* ask me to dance, won't you, Roger?' Rivka wiggled her hips at Roger, who inclined his head obligingly as though marking his card. Further back in the queue, Wolfgang hid behind Jim. Wolfgang had had enough of dancing for one day.

A salmon with an artichoke in its mouth lay beside a turkey with an eggplant in its bottom. Next up were stuffed peppers, spicy bourekas and things I didn't recognise. I put a couple of hot dogs, some chicken wings, a portion of Israeli salad and a carton of chocolate mousse on my tray, beside my bottle of Nesher, and looked for a vacant seat.

'Winston Churchill! Winston Churchill!'

'Hey, Boris! How are the turkeys?'

'May I present to you Svetlana, my wife, and Anna, our daughter.' Boris stood aside to reveal a stern-looking woman with short peroxide hair who was adding pickled herring to her red cabbage and cauliflower, and a little girl who evidently didn't want to be there. Boris had a plaster stuck over the crook of his elbow. 'Today I give blood. Svetlana, she can do transfusion, but they tell her, stay in kitchen, we have special nurses for blood-donation day. You give blood, my English friend?'

'No, I must have been asleep.'

'You can sleep when you are dead.' On Svetlana's call, Boris returned to his family.

Herbie and Abdullah were eating at a table by the five-foot line. Faces washed and hair gelled, wearing identical white polo shirts and blue denim jeans, they could have been dressed by the same mother. Both were on their best behaviour.

'Hi, chaps.'

'I was there in the Sixties, when it was all going down.' Herbie was reminiscing.

'What was going down?' asked Abdullah, between mouthfuls of baked fish and couscous.

'The USA was turning on, tuning in...,' Herbie paused over a forkful of lamb tagine. He reached for a napkin, too late to catch a drip of apricot marinade that stained his white shirt. 'And dropping out.'

'I turned on, tuned in and dropped out,' I said. 'But I was born too late. Simple Twist of Fate.'

Herbie was awestruck. 'Hey, man, that's Bob Dylan. I got a poster of Dylan on my wall. "Protest against the rising tide of conformity," it says. Those were the days. Every night we partied like there was no tomorrow. And when we weren't partying, we were marching against the war in Vietnam.'

'There are marches in Ramle, on Fridays,' said Abdullah, in case Herbie wanted to turn on, tune in and drop out all over again.

'We marched in Washington, DC, yes siree Baab. Right outside the White House. "One, two, three, four, what are we fighting for?"' Herbie jiggled his shoulders in time to the song.

'You should drop by my place, Abdullah. We could listen to some Dylan, drink a few beers...'

A gasp became a murmur, then applause and cheers. A roving spotlight stopped at a table directly beneath the lifeguard's hut to shine on our bride and groom. Bling flashing, Nissim tapped the microphone.

'Guess who?' Someone put her hands over my eyes. I didn't need to guess; she had an aura. She removed her hands and there, adoration written across his face, was Herbie.

'Who is the next cake?' Lottie whispered.

'You mean *where* is the next cake.'

'*Where* is the next cake.' Lottie was drunk.

'Where are you going?' demanded Herbie as I took Lottie to the buffet, for some cake.

'Shhh.' The guests were listening to Nissim's speech.

Lottie stumbled on a grassy bank and pulled me down beside her. She gazed upwards in wonder. 'The stars are so bright when they visit us from their universe.'

'I'm going to go to Jerusalem.'

'I love to sleep under a sky full of stars.' Lottie lay back and closed her eyes.

'*We* could sleep under the stars. When I get back from Jerusalem we could go on a Shabbat *tiyul*, just the two of us, to a secluded beach up north. I saw pictures in a book...'

Lottie was dozing off, oblivious to both my invitation and a third party, who was pissing behind a tree.

'Hey, Danny, what's happening?'

'*Quien a buen arbol Se arrima, Le entran ganas, Y se orina.*' He zipped up his flies and sat down on my other side. 'It is time to say goodbye.'

'Why, where are you going?'

He lay on the ground, glanced at Lottie then turned towards a sky full of stars.

A murmuring drone gave way to hushed anticipation. A circle of light followed a singer to the bandstand. Buxom in a sparkling ballgown, she nodded to a four-piece band then faced her poolside audience.

'*Yerushaliyim shel Zahav*. Jerusalem of Gold,' she announced, to a buzz of approval. A half-moon rippled in the swimming pool.

'*Avir harim zalul kayayin...*'

Her quivering voice wailed and keened. A soft breeze prickled my arms. A lump blocked my throat. Tears filled my eyes. She was rousing the spirits of our ancestors, and their yearning for Jerusalem.

'*Yerushaliyim shel zahav...*,' she sang.

<h1 style="text-align:center">Letter 30</h1>

The venerable citadel rose above a barren valley in a city that reeked of traffic fumes and garbage slowly roasting under an all-powerful sun. Tourists roamed the Old City's ramparts over masonry pockmarked by bullet holes. I entered through Jaffa Gate, not a gate so much as a turret so immense it was almost a tunnel.

Ice cream parlours and pizza joints lined a bright castle keep. Street vendors lounged alongside watermelons stacked in pyramids, a beggar and his dog slept by a wagon loaded with dough sticks. A youth-group leader was addressing a flock of bored American teenagers. A donkey trotted up a hill towards a modest church, whose whiteness stood out in a city of sand-coloured uniformity. Jerusalem was shaped by the desert.

I had set out, after an early lunch granted by Moshe and facilitated by Lottie, to discover my heritage. I had a bottle of water, a Jerusalem Post and a map of the Old City that I consulted as the bus ascended a ravine between sparsely forested hills on the road to Jerusalem. To travel light, I had stuffed a change of undies, socks and T-shirt, as well as my toothbrush and a tube of toothpaste into the voluminous thigh pockets of a pair of army-style trousers I'd bought at the *kolbo*, along with a T-shirt sporting Galuyot's logo on a small crest.

Now I found myself in a dusty souk, wondering what time it was. At Galuyot, the sun marked time by its position in the sky; here the sun was hidden by overhead carpets like the world was upside down. At Galuyot the humidity was oppressive but you got used to sweating it out. Here the heat was dry and sneaky, it crept up on you and played havoc with your mind.

Jerusalem was not what I expected. There was no sign of my ghostly ancestors, no spiritual utopia and no buzz of crazy personal delusions. I beheld only families on holiday, youth groups on tour and dawdling pilgrims, all holding me up as they contemplated T-shirts and baseball caps, ceramics, amulets and other tourist tat on a downhill drag flanked by proprietorial Arabs in black-and-white keffiyahs and white dishdashas who sat smoking nagilas and playing backgammon between sacks of colourful spices and soldiers stationed in pairs looking bored. A *charedi* man pushed through the crowd as though late for a very important date. I stepped back to let him pass, and knocked down a rack of postcards.

Crash!

Western Walls. Tombs of Christ. Domes of the Rock. Images of Jerusalem's holy sites lay scattered at my feet. A human barrier halted the flow of tourists to prevent any further desecration. A nun saw the pictures too late and jumped up and down as though dancing on hot coals. Faces turned angry.

I picked up the postcards and felt a surge of responsibility. My duty here was to assign holy places to devotees, to give every Jew a Western Wall, every Christian a Tomb of Christ and every Muslim a Dome of the Rock. A young stallholder's glare made me think again. Not wanting to cause trouble, I replaced the postcards in their revolving paniers. But in my rush to do the right thing, I left the holy sites of Judaism, Christianity and Islam all shuffled together.

The stallholder had a mullet haircut, a keffiyah worn as a scarf and hosepipe jeans – the uniform of rioting Palestinians. 'How dare you knock down the Dome of the Rock then mix it up with Jewish and Christian sites?' said his face. He looked like he was going to kill me. It would make headlines throughout the world, there would be a military clampdown in the Old City, debates in the Houses of Parliament, rioting on the streets of capital cities and, in all likelihood, war between Israel and its Arab neighbours, if not a greater global conflict. Then I realised, he wasn't bothered.

'Come, come,' he said, though not in the British sense. 'I have something for you. I give you very good price.'

Enormous African bongos jostled with classical Greek amphorae in a cool, cavernous grotto of jagged whitewashed walls under a high vaulted ceiling. Assorted chess sets, silver jewellery and blue *Hamsas* posed in glass cabinets. A rotating ballerina rose from a wind-up music box.

'What you want?' he asked. 'You choose. I give you very good price.'

'I don't want anything.'

'You don't like nothing?' He stood between me and the door, hands on hips.

'It's not that I don't *like* anything. Everything's very nice. It's just that I don't *need* anything.'

'You want a carpet? I have a friend who will give you very good price on a beautiful, hand-woven carpet. Whatever you want.'

'How much are they?' I nodded at an array of cigarette lighters. All had a picture of Jerusalem on one side.

'These are very good quality.' He sparked up a lighter. 'How much you want to pay?'

'Do you know how many shekels are in a pound?'

'I give it to you for fifty agurot. Is very good lighter.'

'Okay.'

I paid the vendor, who seemed surprised by my acceptance of his starting price, and lit a Time with my new lighter, which depicted the Old City walls illuminated at night.

I had to raise my cigarette above my head as though leading a mission of smokers, so densely packed was the souk. Gradually the torrent of tourists thinned and moved at a faster clip, giving me space to unfold my map. I tried to find my location in this semi-subterranean labyrinth of drags and alleys, of twists, turns and dead ends, but the map's network of multicoloured lines made no sense and its symbols could have been hieroglyphics for all they meant to me. A progression of aromas formed a more immediate guide: a urine-stained wall behind me, a tang of new leather to the left, greasy kebabs to the right. A whiff of hashish emanated from an alley so narrow, opposing balconies almost touched.

Roman centurions were marching under military banners. Jesus was delivering a sermon on a hill. Eve was tempting Adam to bite an apple. In place of the sky or a ceiling, embroidered tapestries pictured scenes of local history.

'Which way to the Western Wall?' I asked a couple of blond backpackers, who were loitering in a doorway under a carved wooden sign for St Christopher's Hostel for Travellers.

The backpackers raised their chins in the direction I was taking and within minutes I arrived at a military checkpoint. A soldier patted me down and let me pass into a plaza too bright to be seen.

The sunlight was dazzling. A new, unfiltered heat bore down from above and rose from a vast floor of flagstones. On the plaza's far side, the golden Dome of the Rock stood radiant and aloof above a high ruin, a giant fragment of a relic spouting brigs of moss in its cracks. The Western Wall was so humble, discreet and indistinguishable from the prevailing run of sand-coloured walls, I would scarcely have given it a second glance but for a groundswell of tourists and supplicants in black hats and gabardine coats that defied the Middle Eastern sun.

Papa accompanied me across the plaza. The older he became, the more Papa regretted his failure to visit Jerusalem and now he was here, facing a reality he had known only in his heart. '"*Shema Yisrael, Adonai Elohanu, Adonai Ehad,*"' he intoned. 'This is all you need to know.' Then he recited the prayer in English and it sounded like his words were addressed to me personally.

I repeated, after Papa: '"Hear O Israel. The Lord is God. The Lord is one."'

'Hey, buddy. Howya doin,' man?'

A bespectacled, bearded character wearing a baseball cap, a rumpled suit and grubby sneakers was standing beside me. He was holding a blue velvet clutch bag adorned by a gold Star of David. Knotted tassels dangled over his belt.

'Watch out!' warned a bell in my head. 'He's a missionary. Just ignore him.' Old warnings rang faint.

'I'm going to the Wall,' I said. 'To honour my grandfather.'

'You're a Brit! I got friends in Britain, *baruch hashem.* You know a guy called Asher Felixbaum?'

'No, I've never heard of him. And I never met the Queen, either.' It was too hot for chitchat. I wanted to touch the Wall for Papa then sit down with a cool drink under a café's protective awning.

'Asher's a great guy. I think you'd like him. His brother Menashe not so much, but that's another story. He lives in Hampstead Heath. That's in London, right?'

'Right.'

'You know it, huh? I'm Abba Ben-Abba, the poet.' He gave my hand a vigorous shake. 'You might have seen some of my work. I leave samples around the city, stuck on billboards and bus shelters.'

'No, I've only just got here.'

'You a stoodent?'

'I *was* a philosophy student, of Nietzsche in particular.' As a student of Nietzsche, I was impervious to the blandishments of missionaries.

'You're a philahserfer!' He shook my hand again. 'What *nachas* for your parents! What do they call you?'

'Jacob.'

'Jaaay-kaab,' he repeated in his booming Brooklyn baritone. '"Your name will no longer be 'Jacob,' but 'Israel,' because you have struggled with God, and with humans, and you have overcome".'

He was overstating it, as is the American way, but Abba Ben-Abba seemed to know my story.

'The *midrash* says Jacob's struggles begin before he is born. He's in the womb with Esau, his twin, and already they're fighting to be first out. And their fighting continues as they grow up. According to some sources, it's in fear of Esau that Jacob runs away. Anyway, he lands up in Mesopotamia, where he falls in love with a girl, who is his beautiful and lovely cousin. Her father, Laban, tells Jacob he must work for him for seven years before he'll let them marry. "And they seemed to him but a few days, due to the love he felt for her."'

'What was the girl's name?'

'Rachel.'

'So Jacob married Rachel?'

'It wasn't that straightforward. On their wedding night Laban puts Leah, his elder, less attractive daughter, in Rachel's place and Jacob doesn't find out until the following morning. You gotta feel for Jacob. There he is, expecting to wake up beside the beautiful and lovely Rachel, for whom he's waited seven years, but he rolls over in bed only to find the ugly sister! Then Laban makes him work for *another* seven years to win Rachel's hand all over again. Yada yada yada, fast forward and Jacob and Rachel are finally married. Jacob has already had four sons with Leah, and Rachel wants children of her own. But it doesn't happen. She's barren. In desperation, she tells her maid, Bilhah, to sleep with Jacob so that she, Rachel, can adopt their children. Bilhah gives Jacob two sons. As does Leah's maid, Zilpah. Then, it says in the Torah, God remembers Rachel and He gives her a son, Joseph. After Joseph is born, they decide to move back to Hebron. Jacob, his wives, their maids and their children all head for Jacob's home town. They're still on the road when Benjamin, the twelfth and last of Jacob's sons, is born. Rachel dies giving birth and is buried on the road to Bethlehem. Her tomb is still there. You should go see it. Hey, buddy... I said you should go see Rachel's tomb.'

'Who am I?'

'You are a pilgrim in *Yerushalyim*. That's a sure sign of a *tzaddik*. You know what a *tzaddik* is, don't you? According to Rambam, a *tzaddik* is one whose merits outweigh his iniquities. In other words, a righteous person.'

'I'm not a pilgrim. I'm a volunteer on a kibbutz.'

'That's wonderful. Where you at?'

'Kibbutz Galuyot.' My commune's name had the comforting ring of home. 'See?' I thrust out my chest to show him Galuyot's crest. 'I work in a banana plantation.'

'I've heard of Kibbutz Galuyot. I used to have a friend in Rehovot, at the Weizmann Institute. Rehovot's a wonderful town. Here, put it on.' He handed me a crocheted *kippa* like those worn by some kibbutzniks, a modern version of the silk *yarmulkes* we put on for *kiddush* on Friday nights when Papa was alive.

'You *are* a Jew, right?'

I must have put it on upside down, or inside out. I turned it round and he gave me a hairclip to keep it in place. 'Yes, I am. Though I must admit, I used to think being Jewish was mere chance, that I could just as easily not be.'

'"I could just as easily not be,"' he chortled before adopting a thespian's full-breasted posture. '"To be or naaat to be,"' he boomed. '"That is the question."'

I wasn't expecting to hear Shakespeare at the Western Wall, from an Orthodox Jewish missionary, in a Noo Yawk accent. My head was spinning.

'"To be" means "to be with God,"' said Abba. 'Have you ever thought about becoming *ba'al teshuvah*? That means being born again, returning to righteousness. Literally, it means "master of repentance".'

'*Ba'al teshuvah*' had a magical resonance, like 'open sesame'. The phrase promised a whole new future. Instead of working on a kibbutz, I could be returning to righteousness in Jerusalem.

'How does one return to righteousness?' I asked.

Abba took from his clutch bag two black leather balls, which he unravelled into long, thin strips, each attached to a small black box. 'You never seen *tefillin?*'

Bells of apprehension rang again. Inasmuch as I could hear them, the chimes referred me to lessons learned from infancy onwards, at home, at school and at university. But my new reality was informed not by experiences in this life but by traditions that dated back to time immemorial.

'We have laid *tefillin* every morning for thousands of years, except on Shabbat, when we don't need *tefillin* to remind us of our relationship with God.' Abba held up the two black boxes. 'Inside each of these is a scroll of parchment inscribed with the Torah portion that relates the Israelites' exodus from Egypt. We were slaves, man. Don't you remember? "Once we were slaves and now we are free."'

'Once we were slaves and now we are free.' The refrain sounded familiar, like a forgotten melody I'd once known by heart.

Abba placed a black box on my left bicep. 'One box goes on your arm, facing your heart, to protect you from its desires.' Muttering prayers in Hebrew, he wound a leather strap around my arm seven times, then round my finger, 'like a wedding band. This is to show you are married to God and will respect that marriage covenant, which is the Torah. This goes on your forehead, to connect your mind to God.' He positioned a box between my eyes and tightened a strap around my head to keep it there.

'What convoluted paraphernalia! What a superstitious ritual! It's mumbo-jumbo designed to subjugate people into senseless conformity. The Western world's most cherished traditions of rational philosophy, insightful psychology and creative literature all stand against such submission. It's preposterous.' The voice of reason faded away, taking scepticism with it.

'It has been said that the daily act of laying *tefillin* has done more to express the high morality of our people than all the books on ethics ever written,' said Abba. 'How, you might ask, can such a claim be made?'

'How *can* such a claim be made?'

'Laying *tefillin* is our greatest *mitzvah*. That is to say, our greatest deed to please God.'

'How does laying *tefillin* please God?'

'The truth is, I don't know. I'm not an expert. Some say *tefillin* represents a unity of mind and heart. Some say it represents obedience to the Almighty. Some say it's only in the symbolic nature of words and actions that virtue resides. In laying *tefillin*, we stamp God's truth on our soul. Now you're wearing *tefillin*,' he said proudly, 'you can go pray at the Wall, maybe leave a letter to the Almighty between the cracks.'

I took a step towards the Wall, towards a long, black line of supplicants. The sun glared down and I was overcome by dizziness. Flagstones became tombstones rising from the ground. The dead were returning, to hail the Messiah.

Then everything went dark.

A flight of steps ascended through pure, still air towards a brilliant blue heaven. Down below, in downtown Jerusalem, gold tributaries snaked between Ottoman towers and Mandate-era masonry. Western hills threw up tired scrubland and brown patches of earth. A hazy horizon shimmered in the east.

A bright, paved square surrounded an elaborate water fountain. A few isolated saplings provided a small measure of dappled shade. A pregnant woman in heavy clothes was sitting on a bench, a pram by her side. A tramp in a beanie hat and prayer shawl was striding towards a gated institution.

'Ben-Bazak!' hollered Abba.

The tramp pulled up as though tugged by a leash.

'Howya doin,' man?' Abba held up his fists, ready to spar, though Ben-Bazak hardly seemed the pugilist type. 'Say, this is Jacob. He's just off the boat from London.'

'I have seen you before,' said Ben-Bazak. Squinting through raisin eyes half-buried in fleshy creases, he did well to see me now.

'Do you recognise me from a previous life?' If he recognised me, he might recognise you, I thought.

'I see you every day. You shoot us with your cameras, even as we pray. *Hashem* sees how *Yerushalyim* is defiled and profaned, like a whore.'

'Jacob's not a tourist. He's going to be *ba'al teshuvah.*'

'You leave home and search for your self,' Ben-Bazak told me. 'You fall into the hands of a beautiful woman. You succumb to the *yetzeh hara.*'

'Ben-Bazak has the gift,' said Abba. 'It's kinda like second sight. It's not uncommon among Yemenites.'

'*Hashem* has drawn His bow and made you a target for His arrows.' Ben-Bazak was still applying his second sight to me. '*Hashem* is like an enemy.'

'Ben-Bazak's going to the *bet midrash,*' said Abba. 'He's there every day, studying Torah from early in the morning till late at night. Except on Shabbat, when...'

Ben-Bazak motioned Abba aside for a word, which soon became a heated argument. Interpretations of Jewish law were, it seemed, a matter of personal honour. They circled each other like boxers, gesticulating like actors, their faces red in angry concentration. Abba had the louder voice but his halting Hebrew left him searching for words and their dispute smouldered into random pot shots. Ben-Bazak turned his back and we crossed the square into a warren of neatly paved paths and adjoining sandy-brick residences.

'Uphold the tradition, man!' Abba was seething. 'Do the right thing! I gotta say, it's unprecedented. I wanted to say that but I think I got the word wrong.'

'What were you arguing about?'

'There's four of us. Yariv from the *makolet,* Lenny the violinist, Ben-Bazak and me. We go to Ben-Bazak's on Thursday evenings, when Abichayil is doing ritual-purity supervision at the *mikveh* and their kids are at the neighbours'. Only *this* Thursday...,' Abba drew a circle in the air, '...*this* Thursday, Abichayil's gonna be home, with the kids. And Abichayil don't approve of poker.'

'Poker?'

'She's a piece of work, that one. Always complaining. She says we make too much noise, and eat too many munchies, and she's sick of cleaning up our mess.'

'I don't get it. I thought you were a missionary.'

'A missionary? That's funny. I'm just a lunatic, man.'

'I thought you were born again.'

'Sometimes I am and sometimes I ain't. To be or not to be, right? Say, man, you wanna try our local hashish?'

We had turned down a flight of narrow steps lined by an inclining terrace of austere institutions and immaculate homes and emerged into a quiet courtyard of shops full of religious or bohemian headwear, kaftans and accessories, then stopped to view a skyline cluttered by water tanks on stilts, naked girders sticking out of half-assembled breeze blocks and TV aerials angled like giant craneflies. I must have misheard him.

'Hashish?'

'Shhhh! You gotta keep it under your hat, you know what I'm saying? I call it yo-ghurt.'

'Religious people smoke hash, I mean yo-ghurt?'

'Sure. Ben-Bazak has a bong for breakfast.'

'You got some on you?'

'Not right now. But we could go see Ne'eman, my man in Mea Shearim. That's an ultra-Orthodox neighbourhood. You gotta behave yourself there.'

'Yeah, let's go! Let's get high!' I danced a jig and Abba danced too, adding a song whose every other line was, '*baruch hashem*'.

'I helped Ne'eman move into his apartment,' he said as we resumed our stroll. 'He's a yeshivah *bocher* of the old school. But first I gotta go home to see Batya. I'm a married man.'

'Okay. We could meet up later. I was thinking of staying at St Christopher's Hostel for Travellers. I passed it in the souk.'

'You don't need no fucking hostel. You can hunker down at mine. My place is your place, man.'

'Are you sure?'

'You're so British. Stay for as long as you like, *habibi*.'

'Thanks, Abba. But I'm due back at Galuyot by tomorrow night.'

'We'll have Botz for breakfast. That's Turkish qwaafi. You drink that stuff?'

'We have it in the banana plantation. I don't like it. It's too strong.'

'"It's too strong,"' chortled Abba.

We entered a neighbourhood of formidable stone buildings that could have been synagogues, seminaries or libraries, then turned towards the citadel's high wall under a sign saying, 'Armenian Orthodox Patriarchate Road'. The sunny side of the street was lined by shops displaying identical olive-wood nativity scenes, last suppers and crucifixes. There weren't any customers, or even window shoppers, only a pair of pedestrians in high black hats and black dishdashas strolling arm in arm like a beast with two heads.

'Armenian monks,' said Abba. 'The Armenians get their own quarter because they've been here since the fifth or sixth century. If we had more time, I'd show you the tourist sites. The Church of the Holy Sepulchre is just round the corner. Those Christians, they got more denominations than I have fingers and toes. Russian Orthodox, Greek Orthodox, Syrian Orthodox... Armenian Apostolics, Egyptian Copts, Roman Catholics... Nobody dares leave the building lest the locks are changed while they're gone. Sometimes their fights get outta hand and the cops have to break it up.'

The road fed into Jaffa Gate's quadrangle, scene of ambulating tourists and al-fresco fast food. I had been here before. I found a tree stump on which to rest and drink from my now warm bottle of water.

'Oh, God!'

Abba had disappeared. I jumped to my feet, checking baseball caps and faces in the crowd. None belonged to Abba. I was on my own.

A taunting voice was there to apportion blame. 'It's your own fault. Why did you have to go find a tree stump? You couldn't drink where you were? You should have stayed by his side. And you should have taken his address and phone number, just in case something like this happened. As it is, you have no idea where he lives, you don't know anyone else and you don't know where you're going.'

Maybe he hadn't been there at all but was just a hallucination. Zehava had warned me that Jerusalem can play tricks on your imagination. Yet he seemed so real. Maybe he was an angel sent by God who could appear and disappear at will. Whatever the case, there was no sign of him now. I lit a cigarette and turned towards the drag that led to St Christopher's Hostel for Travellers.

'Here's the place. They got the best falafel in *Yerushalyim.*'

The sound of Abba prompted a rush of gratitude to God. He was on a cobblestone path round the corner, studying a menu. Abba, that is.

'How do you take your falafel? I like mine with french fraaas. And a little salad.'

'Sounds good. I haven't tried one, though they do sometimes have falafel in the *cheder ochel* at Galuyot.'

'And some hot chilli sauce.'

'Mixed with mayonnaise.'

'They ain't got no mayonnaise. But you gotta have hummus, right? And tahini. You'll love it. You got any moolah?'

We took cans of Coke from the fridge and bulging pittas from a vendor with whom Abba shot the breeze in a mixture of Hebrew, English and Arabic. Once we were seated under a striped awning at a wobbly table, Abba put down his velvet bag of *tefillin* and made a blessing.

'That's just approximate,' he said. 'There ain't no *b'rachah* for falafel. Whaddya think of our national dish?'

'I could eat one of these every day.' Not even pink Israeli salad was as delicious as this savoury, Middle Eastern concoction of mashed chickpeas in fried breadcrumbs, with salad, hummus, tahini and chips in an open pitta.

'My old man ate pistachio ice cream every day,' recalled Abba as we smoked post-prandial cigarettes and sat back to watch the Old City go round. 'It didn't matter where we were – and we were always moving, from city to city, from Pittsburgh to Charlotte to New York – he had to have pistachio ice cream. Oy! He drove my mother crazy. Eventually we settled on Long Island. Then just before my barmitzvah, he had a heart attack. Dead, just like that, at the age of forty-seven. That was when I started getting religious and going to a yeshivah. I wasn't the best stoodent but I stayed for a number of years, and might have stayed longer if the rabbis hadn't expelled me.'

'Did they catch you smoking yo-ghurt?'

'They caught me visiting a lady of the night, though I still don't know how they found out. "It's my old man's *yartzheit*," I told them. "Three years to the day since he passed." I needed comfort, or a hand job at least, you know what I'm saying? The irony is, of all the whorehouses I've been to, from here to Honolulu, it was only a classy broad on Long Island who gave me the pox.'

'What did you do?'

'I had to see three doctors, man.'

'After being expelled from yeshivah.'

'I hit the road. Wherever I went, I taught literature to the poor and uneducated. Whitman, Faulkner, Hemingway, Kerouac... The great American pantheon. Then I went abroad and that's when I started writing my own shit. I travelled across Europe, to Greece, and fetched up in the Sinai, where I gave toiletries to fine young men in *gelabeas*, receiving a conch in return from Sheikh Ali. That was in '77, before I visited Grandma. It was at Grandma's that I met Batya. I knew we'd be married from the moment we met, even though Batya wasn't interested.'

'Batya wouldn't melt.'

'When Batya was growing up in Copenhagen...' He threw back his head in laughter. 'That's very good. Batya wouldn't melt. Wait till you meet her, ha ha ha. Where was I?'

'When Batya was growing up in Copenhagen...'

'She was squatting in a hippy commune. She thought she was a Christian called Mathilde, and it was only after her mother died she found out she had been adopted. Turns out her birth mother was Jewish. (Batya says she always knew it, in her subconscious or whatever.) And you know what? She fell in love with Judaism. Became *ba'alat teshuvah*. Now she's a zealot. There's nothing a religious woman will not do for her husband. "Charm is deceptive and beauty is vain,"' he boomed. '"But a woman who fears God should be praised."'

There was more to Judaism than met the eye. As we got up to leave it seemed like the earth had moved. The sun was so low it could have rolled through the alley.

We left the Old City through Jaffa Gate and descended a desolate wadi, a wasteland furnished by odd acacia trees, hairy clumps of grass and ankle-high rocks. There were no lights and it was getting dark. A distant dog barked incessantly.

'This is hell,' said Abba, like a tourist guide. 'The valley of Hinnom. The original Gehenna. All-consuming fires used to break out right here for no apparent reason. The rabbis said the area was cursed. Modern science tells us the fires were caused by underground sulphur deposits. But to the pagans who lived here, fire signified the wrath of their gods. So what did they do? They threw their children into the flames. Can you dig that shit?'

The descent was easy enough but we huffed, puffed and stumbled over half-visible obstacles as we ascended the valley's far side. The rim at the top met a winding residential street signposted as 'Rehov Ein Rogel'. I made a mental note, in case I needed to know where I was.

A panoramic view showed a land fading into dusk. Abba pointed to the Old City, to a bell tower and adjacent cupola. 'That's the Dormition Abbey over Mount Zion.' A rippling twilight further east was so opaque, land could have been sea. 'That's Judea, home of our ancestors. That's why we're called "Jews": we originate in Judea.'

A red sun was dipping between hills to the west. Lights twinkled like fireflies in the new city below. I could see a road I had travelled by bus just hours earlier. Now under parallel lines of orange lights, it was flanked by a limestone palace on one side, a sandy-brick tower on the other.

'You see the King David Hotel?' Abba pointed at the limestone palace. 'The Brits used it as a military base when they were sending Holocaust survivors back to internment camps in Germany and Cyprus. So the Irgun bombed them out. They called in a warning, twenty minutes in advance, told them to evacuate the building. But did the great British army of occupation listen? No, they stayed in the hotel and some of their soldiers got killed. The Brits called it terrorism,' Abba chortled.

We passed a miniature castle of thick Jerusalem stone built into a hill between gnarled sycamore trees. A neighbouring villa displayed a courtyard styled in sensuous Arabic curves. Then came an intrusion from the 1970s, its perspex and plate-glass panels barely rising above high compound walls and electronic gates.

'This neighbourhood's called "Abu Tor,"' said Abba. 'King David's spies hid here, it's in the Bible. These days it's a mixed neighbourhood. Jews and Arabs, religious and secular, Ashkenazi and Sephardi. We got a train station round the corner, and the Cinematheque is just down the hill. I think you'll like it here.'

'Aaaargh!'

Someone was screaming in a discreet institute set back from the road. There was no front door and its windows were closed behind shutters. Flower baskets hung low from wrought-iron balconies. I assumed it was a lunatic asylum.

To my surprise, Abba turned to climb the building's side-steps, which led to an overgrown bower. I followed, right behind, lest I lose him again. He rang a doorbell and rattled a grille. Dogs yapped, heels clattered on a stone floor. A heavy front door creaked open.

'Heeey, Grandma. *Shabbat shalom.*'

'It's not Shabbat, you dunderhead.'

Grandma reeked of alcohol. Her hair was tangled, her mascara smudged, her dress was dishevelled and one of her red mule slippers was missing a pompom. Nonetheless, Grandma maintained the hauteur of a grand chatelaine. A pair of Chihuahuas ran rings round her ankles.

Cracks and missing pieces marked a gloomy vestibule's mosaic floor. Shrouded lamps barely illuminated rows of antiquarian books. Kiddush cups, candelabras and menorahs were jumbled together, dusty Judaica sleeping on shelves and cabinets. Cobwebs formed nests in overhead cornices and dark corners. A brighter light slanted between a pair of double-doors that Grandma had left open. Grandma's quarters had gold and purple cushions, thick rugs and drapes, a chaise-longue and a footstool inlaid with sparkling stones. Grandma's residence could have been a harem bequeathed by Ottoman invaders.

'Where are your keys?' she asked Abba as he put his velvet bag on a cabinet's jutting ledge.

'I've been asking myself the same question.' Abba patted himself down. 'Great minds think alike, right? I must have given them to someone.'

'Don't look at me,' I said.

'Who's this? One of your pickups from the Wall?'

'This is Jacob. Jacob's a philaserfer.'

'Oh, you're all philosophers. But when something needs fixing...'

'Grandma has a jewellery store, on Emek Refayim, not far from here. And she has some associate stores, in...'

'Aaaargh!'

Behind a small doorway carved into a recess at the vestibule's end, someone was suffering appalling agonies. Neither Grandma nor Abba took any notice until another ghastly scream interrupted Abba again.

'Shaddaaap!' yelled Grandma. 'It's getting worse,' she told Abba.

'Mendel's a Holocaust survivor,' said Abba, his head bowed. 'Grandma's been trying to get rid of him for years.'

'You make me crazy.' Grandma turned on her yapping Chihuahuas. 'Do you know what it's like to be crazy?'

A door opened to the sounds of a party. Out came a pregnant woman in matching headscarf and apron, swinging her beefy arms like a farmer's daughter.

'Abbaaah. Where have you been?'

Abba pecked her cheek. 'I ran into Ben-Bazak.'

'Your friends are waiting for you.'

'They're not *my* friends, they're *our* friends. Hey, meet Reb Jacob.'

'Hello, Jacob.' She shot me a long-suffering look. 'I am Batya. Welcome to our home.'

'Pleased to meet you.' She wasn't one for kissing, or even a handshake, so I made do with a bit of a nod.

'Where's Gingie?' demanded Grandma.

'I told him to go home.' Batya reddened. 'He worked very hard today, reconnecting the boiler and...'

'I need Gingie,' said Grandma. 'Tonight. Where is he?'

'He's gone home, Grandma,' said Abba. 'Gingie's a Palestinian from Azariya, on the other side of the Green Line,' he told me. 'They have curfews after terrorist attacks but somehow Gingie always seems to get through. If he doesn't fancy going home, he hunkers down at my place.'

'*Our* place,' said Batya.

'Get inside!' Grandma kicked the Chihuahuas into her Ottoman apartment.

Abba and Batya lived in a baronial hall with walls of huge stones and thick mortar. A spiral staircase in the corner ascended to a curtained-off mezzanine floor. A pair of French windows looked out to the Old City, now coloured pink.

The room was full of Deadheads, all spaced-out eyes and beatific smiles, hairy faces and loose cotton threads. Beyond their acid-casualty frills, they seemed to share a deeper tribal bond. Everyone's head was covered. Everyone's head had been turned by Jerusalem.

'*Hevrai, hevrai.*' Abba cut through their chatter. 'I want you to meet Jacob. He's just off the boat from London.'

'*Avenu shalom aleichem, avenu shaaaaalom aleichem...*'

They clapped, danced and sang a traditional song of welcome. In Jerusalem, the return of one of their own was a call to celebration. In Jerusalem, reverence and exuberance danced hand in hand.

I too clapped, danced and sang, in Hebrew, like a groom at his wedding. Still wearing Abba's *kippa*, I felt at home with the happy *hevrai* and looked forward to making new friends.

'*Avenu shaaaaalom, shaaaaalom, shalom aleichem.*'

'*Hevrai, hevrai!*' Abba squeezed through to stand at the French windows, facing the congregation, pamphlet open in his hand. I thought he was going to recite some words from the Bible or lead us in prayer.

'The Train Station Angel in Athens,' he boomed.

'The Train Station Angel in Athens' didn't sound very biblical. 'I thought you were going to say a prayer.'

'In Hebrew numerology, "prayer" and "poem" are the same,' a *haver* in a Lenin cap told me.

'Abbaaah,' said Batya. 'Must you read your poem now?'

'The Train Station Angel in Athens. *

> "*She's breathing the roof-top air,*
> *Across the gravel and railroad tracks,*
> *Sitting there, her surprising wings*
> *Seem to be fluttering as I move*
> *To see her more clearly...*'"

---

* The Train Station Angel in Athens is by Adam Schonbrun, who kindly offered it to be used as Abba's party piece before he died in 2014. Adam's memory will always be a blessing.

Abba looked up, to see her more clearly. 'Oh, fuck.' He had lost his place.

'Start again, from the beginning,' said a *haver* in a fez, like a film director encouraging a temperamental actor. 'Take your time, don't worry. Enjoy yourself. Do it with love.'

'The Train Station Angel in Athens.' Abba started again.

> *"She's breathing the roof-top air,*
> *Across the gravel and railroad tracks,*
> *Sitting there, her surprising wings*
> *Seem to be fluttering as I move*
> *To see her more clearly.*
> *Could she be the blonde Irish girl*
> *Whose address I lost?*
> *Sun-burnt and beautiful,*
> *With sculptured wooden-eyes,*
> *Watching the travelling back-packers*
> *Saying their hellos and goodbyes...*
> *Not moving,*
> *But that she is human I am convinced.*
> *O this, her petite, carved breasts,*
> *While I pass on my way to 'Paradise*
> *Youth Hostel' among crushed and rotten*
> *tomatoes on this dingy street...'"*

The phone rang. Abba picked up the handset, which he held at arm's length.

> *"...At the station, innocence*
> *In the summer rain, drizzle*
> *Healing us... And she up there,*
> *Meaning more to me than any Acropolis*
> *Or Satyr,*
> *Enjoying the mad Retsina, Goddess above*
> *The train's smoke*

Angel at the Peloponnese."'

Abba blinked behind his glasses and the *hevrai* broke into a smattering of applause.

'Awesome.'

'That was great.'

'*Kol hakavod.*'

'Abbaaah,' said Batya. 'There is someone on the phone.'

Abba put the phone to his ear. 'I met Ginsburg once,' he said into the mouthpiece. 'He was giving a reading in the Village. The yeshivah's *rosh g'dol* didn't want me to go. Said I was too young. It was just after... Who? No, I never heard of him. *Shabbat Shalom,* man.'

The *hevrai* rose to their feet, men to the fore, still facing the French windows. Then they began, buzzing piously, everyone intoning and swaying to a rhythm of his own, with Abba providing baritone murmurs where appropriate.

An illiterate foreigner unable to speak Hebrew or recite prayers, I watched from the sidelines, wishing I could participate. As it was I could only wait to set out on the road to becoming who I truly am. My parents weren't going to see it that way. They could cope with 'Jacob is volunteering on a kibbutz,' which implied merely a phase in growing up, but 'Jacob is being born again in Jerusalem' said I found something missing in my original birth, when what was missing was my common sense.

'Ahhhhh-men.'

After prayers, while Abba toured the room, still basking in acclaim for his poetry reading, and Batya bustled away in a spartan, dimly lit kitchenette, organising refreshments, the *hevrai* sat on the floor in little circles and spoke over each other.

The fez spoke loudest. 'You all have to make a decision. What does Rosh Hashanah mean to you? Do you want to go to Uman to pay your respects to Rebbe Nachman – may his name be a blessing – while supplying much-needed Judaica and samizdat literature to our brothers and sisters behind the Iron Curtain, or do we go to New York for the Madison Square Garden shows? Pilgrimage to the dead or pilgrimage to the Dead?'

'I saw the Grateful Dead in London in '81,' I said.

I wanted to tell them about the shows at London's Rainbow Theatre, and my collection of bootleg tapes, but I was helping Batya put out bottles of soda and platters of warm *barekas*. And a woman in an oversized *kippa* was reminiscing about her escapades in a Chevy that ran out of gas in a tailback on a highway, thirty miles short of Ithaca, where the band was about to play one of the legendary Cornell shows of '77.

And a girl wearing a black beret and a Star of David necklace had arrived.

Letter 32

You sat on a chair beside mine, a prim, dowdy figure in a cardigan and ankle-length denim skirt, sucking a fizzy drink through a straw. Your bowed head and quiet, virtuous air bespoke an introspective devotion quite distinct from the excited zealotry all around us. I recognised you on first sight but didn't want to mention our previous meeting lest you think me crazy. To break the ice, I opted for some local gossip.

'So, what do you think of the binding of Isaac?'

I remember every word of your response.

'You know, I've never quite managed to understand it. I've always thought it a guy thing, something to do with fathers and sons. I mean, it's ridiculous. Abraham must be crazy if he's ready to kill his only son on the basis of a message from a disembodied voice, right?'

You were challenging me to an argument, as though inviting me to dance. Were I to agree with you, saying, 'Yes, Abraham must have been crazy,' there would be no dance. You wanted to hear me justify our patriarch's brush with filicide.

'Abraham isn't crazy,' I said. 'This is the Bible. We're dealing with moral paradigms, not real people. Abraham passes God's test of his faith, thereby becoming an example to humanity.'

'"Now I know you fear God,"' you said, before tutting in frustration. 'That's so typical. I can recite quotes from the Bible and *midrashim*, but from secular sources, never.' You glanced at me surreptitiously as if gauging my trustworthiness. 'Sometimes I think the Bible is addressed to me personally. I wouldn't be able to make sense of life without it.'

I was well versed in talking about books I hadn't read. But in my student days, books were either fictional literature or speculative philosophy, or interpretations or analyses of such texts. In Jerusalem, the Book was reality.

'The Bible is totally relevant,' you said. 'It gives me a sense of belonging.'

'What about the Book of Job, *habibi?*' asked Abba. 'I have a version of the Book of Job with illustrations by William Blake. It was given to me by...'

'I could do without the Book of Job, thank you very much.' Your tone said you could do without Abba, too, thank you very much, and he promptly moved on.

'The Bible is authentic, and true,' you said. 'It's through the Bible that God breathes.'

'No it isn't,' I argued, just when you weren't expecting to be contradicted. 'It's only through the spontaneous words of people, of humanity's living representatives, that God can be said to breathe.'

'That's beautiful,' you replied. 'Who are you quoting?'

'I'm not quoting anybody. It just came out. Maybe it was something you said.'

'You must have been a prophet in a previous life. Who *are* you?'

You raised your eyes for the first time. They were dark, soulful and defiant. You didn't want my admiration but I could hardly ignore your pretty, vivacious face and scarlet petal lips, your perfect pearly teeth and ironic, dimpled smile. Your pulchritude expressed the love in God's mind when He set down the laws of monogamy. (So too it explained the licentious jealousy of antisemites down the ages.) In you I beheld the history of our people. You were Rachel in Mesopotamia waiting seven years then seven more years for her husband's hand. You were the lovely Sephardi girl from Haifa whom Papa intended to marry. You were a sophisticated mademoiselle lending your allure to France. You were a paragon of Jewish womanhood and I had caught a glimpse of your soul.

'Jacob Green.' My old name, the names I'd had since birth, felt like a child's two-piece suit, outgrown and surplus to requirements.

'I'm Rachel,' you said to your drink.

'You're French, aren't you?'

'I'm from Marseille, actually. How can you tell? Grassed up by my accent, I suppose.'

'You know we've met before?'

'*Déjà vu*, huh? I get that every now and then.'

'You're Sephardi, right?' You had the mysterious grace of 'that exotic subspecies,' as Papa called Sephardim.

'I am, as a matter of fact. At least I am on my father's side. He's Algerian. His family, a branch of the eminent Abouflika dynasty, immigrated to France during the war.'

'Why would you immigrate to France during the war?'

'France's war in Algeria. Have you heard of it?'

'Yes, I've heard of it. And I saw Pontecorvo's movie, Battle of Algiers. Have you heard of it?'

'Touché.'

'How barbaric were the French in Algeria?'

'*Ooh la la!* What a low blow!'

You put on a show of Gallic pride and I appreciated your irony. You weren't rooted in France any more than I was in England. We both belonged right here, in Jerusalem.

'My father is a typical Sephardi. Everything revolves around family, and the patriarch's word is law. When I'm at home, I can't go out without a chaperon, for example. And even then I have to wear a long dress that covers my arms. My brother, on the other hand, can wear what he likes.'

'I bet he can't wear a long dress that covers his arms.'

Your frown of confusion turned into half a smile. 'I thought you were going to say it's a double standard.'

'You don't *have* to obey your father, you know. I don't want to sound like Jesus but...'

'*Sacré bleu!* I owe everything to my father. It wasn't easy for him to let me come to Jerusalem, unaccompanied. In our culture, a girl doesn't leave home until she marries, God willing. Yet here I am, away from home, on my own, with my father's blessing.'

'I'm glad he did let you come.'

My honesty fell on stony ground. You didn't accept compliments or flattery because you yourself would never be so insincere. You didn't deviate from the straight and narrow path of virtue. Whereas I was brought here by chance, you were driven by your own high morality.

'He wanted me to go to the Sorbonne, which was kind enough to award me a scholarship. I could be staying with cousins in Paris, studying international law and looking forward to a career as a barrister, or a diplomat. But he knew my heart was set on Jerusalem.'

'Here's one for Jerry,' announced a bearded guitarist, to whoops and whistles from a semicircle of *hevrai* at his feet. A sticker on his guitar said, 'Jews for Jerry'.

'*If my words did glow, with the gold of sunshine...*'

The *hevrai* sang along while swaying from side to side, shoulder to shoulder, though none as loud as Abba when it came to, '*Let there be songs... to fill the air*'. You clapped on the down beat and I clapped beside you while singing with the *hevrai*. All Deadheads knew the words to Ripple.

'Jerry Garcia,' I told you. 'He's the lead singer, guitarist and spiritual centre of the Grateful Dead.'

'What was that?'

'It was a long, strange trip.'

You couldn't hear me and wouldn't have known what I was talking about if you could.

'This one you'll know from our beloved teacher, Reb Shlomo,' said the guitarist.

'Rabbi Shlomo Carlebach,' you told me. 'He's the lead singer, songwriter and guitarist for *ba'al teshuvah* hippies.' You added something about '*niggunim*' but I couldn't hear you and wouldn't have known what you were talking about if I could.

The guitarist strummed an introduction to 'a *niggun neshama*, a soul rap. Please get up and dance.'

The *hevrai* rose as one.

'Give us your energy, your devotion, your love. Give everything you have to greet the *moshiach*, now, now, now...' He broke into a scat, to a foot-stomping beat and thrashing guitar chords.

'Moshiach! Moshiach! Moshiach!'

The *hevrai* chanted and danced to greet the messiah. As the rap sped up, so did the clapping and the dancers, who swirled as if possessed. The song finished and still we clapped and chanted.

'Moshiach! Moshiach! Moshiach!'

Abba was heading in our direction, all set to take me to see his man in Mea Shearim. His timing could not have been worse. I was already worried lest you start talking to someone else. Any moment could have been our last.

'Let's go outside,' you said.

We stepped out to the balcony, and your thigh brushed mine as we passed through the French windows. I pretended not to notice, to be numb to your touch and insensitive to my racing heart. I offered you a cigarette and you cupped your hand around my lighter's flame. We leaned on a railing facing the Old City walls, so close we could feel each other breathe. We gazed into a violet sky, flicking ash into a warm breeze, both pulled by a weird gravity.

'I went to the Western Wall today,' I said.

'What for?'

'What do you mean, "What for?" That's where I met Abba.'

'It's such a tourist site. It isn't even a wall of the actual Temple so I don't know why people worship it and stick notes in its cracks. That's so superstitious. Maybe it's a guy thing.' You laughed self-mockingly. 'Are you here on holiday?'

'I'm a banana farmer on a kibbutz, actually.' I was, I wanted you to know, contributing to Israel's agricultural output.

'I see.'

When my mum said, 'I see,' it was to register her incomprehension. Your 'I see' meant you saw through me. With anyone else, I would have been embarrassed. With you, I was elated: you knew me.

'Sorry.' You put a hand over your mouth. 'It's just that you don't really look like a banana farmer.'

'What do I look like?'

'A nice Jewish boy.' The slightest of smiles brought out both dimples. 'You know what Nahum says...'

'Who's Nahum?'

'That is the question. Nahum says, "When I appear before the heavenly tribunal and I am asked, 'Why did you not lead your people like Moses?' I shall not be afraid. When I am asked, 'Why were you not a David, who worshipped me and shepherded your people?' I will be calm. When they ask, 'Why were you not Elijah who spoke the truth and brought forth justice?' even then I will not shake. But when they ask, 'Nahum, why were you not Nahum?' I will tremble from head to toe".'

In other words, one should be true to one's self. My self was emerging on that very night, in your intimate company, in the celestial city of Jerusalem. I could feel it coming to the surface, rising from a latent well of darkness.

'When did you make *aliyah*?' I asked you.

You sighed, at my misapprehension and your own shortcomings. 'I'm only in Jerusalem for a year, God willing. I'm on a programme at the Hebrew University. Half of the students in my class are Americans, who treat it as a holiday. A few weeks ago we had to vote on a *tiyul* to a site of national significance. "Let's go shaaapping in Dizengaaaff,"' you drawled. '"Let's hit the beaches in Eilat".'

Your impersonations made me laugh. 'What did you vote for?'

'The Cave of Machpelah. "Not the Cave of Machpelah! It's in Hebron. It's in occupied Palestinian territory. It's not safe." For days I pleaded with our *madrich* and eventually we went, at least some of us did, in an armoured bus. When we got there, I cried and cried.'

'What were you crying about?'

'It's Abraham's burial place. All the patriarchs and matriarchs are buried there, except Rachel. I was just overwhelmed by a sense of continuity. To find my place in the world, to know where I come from... I thought everyone would be affected the same way. But it was just me.'

Like the provincial heroine of a nineteenth-century French novel who fetches up in the big, bad world of high society quite unaware of her beauty (which would in any case mean nothing to her) and its effect on hot-blooded men (which would mean even less), you had no idea that your noble ideals went unobserved in modern life.

'As for Jerusalem...' You looked on the verge of crying again. 'Do you feel God's presence?'

'I do.'

'I don't want to go back to France,' you said.

'Then don't. You're a free person.' I laughed at this deployment of my old line of reasoning.

'What's so funny?'

'Well, we're not free, are we?'

'I suppose not,' you said. Then you looked across the valley at the Old City. 'This is where I belong.'

'Me too.'

Fireworks burst and shattered. Pinks and purples lit up an enchanted castle. The movie was about to begin. Boy meets girl at a party in Jerusalem. They embark on a giddy new life together, going to the local Cinematheque to see old movies, attending synagogue for prayer services on Shabbat and socialising with Abba and his circle of friends, all the while abstaining from sexual intercourse until their wedding night, when more starbursts foretell a happy ending.

'Sometimes I'm too busy to appreciate where I am,' you said. 'When I'm at work, for example. I have a part-time job at the Jerusalem Post, doing translations for the French edition.'

'That's wonderful. Do you reckon they might give me a job? I could review the latest film releases...'

'Have you seen many films lately?'

'The Sound of Music. Dr Zhivago. The Graduate.'

'*Wah wah zzz waaaah zzzz.*'

A rock band was soundchecking feedback in a valley to the west. Then drums and bass laid down a Middle Eastern beat. An electric guitar wailed. A sneering singer exercised his vocal cords while an orderly crowd of punters thickened.

'Concert at the Sultan's Pool,' you said.

'I don't see any pool. Just a crater in the ground.'

'Well they have good concerts in that crater in the ground. Especially now it's summer. Last week there was a jazz festival with BB King, Freddie Hubbard and McCoy Tyner.'

'Did you go?'

'*Oui, oui.* We had free tickets. McCoy Tyner played solo piano and Freddie Hubbard played in front of quite a big band. BB King was the headline act. He introduced us to Lucille. That's what he calls his guitar.'

'Was it a good gig?'

'Depends who you ask. McCoy Tyner's a bit modern for me. And Freddie Hubbard was more hard-rock fusion than jazz. But you have to love BB King. He's such a sweetie. I only knew one of his songs. The Thrill Has Gone.'

'The thrill has just begun.'

You smiled modestly.

'Do you like jazz?'

'I do when I'm in the mood,' you said. 'Though it's hard to tell when that will be.'

You were so right. One day's music was another day's noise, depending on your mood. I was going to admire your wisdom out loud when a second thought stopped me. If I wasn't careful, I'd give the game away.

'Don't worry,' you said. 'Mood swings are normal. At least that's what my psychoanalyst tells me.'

'You see a psychoanalyst? I always wanted to see a psychoanalyst. My ex-flatmate Vincent used to say I'd wind up in a lunatic asylum.'

'Why?' you asked. 'Are you crazy?'

'Well, I did some crazy things in my student days.'

'That's so typical,' you said.

'Anyway, that's all in the past. I'm not crazy these days.'

'I'm glad to hear it. I'm not crazy either. It's just... sometimes I need someone to talk to. My psychoanalyst hears things that other people don't.'

'What about friends?'

'I don't really have any, at least not close friends I can confide in. Why, do you have friends you can confide in?'

'I did have a friend called Skunk. We were like doppelgangers – people thought he was me and vice-versa. And I confided in my girlfriend, too. Diana and I lived together, "in sin" as they used to call it.'

You didn't know about doppelgangers and living in sin. That's why I have been trying to explain myself to you in these letters. Sometimes I wonder whether you will read them.

You sighed and rested your head on my shoulder.

I could have gathered you in, to gaze into your eyes, to kiss your mouth, to feel your warmth. How offended you would be by the tasks of desire. I wiggled my shoulder free, as though disapproving of our physical intimacy on your behalf.

'I'm so sorry!' you said. 'That was so inappropriate.'

'No, it wasn't.' I was on your side. 'Just a bit uncomfortable.'

'I thought you were getting bored.' Your coquettish laughter hid a greater truth. I wished I knew what it was. 'It's getting cold,' you said, before heading back inside.

I listened to the gig below and heard nothing. My senses were numb, like I'd been tranquilised, until a burning sensation in my fingers made me drop my cigarette's glowing butt. My calmness surprised me. I associated love with fraught infatuation but now it seemed perfectly natural, *baruch hashem*, appropriate and preordained. Still, I didn't want to bring up the L-word. Everyone was scared of the L-word. And, superficially at least, I was still a stranger.

The *hevrai* had departed and you were helping Batya do the washing up. Beret tilted just so, cashmere cardigan draped over your shoulders, you cut an image of Gallic chic. At the same time, you radiated humility. On seeing me, you checked your watch.

'So, tell me, Racheli...' Abba was flat out on the sofa, taking his rest after a long day in the city, unaware of my presence behind him. 'What do you think of Jacob?'

'He's quite the expert in *pilpul*, isn't he?' Somewhere beneath your praise, you were being ironic.

'An expert in what?' I asked.

Abba spun round. '*Pilpul* is the art of talmudic disputation, of interpreting interpretations of the Bible. The greatest scholars and rabbis devote their lives to *pilpul*.'

'There's nothing in Western philosophy that you won't find already written by our great Jewish sages,' you said.

'What about dialectics?' I was up for another dance. 'That's Western philosophy. It's Hegel and Marx and Sartre.'

'Dialectics is the most Jewish thing!' you exclaimed.

'Is it? Give us an example.'

'Okay. Take the story of Rebbe Nathan of Korets. One day the rebbe noticed that his students were worried. "What's wrong?" he asked them. "We are scared of being pursued by the *yetzeh hara,* the evil inclination," they said. The rebbe told them not to worry. "You are young, you are still in the foothills," he said. "The truth is, *you* are pursuing *him*!"'

'Y*etzeh hara, yetzeh hara...*' Batya wiggled her hands above her head like a peasant casting off a curse. 'Tfuh, tfuh to the *yetzeh hara!*'

'That reminds me of a Zen parable,' said Abba. 'A monk and his student see a well-dressed lady unable to cross a huge puddle in the street. The master picks her up, crosses the street and puts her down. The student says, "But master, isn't it forbidden to carry a lady like that?" The master answers, "I put her down yet you are still carrying her".'

'Good one,' I said.

You rolled your eyes, at Zen parables, Abba's comparison or my approbation.

'It is a terrible thing, the *yetzeh hara,*' warned Batya. 'It is not to laugh or make jokes, I tell you. One time God was not liking people's behaviour. So He took away their evil inclination.'

'Then what happened?' asked Abba.

'Then there were no more children being born, so He had to give it back again,' said Batya, prompting prolonged laughter, from Abba and me at least.

'*Au revoir, mes amis,*' you said as you gathered yourself to leave.

'How are you getting home?' I asked.

'Walking.'

'Where do you live?'

You shot me a sidelong glance. You weren't in the habit of divulging your address to strange men.

'You're on Rehov Yishor, right?' Abba was quite oblivious. 'Baaka's a nice neighbourhood.'

Batya apologised for Abba and ushered you out. Chihuahuas yapped, a heavy door creaked on its hinges. The door slammed shut and you were gone.

'So, Reb Jacob,' said Abba. 'Are you ready to go see my man in Mea Shearim? Hey, what do you think of Rachel? She's a great girl, isn't she?'

'Abaaah!'

'What?'

'Abba sometimes forgets what he is saying. He needs me to remind him.'

'I've always liked Rachel.' Abba ignored her. 'From the first time we met at the *Rabbanut...*'

'We met her at the *misrad hapanim*, Abaah.'

'"*Hapnim*," not "*hapanim*".' Abba smiled indulgently. '"*Al hapanim*" means "all fucked up".'

'It *is* all fucked up,' said Batya. 'The bureaucracy here is terrible. You can wait in government offices like the *misrad hapanim* all day. I do not like those places. They stink so bad, and the magazines are six months old.'

'You can't read Hebrew magazines,' said Abba.

'I can look at the pictures.'

'*Nu?* Is an old picture not as good as a new picture?'

'I don't want to see pictures of that Madonna flaunting her body.'

'So bring your own magazines.'

'My magazines are also old.'

'Then throw them out and buy new ones.'

'With what? We don't have money to pay our bills, so where's there money for Dutch magazines? Did you pay Grandma for the gas and electricity?'

'I was gonna do that. I went to the bank earlier.'

'*Nu?*

'The girl behind the glass wouldn't give me any money. "I don't want your money," I said. "You're beautiful."' Abba sat up and pulled a shoulder bag out of the cushions. 'Is this yours?'

'It is a woman's bag,' said Batya. 'It is Rachel's bag.'

'She can come pick it up tomorrow,' said Abba.

You had left it behind for a reason, that's what Freud would say. You were giving me a pretext for coming after you. There again, Freud wasn't what he was, and you wouldn't be so cunning. Besides, I had to go see Abba's man in Mea Shearim.

Letter 33

Abba gave me directions. I was to turn left at the end of Ein Rogel onto Derech Hebron, a highway that went to Talpiot. I wasn't to turn right or I'd be back at the Old City, where I didn't want to go on my own after dark. I was to look for a sign pointing left to a *tayelet* that was under construction and right to Baaka then, all being well, I would head you off at the pass. At Batya's suggestion that you might have gone via Beit Lechem, Abba stroked his beard and recalled a time when Beit Lechem was surely inhabited by bakers, on the grounds that 'Beit Lechem' means 'House of Bread'. In biblical days...

I didn't have time for a discussion. The following few minutes would be crucial. If I didn't find you on Derech Hebron or Beit Lechem, all would be lost. I slung your bag over my shoulder and let myself out.

A demure, self-possessed figure was waiting obediently at a set of traffic lights. Even from a distance you were easy to spot. I was about to jump out, saying, 'surprise!' when you stuck an arm across my chest to save me from a speeding car.

'Thank you. I forgot which way the traffic goes. You saved my life.'

'Thank *you*,' you said, for your bag.

The traffic lights turned red and you set off at quite a clip, as though accustomed to walking alone. I tagged along like a stray dog accompanying a new mistress on the understanding it doesn't become too attached. I showed persistence, you feigned indifference. Such were the universal traditions of a boy-meets-girl romance.

'You can go now,' you said.

'No I can't. I want to make sure you get home safely.'

'Yeah, right. There's no street crime here, you know. We're not in New York.'

'Have you ever been to New York?'

'Yes, I have, as a matter of fact. We went there for a holiday last year, to coincide with my cousin's barmitzvah. We've been there a few times.'

Shopfronts, residences and landmarks whizzed by. We could have passed the Hanging Gardens of Babylon and I wouldn't have noticed a flower. Nor could I feel the ground beneath my feet.

'Have *you* been there?' you asked.

'Have I been where?'

'Keep up. New York.

'No, I've never been anywhere. Except here.'

'On previous trips we couldn't get away from our family in Brooklyn but last year my father took me to see the sights. Empire State Building, World Trade Center, Museum of Modern Art...'

'Which was your favourite?' Every detail of your life was there to be learned, a treasure to be savoured, a memory in the making.

'Well, we were both very moved by the immigration museum on Ellis Island. They have first-person testimony from Jews who fled from pogroms in Russia and eastern Europe. My father found it heart-rending.'

'You're close to your dad, huh?'

'You don't miss a thing, do you? We went to New York a few days in advance to have some time *à deux*. My mother came later, with my brother, just to ruin our holiday. My mother and I don't get on.'

'Does she see you as a rival?'

'She's a typical American. In fact, she's just your type.' You must have thought I liked American women. Or my girlfriends' mothers. Or you were trying to deflect my attentions. Maybe you were just teasing me.

'New York reminds me of my favourite movie, actually,' you said.

'Don't tell me. Let me guess. Fiddler on the Roof?'

'What has Fiddler on the Roof got to do with New York?'

'Well, when they leave Anatevka, they probably head for Ellis Island.'

'You're so funny, aren't you?' Smiling despite yourself, you gave my shoulder a barge. 'Just for that, I'm not going to tell you what it is.'

'Annie Hall?'

'Not even close. It's The Godfather.'

'The Godfather?' I was amazed.

'Uh huh. I adore Michael Corleone.'

'You mean you fancy Al Pacino.'

'Not at all, though he is excellent in the role.'

'Why would you *adore* a Mafia don?' I was jealous of a character in a movie. 'He's a ruthless murderer, a cold-blooded killer.'

'He's not cold-blooded. Everything he does is for his family. He's a model son, loyal and devoted. And as a husband he does whatever it takes to protect Kaye from his illegal businesses. He even tries to go legit. Meanwhile, Kaye betrays him.'

'She doesn't betray him.'

'Yes, she does. She has an abortion, without even discussing it with him or telling him, even though it's *his* baby. What does he say to her when she says their marriage is over?'

'"You won't take my children."'

'Exactly.'

A building site gave way to a row of Jerusalem-stone villas. Art-deco designs and red-tiled roofs appeared and disappeared. Our pace slowed and every so often our hips bumped.

'What's *your* favourite movie?' you asked me.

'You probably haven't seen it. It's called "The Passenger".'

'Isn't that the one about Jack Nicholson getting lost in a desert? Is that who you identify with? A guy who travels around aimlessly before killing himself?'

'He doesn't kill himself. He just dies for no apparent reason. Anyway, who says I identify with him?'

'Of course you do. You're the existential hero, lost in a foreign land, detached from his past, becoming someone else.'

'And you're The Girl. A solitary French traveller abroad, always reading a book, yet open to the possibilities of a chance encounter.'

'I don't think so.'

'You even look like Maria Schneider.'

'And you look like Al Pacino.' You bit your lip but the words were out.

'When I was a student, our local arts cinema used to screen The Passenger on a double bill with Last Tango in Paris, in which Maria Schneider is The Girl once again.'

'Oh, your hero dies at the end of that one also. It's Marlon Brando, isn't it? What a big, fat, middle-aged *mamzer*.'

'Have you seen it?'

'Certainly not. But I know The Girl shoots him dead at the end. And quite right too after he imposed himself on her, sexually. Do you identify with him too?'

'I'm not big, fat and middle-aged.'

'No, you're small, slim and young.'

A car pulled up in a brightly lit forecourt beneath a neon 'Esso' sign. An attendant in overalls inserted a rubber pipe's gun-like nozzle into an orifice in the car and the driver crossed the forecourt to a kiosk, where he paid a cashier through a window. He returned to his car, exchanged guttural words with the attendant and drove off. Twin rear lights became pinpricks then disappeared in the night.

'Where are we?'

'Well, Baaka is over there.' You nodded at a side street. 'There's an absorption centre for new immigrants on my street. It's a place to stay while they give you Hebrew and history lessons and help you find work and somewhere more permanent to live. Do you speak Hebrew?'

'No, not at all, apart from a few words I've picked up at Galuyot. I'll have to learn it.'

'It's not difficult. Related words all share a root. For example, "*sefer*" is "book," "*sofer*" is "writer" and "*sifriya*" is "library". It's not like English, where those three words have totally different roots.'

'But the words go backwards, from right to left. Look at that.' I nodded at a sign that said 'Talpiot' in three alphabets.

'Talpiot's an industrial zone. It's a bit of a rough area.'

'We're not in New York, you know.'

'I'm glad you're paying attention.'

'Are we nearly there?'

'You sound like a little boy on a long car journey.'

I wished I was that little boy, aching to arrive. My predicament took the opposite form: I dreaded our journey's end. Every step brought us closer to goodbye.

'You know, this is all new to me.' You shot me a sidelong glance. 'I mean, I've never been in this situation before.' Romance happened only to other people, or in movies and books. 'You wouldn't think we've only just met.'

'I know. It's like we're characters in a novel.'

'It is! I was thinking the same thing. What novel would it be?'

'Nausea. By Sartre.'

You frowned before breaking into a laugh. 'God, you're funny.'

'What do you think of Sartre?' I asked. As a religious student and a scholar of the Bible, you were bound to dislike your compatriot, the godfather of existentialism.

'I hate him,' you said, with admirable passion. 'Did you read his *Réflexions sur la question juive*? What a horrible book! He thinks Judaism is defined by antisemitism.'

'That's why its English title is "Anti-Semite and Jew"'. I didn't care about Sartre or existentialism. But I loved crossing swords with you.

'And even then,' you said, 'he uses antisemitism only to promote his own Hegelian-Marxist model of "the other". Besides which, he published it only after Paris was liberated and the Nazis were defeated. What good was that?'

'Sartre was a speed freak,' I said.

'And that's a good thing, is it?'

'I'm just saying you can see the writer's addiction in his work. Sartre's prolixity was due to speed. Same thing with Freud. I mean, you're bound to become obsessed with sex if you're jacking up cocaine. And what about the Romantic poets? All that dreaminess after smoking pure opium.'

'*In vino veritas*. Is that what you're saying? Intoxication leads to truth?'

'You don't *have to* be intoxicated on a quest for truth. But you'll probably drive yourself crazy *en route*. Take Nietzsche, for example. He went crazy and spent the last years of his life in a lunatic asylum.'

'Sounds about right,' you said.

'Nietzsche is like the Bible.'

You stopped still, hands on hips. You had heard enough. Then your face softened. I was winding you up. We were back on the move.

'Go on, then. How is Nietzsche like the Bible?'

'They both hold up a mirror to your prejudices. You can only get out of a book what you already know, you know. Who said that?'

'Maimonides.'

'Nietzsche.'

'Is that so? Alright then, enlighten me. What are Nietzsche's greatest hits?'

'Eternal recurrence. *Fati amor*. Man's will to guilt...'

'*Zut alors.* If he were here now, I'd give him a slap.'

'What for?'

'For filling your head with such nonsense. Man's will to guilt, indeed. Honestly, *je vais vous présenter la vraie vie.*'

I was touched by your concern. I was also embarrassed by my indoctrination, and seduced by your French. I couldn't wait for you to show me my true life.

'Which writers *do* you like?' I asked.

'Take a guess.'

'Tolstoy?'

'I did read Anna Karenina.'

'I *love* Anna Karenina.' I meant the novel, though now I loved Anna too.

'Not one of my favourite heroines.'

'Why, what's wrong with her?'

'What, apart from being a selfish drug addict who abandons her husband and young child to live out her fantasy?'

'And there was me thinking of her as a role model.'

Your dimples ruined your attempt to look cross. 'Are you staying with Batya and Abba?'

'Yes, Abba said I can stay for as long as I like, though I'm due back at Galuyot by tomorrow night.'

'Well, maybe you should think about going back now. They might want to go to bed.'

'I'm not stopping them.'

'You don't want to wake them.'

'I'll be very quiet.'

'You're being deliberately obtuse, aren't you? How will you get in if they're asleep?'

'Abba gave me a key.'

'I don't believe you.'

'It's in my pocket.'

'You're lying.'

You chased me down Derech Hebron and I let you catch up. I swerved and slipped your grasp, then swerved the other way. After a few more missed tackles you grabbed my T-shirt. You searched my pockets, and your hands rubbed my thighs. Your breast brushed my shoulder. Your breath touched my neck. To you, we were *copains* mucking around, kids having a laugh.

'You're such a liar!' There was no doorkey.

'Oh *dear*! Now what am I going to do?'

'You'll have to sleep under the stars.'

'Maybe a stranger will take me in. People here are very friendly, you know. Not like strangers at all.'

'Do you fancy a falafel?'

'You're not a falafel,' I was about to say, before noticing a busy falafel joint up the road.

Teenage girls in crop tops and mini-skirts, boys with slicked-back hair; hirsute workers in overalls, soldiers wearing Uzis; yeshivah *bochers* too young for their fedoras, Ashkenazi *yekkes*: all milled around the little restaurant and bar. In my crocheted *kippa*, Kibbutz Galuyot T-shirt and army trousers, with a religious girl at my side, I blended right into Jerusalem's nightlife.

Inside the falafel joint, a wall-to-wall mirror gave everyone a double. The proprietor, who looked like Anthony Quinn as he worked an old-fashioned cash register, appeared in framed photos on the wall, his arm around a different national hero in each picture. Here was Moshe Dayan in trademark eyepatch and battle fatigues, beaming at the camera. There was Menachem Begin, in dark glasses and a suit, mouth open while speaking. And there was Yitzhak Rabin, his granite face half-hidden by cigarette smoke. A fast-talking voice on the radio cut off a Middle-Eastern pop song. Everyone paused to listen. Then a brash advertising jingle cut to more zithers and ouds and a resumption of punters' chatter.

You almost flirted with the proprietor and I was almost jealous. You insisted on paying because I was merely a poor volunteer, or to demonstrate your feminism, or to show that we weren't on a date. We took a table for two in a corner from a couple who were leaving and sat facing each other. I gobbled down my falafel, enjoying every mouthful, until I perceived a change in your mood. Head down or glancing over your shoulder, shielding your face or nibbling your falafel, you seemed to fear being seen.

'It's past my bedtime.' You sipped your Coke, dabbed your lips with a napkin and pushed aside your half-eaten falafel. 'Have you got a cigarette?'

I lit our cigarettes and our smokes coalesced in a cloud.

'I was thinking,' you said.

'What about?'

'Us. It must be fate. Being thrown together like this...'

Your thoughts sent me into raptures. Your every word gave credence to my hopes. 'Us' saluted our intimacy. 'Fate' acknowledged our union, one which, far from being a mere circumstantial happenstance, represented a divine alignment. 'Being thrown together' cast us as lovers.

'We're strangers yet I feel like I can talk to you about anything,' you said. 'It's just so... I don't know. It's so unusual.'

'It's not that unusual.'

You frowned at my nonchalance and stubbed a barely smoked cigarette in an ashtray. 'What about the joy? Don't you feel it?'

'Of course I feel it. What I'm saying is, people fall in love all the time. It's natural. It's almost to be expected.'

'*Vous êtes trop mignons.*'

I was too cute. Did you mean 'too sweet,' or 'too cunning'? Either way, you were probably being ironic. You were a mystery inside an enigma inside a Sephardi doll.

'*Ben zona!* A charedi teenager thumped a pinball table, to his mates' amusement. '*Lehitraot,*' they said to the proprietor, who followed them with his eyes as they headed out.

'Let's have a game of pinball,' I said.

'I don't know how to play.'

'I'll show you.'

Deadly Dragon looked much the same as the pinball tables in Wessex University's bars. I inserted a ten-agurot coin and set 'players' to 'two'. You smiled in excitement as Deadly Dragon clicked and flashed into life.

'The ball comes out from here. You press these buttons, to operate these flippers, which you use to hit the ball.' I flipped the flippers to demonstrate. 'See? You score points by hitting the targets. I'll show you how it's done.'

'You're so modest, aren't you?'

A silver ball careered up the chute and whizzed around the table, pinging off taut rubber. It skirted a saucer and snuck into a hole that sent it up a ramp to a higher deck, where it hit a couple of targets then careered down a side chute. I trapped it on my flipper. 'Skull-and-crossbones tunnel.' I let it roll to the flipper's sweet spot then smack! Right up the skull-and-crossbones tunnel. The ball whizzed back and smack! Right up the skull-and-crossbones tunnel. One more for a multi-ball. You had never seen a multi-ball. The ball whizzed around the deck then rolled down the centre, out of my flippers' reach. Now I didn't have a single ball, let alone a multi-ball.

'Wah wah wah,' laughed Deadly Dragon.

'What happened?' you asked.

'It's your turn.' I stepped aside to let you take my place.

'Where's the ball?' You flipped your flippers in unison, smiling in anticipation.

Standing behind you, at the back entrance to your soul, inhaling your essence, I pulled the plunger at your hip. A delicious thrill stirred my loins.

Desire was the night visitor.

'Go away!' I told him. 'I won't have gatecrashers.'

'I'm sure Rachel would like to meet me.'

'No, she wouldn't. She's quite happy chatting with Respect and Affection,' I said, though I doubted it. Respect and Affection were merely associates here to make up the numbers, to kill time in small talk.

'Rachel is one foxy chick.'

'How dare you! Why don't you go pester one of those tarts over there by the mirror?'

'You mistake me for Lust, my illegitimate half-brother. Lust is aroused by every woman he sees. I am the opposite. I want only the one for me.'

'Rachel isn't the one for you. She's not your type. You've never met a girl like Rachel.'

'I can tempt anyone.'

'Not here you can't, not in Jerusalem.'

Desire laughed at my naïveté. 'I'm well-known in these parts. Who do you think was whispering in King David's ear when he saw Bathsheba, his general's beautiful wife, lying naked under a shiny moon? Who do you think gave him the dreadful inclination? David, Israel's greatest king, was powerless over me. He climbed down from his elevated quarters and approached Bathsheba, his heart so amorous not even...'

'Why don't you fuck off?'

Desire wouldn't leave. He introduced himself as 'Love' and everybody fell at his feet, forgetting their own conversations to latch onto his words or to bring him wine and canapés. He put a patronising arm around my shoulder. 'You have done well to keep your ammunition dry,' he said. 'And when the time comes, play it cool. Rein in your excitement until you have savoured every touch of your bodies. I can see you now, kissing her feet and working up her calves, then moving into her thighs, your lips and tongue leading the way as she widens her hips and you open your mouth to enter her moist delight. But stop! She won't want to taste herself on your tongue when you kiss. So you nuzzle into her neck and kiss her long and hard. You caress her breasts and rouse her nipples, you stroke her with your erection. Only then do you go down on her. I see you coming up for air, looking into her eyes and declaring your undying love before hauling her aboard your naked body. You thrust ever higher, rumbling for an eruption, you strain and reach for the highest peak, surging towards a climax. You are all set to explode in ecstasy, when you hear her say...'

'*Zut alors!*'

You had been flipping the flippers, uttering exclamations until the ball dropped down a chute. You smiled wistfully at your turn's premature end. Then you saw the change in me. Your dimples withdrew and you picked up your bag.

'I really ought to be going.'

'Hang on, we haven't finished. You can still catch up. There are two more balls to go.' I stepped up and pulled the plunger. Now thoroughly distracted, I mistimed a flip and lost the ball.

'Wah wah wah,' laughed Deadly Dragon.

'She can't have gone far,' said Hope, who had joined Desire in leading me through a crowd of hot bodies towards Baaka, ignoring a half-dressed girl slouched under a fruit truck half-mounted on the kerb, and a girl who flickered blue and white in a bank's neon lights.

'What a sultry night for young lovers,' said Desire.

We caught up with you as you turned into a side street under a sign for Rehov Yishor. Your expression sent Desire packing. Hope remained to help put things right, but Hope kept quiet for fear of tempting Fate.

'We just have to get through this sticky patch,' I said. 'It's just a minor contretemps. Then we'll emerge all the stronger.'

'Listen, Jacob.' You sounded serious. 'What we had tonight was a connection. I'm not denying it.'

'What we had' was mortifying. Why were you speaking in the past tense when we had a lifetime ahead of us? You acknowledged our 'connection,' but a 'but' was always coming.

'But there is a gulf between us.'

'That's a good thing. It's dialectical, isn't it? Opposites attract.'

'We should honour the connection and respect the gulf.'

What a brilliant formula! Our coming together had inspired a new model for humanity. 'Honour the connection and respect the gulf' could constitute a moral basis for all personal interactions. Except you were talking about *us*. I wanted to cross the gulf, not respect it.

'You can't say that! Our meeting was fate, remember? You said so yourself.'

'I was thinking on one foot.'

'Surely the gulf isn't as wide as the connection is deep.'

You put a hand to your face. 'That's the most beautiful thing anyone has ever said to me.'

Never had you imagined connecting with someone so spontaneously, or feeling so deeply about a man you had met ostensibly by chance.

'I'm so not immune to your words,' you said.

'That's the most beautiful thing anyone has said to *me*.' A stone constricted my throat. Tears welled.

You walked away towards a nondescript block of flats as though that were the end. The romcom had finished, on an ambiguous, postmodern note. It was time to return to our humdrum lives. Apart from each other.

'Aren't you going to invite me in for a coffee?'

You stopped and sighed. 'I think we ought to say goodnight.'

'Surely not. We've got so much to talk about.'

You blew through your lips. '*Si vous devez.*'

We entered a clean, tiled vestibule that had four front doors, each with an eyehole, a ceramic nameplate and a *mezuzah*. A zigzag flight of steps led up to an identical landing, then another. You tipped up a pot plant, picked up a key and opened your door.

A man was glaring at me. Then I recognised my reflection in your hallway mirror. And still it looked like someone else.

'We have to be quiet,' you said. 'My flatmate is asleep.'

We were in a tidy, functional living room. I tried counting the volumes of Encyclopaedia Judaica on a book-lined wall but they all looked the same and I kept losing my place. Your flat seemed too small for two. Maybe you shared a bedroom. Or your flatmate didn't exist. Either way, the quiet was conducive to intimacy.

'Listen, Jacob,' you said from a distance.

'Why don't we sit down?' I plonked myself on a small sofa and patted the vacant cushion.

'I can't be responsible for your happiness,' you said.

You were way ahead of me. It wasn't as if I had asked you to marry me. Not yet, at any rate.

'Why not?'

'I am engaged to a man in France.'

The world turned dark. 'Oh, fuck!' I scrambled around for a cigarette. 'Oh, God!'

'I didn't want to tell you, in case you were upset.'

'I knew it was too good to be true.'

'We can still be friends. I've never had a pen-pal.'

'You can't be engaged.' I lowered my voice. 'You can't be engaged. Look, you're not wearing an engagement ring. And you're too young. How old are you?'

'Eighteen.'

'How can you know your own heart at eighteen? You haven't lived yet. Don't tell me: it was all arranged by a matchmaker or some other busybody. You're going to marry a man you don't even know, aren't you?'

'We're planning on a wedding next spring.'

'Next spring' sounded like a death knell.

'I'm worried about my in-laws to be. They disapprove of me. Apparently I'm not good enough for their son. I wouldn't put it past them to ruin what is supposed to be the happiest day of my life.'

'You can't get married. I mean... why?'

'Love.'

It was a half-beat too fast, and too pat, too rehearsed, too joyless. You didn't love him, I could hear it in your voice. You couldn't act to save your life. You needed me to direct you.

'Who is he?'

'He's a yeshivah student. He's going to be a rabbi.'

'And you'll be a rabbi's wife.'

It all sounded fishy to me, like a ruse to dismiss unwanted suitors. Maybe you had a psychological condition. That at least offered a chink of light.

'The sages say we choose our spouse before we are born. That's what is meant by "*beshecht*". A *beshecht* union is one that's meant to be.'

'*We* are *beshecht*.'

'I'm sorry if I misled you.'

Your apology was final. I had served my purpose and you no longer required my services. You put down your bag and went to the toilet, or to check on your flatmate.

A leaflet stuck out of your open bag. It pictured Catherine Deneuve tied to a tree by her wrists. I thought it was promoting the movie Belle de Jour before realising, to my shock and horror, that it was promoting a bondage club. I couldn't believe it. It must have fallen into your bag by accident, or was put there by a person unknown as a prank. Maybe it was Abba. Or you saw only its blank side, which you intended to use as notepaper. Unless I had failed to recognise in you a side that came out at night, at bondage clubs. How could such places even exist here in Jerusalem? How could God tolerate such perversity in His own back yard? He was probably going to send a prophet to liberate Jerusalem from its degradation. On hearing your footsteps, I stuffed the flyer back in your bag.

'I want you to leave, please.'

'What, now? What happened to coffee? What's a flyer for a bondage club doing in your bag? When will I see you again?'

'I think we should say goodbye.' Not '*au revoir*' but 'never again'.

'How can you be so cruel?'

'I don't want you in my life.'

'But I'm in love with you.'

'How dare you? What gives you the right?'

Base human passions are best left undisturbed, or experienced second-hand, in books or movies. You knew it all along. I wish I hadn't introduced you to Desire.

Letter 34

I couldn't find my lighter. I must have left it in your flat. So I held an unlit cigarette as I roamed the streets of Jerusalem, where every whir and flicker prefigured a vision of you. I saw you cause a car's screeching halt. I heard your voice through a second-storey window. I watched a cat that was sitting in a doorway, waiting for you and your saucer of milk.

'Rachel!' I screamed, to make you appear.

'Rachel!' I screamed, to beg for forgiveness.

'Rachel!' I screamed, willing God to rewind time.

But you weren't going to appear, you weren't going to forgive me and God wasn't going to rewind time. There was nothing left except dashed hopes and memories.

'God, you're funny.'

You had never had such a funny encounter. Our humour belonged to us alone, created by you and me together. Neither of us will find again what we found in each other.

'If Nietzsche were here now, I'd give him a slap.'

You were like a protective mother wanting to upbraid a local free-thinker for tempting your boy from the path of righteousness. Back then, I was your boy. Back then, you loved me.

'That's the most beautiful thing anyone has ever said to me.'

The sadness of a parting to come cracked your voice. The sadness and the pity.

Then came the fall. For one everlasting moment, hatred burned in your eyes. 'I am shocked by the turn in your behaviour,' you said. 'Never try to contact me again.'

I was the bogeyman lurking in your woods. I was the predator stalking your nightmares. I was the *yetzeh hara* itself. Now you knew your enemy as 'Jacob Green'. My name had joined the infamous ranks of your persecutors, may their names be erased.

'And you'll be a rabbi's wife.'

You take your place in the second row of the ladies' gallery, your face hidden by a wide-brimmed hat, behind your Orthodox community's most distinguished wives. In previous years you sailed through Yom Kippur, fasting and praying in synagogue without a second thought. This year you have a genuine need to atone. Since returning home, you have been too ashamed to divulge the events of that night to anyone and too scared to admit to yourself the secret in your heart. You have been introspective and reclusive, shunning your fiancé, refusing to see your psychoanalyst and averting your eyes from your father's concern. Music and literature too you have avoided for fear of their passions. Only today can you bring yourself to face the sins you set in motion in Jerusalem. 'Don't be so friendly,' your intuitive caution warned you. 'Don't encourage him,' said the traditional nous of your culture. 'Yet still I went ahead,' you confess to God. You tell Him how blithely you flaunted your virtue, how proudly you mocked your innocence, though of course He saw everything. That night you called your fiancé to tell him of my assault, but instead of comforting you or cursing me, he accused you of complicity. So you changed your story and said, not to worry, it was just a nightmare. You apologised for waking him and begged him not to tell your father. Only now, on the holiest day of the year, here in God's house, do you recall the truth. 'I let him touch me, I let him expose himself and, for just a moment, one that I'll always regret, I took pleasure in his love.' You thank God for His deliverance, for here you are, safely home in Marseille, none the worse but much wiser for your experience. You thank God for accepting your prayers and illuminating the path of righteousness. You have no inclination to linger on a bad memory. Time has passed and your future is laid out ahead of you. Yet something rankles. You wish you understood our joy. The mystery yields to a familiar drone, a prayer you know by rote. 'What doesn't kill me makes me stronger,' you say to yourself, not knowing the line's secular source. You sing the prayer's refrain while looking down at huddles of men holding prayer shawls over their heads. They let their shawls drop over their shoulders, exposing no heads but only a mass of identical fedoras. One of the hats – you can't identify which – belongs to your fiancé. You thank God for such a pious man and resolve to love him to the limit of your abilities, while secretly hoping that marital harmony will restore your virtue in God's eyes. Your fiancé is a fine catch by anyone's estimation. He's not objectionable to look at, he has no apparent bad habits and, as a scion of several generations of eminent rabbis, he's destined for a senior position in one of Paris's most prestigious synagogues. You harbour no ambitions for yourself and would no doubt prefer a simple life in a remote country outpost, to better immerse yourself in pastoral duties, as befits a God-fearing *rebbetzin*. In other circumstances you would regard high office and its trappings a fit subject for satire but now you are a serious woman, one betrothed to an important man. You look forward to keeping a kosher home and devoting your life to virtue. You vow to avoid social situations that might lead to misunderstandings and to keep your beauty hidden from everyone except your husband.

After a while, your husband, the rabbi, will take you for granted. He'll treat you like a glorified servant, then he'll grow to despise you. One day you'll leave a button unfastened or your dress will rise on the wind, you'll linger too long in a smile or overstate a kindness, and a lonesome parishioner will suffer a night of unwonted fantasies. In the morning your admirer will write an anonymous letter, saying, 'Your wife is leading me into temptation. She must be punished for her wickedness.' The rabbi will show you the letter and remind you of our night in Jerusalem.

Then you will remember me.

Letter 35

'Why are you screaming in the street?'

He came in the guise of an ordinary citizen, wearing a standard-issue *kippa*, khaki shorts and army boots. His defensive posture and martial air were those of a gunslinger confronting a suspicious stranger. He slid his fingers towards a holster on his hip, ready to draw his pistol.

'Go on then, shoot me!' I had fallen in love and was ready to die. God wanted a word and I was at His disposal.

The gunslinger maintained a wary distance, his hand hovering over his holster. 'What are you doing? I have been watching you for a while.'

'I'm on a mission from God.'

On hearing this, he decided not to shoot but reached instead for the walkie talkie clipped to his belt. Keeping his eyes trained on me, though now they were more admiring than hostile, he spoke into his palm, eager no doubt to spread the good news. I wasn't a suspicious stranger, I was God's messenger.

'Where are you going?' he asked, as though wanting to offer me a ride.

'Good question. It depends on what God wants me to do. I thought I was going to Baaka for a reunion with Rachel.'

'And you are Jacob, I suppose?'

'Ah, you recognise me. But my name will no longer be "Jacob," but "Israel," because I have struggled with God, and with humans, and I have overcome.'

The man nodded, clearly impressed by my historic struggles, and the tasks that lay ahead of me. 'Don't tell me: you waited seven years, then another seven years, for Rachel. Is that right?'

'And another seven years after that, until I was twenty-one. We were reunited at a mutual friend's place in Abu Tor. That was when I fell in love.'

'You can't go around falling in love with random strangers,' he said. 'Everyone knows that.'

'We were lovers in a previous life. God brought us to Jerusalem to reunite us, if only for one night. Not even that, actually.'

'Listen, I am Dr Yehezkel Levy and I have many years' experience of treating such attacks. We see cases like yours at my facility quite frequently. You need help.'

'Thank you, but my help comes from above. God granted me a special power.'

'We have the world's best specialists in the field, right here in Jerusalem. Now if you'll come with me...' He stepped forward and extended an arm.

'Not now! I have work to do. I'm waiting for a sign.'

A herald of flashing blue lights marked the arrival of an emergency service. Ambulance doors flew open, paramedics jumped out. It looked more like a traffic accident than a divine sign. I wondered why they needed a stretcher, till I realised it was for me.

'Is there someone we should contact?' asked Dr Levy while the paramedics strapped me down. 'Do you have family here? Or friends who will be asking where you are? Who knows you?'

'Only Rachel knows me. And Rachel doesn't want to see me again so I don't think she'll be asking where I am.'

A paramedic injected my arm when I wasn't looking. It was, he said, a sedative. I would be asleep by the time we arrived, he said. Lying in the back of an ambulance, hearing gears grind and brakes screech on a bumpy, hilly road, I drifted in and out.

'I brought you out of exile,' said God. 'I gave you life among the heathens then returned you to the Promised Land.'

'I knew You would come. What's the plan? What must I do?'

'Soon you will reveal yourself to the people.'

'How will they recognise me?'

'They will know the Messiah,' said God. 'For you are Israel, My anointed one, and they will be redeemed by your presence.'

'Moshiach! Moshiach! Moshiach!' They were already chanting on the streets. 'Moshiach! Moshiach! Moshiach!' Their voices grew louder and the ambulance drew to a halt, surrounded by ecstatic revellers.

They already knew who I was. And they knew I was in this particular ambulance. So late at night, when they should have been sleeping in their beds, they were out in droves to celebrate my arrival.

'Moshiach! Moshiach! Moshiach!'

I had returned as a temporary volunteer, then a tourist in Jerusalem, not understanding the real nature of my trip. Only now could I see my life in perspective. The time had come to meet my destiny.

That was days, or weeks, ago. Since then the doctors have expressed reservations about my mission to redeem our people by my presence. And when I ask them when I will be released, they shrug their shoulders and say it's in God's hands.

At times, everything is clear. Then I know who I am. I know who you are. And I know who God is. At other times, it's all foggy. Then I don't know where I am. I don't know where you are. And I don't know where God is. But I never lose faith: God will reunite us once again, even if it takes another twenty-one years.

In the meantime, I remain yours, in love,

Israel

www.ingramcontent.com/pod-product-compliance
Lightning Source LLC
Chambersburg PA
CBHW071416300726
48976CB00006B/2121